Father

PAUL BURKE

PLEASE NOTE THIS IS AN UNEDITED, UNCORRECTED BOUND MANUSCRIPT – NOT FOR QUOTATION

FLAME

First published in Great Britain in 2001 by Hodder and Stoughton
A division of Hodder Headline

10 9 8 7 6 5 4 3 2 1

British Library Cataloguing in Publication Data

ISBN 0 340 79344 9

Hodder and Stoughton
A division of Hodder Headline
338 Euston Road
London NW1 3BH

PART ONE

I

The church was packed. Of course it was. This was Kilburn, 1970, home to the largest Irish community in Britain and the big Catholic Church in Quex Road was its epicentre.

It was a huge church, bigger than most cathedrals – high gothic arches, acres of stained glass. Such was the concentration of Catholics in Kilburn that Quex Road needed eight full-time priests to cope. Every Sunday, more than 10,000 people attended mass there, requiring services on the hour in the church and on the half-hour in the church hall to accommodate them. A total of fourteen Sunday masses in all, standing room only in each.

This was the 11 o'clock mass – particularly popular, as it finished rather conveniently at ten to twelve which left just enough time for a fag and a cough in the car park before the pubs opened at noon.

Back inside, the smell of incense was floating down from the altar, along the aisles and into the furthest recesses at the back. Right down into the corners it wafted so that the slackers who stood there rather guiltily, the ones who had shuffled in just before the gospel and would shuffle out just after Communion, were aware that they were attending Sunday mass. Aware that mortal sin had been avoided and their weekly obligation fulfilled.

Most of the congregation, were just going through the motions – mindlessly mumbling the words of prayers they'd mumbled a million times before. Prayers they knew so well that they didn't know them at all.

There was, however, one parishioner, seated six rows from the front who was considering the broader picture, asking himself the bigger question – why are we here?

Not "why are we here?" in the deep, philosophical sense Why were we put on Earth? What is our ultimate purpose? What is the meaning of life? No, no, nothing like that. When eleven-year-old Francis Dempsey asked himself "Why are we here?" He meant why are we here in the Church of the Screed Heart, Quex Road, Kilburn, spouting what sounded to him like complete and utter rubbish?

Francis, you see, was breaking the habit of a lifetime. He was paying attention. His father Eamonn, having seen the boy gazing vacantly into space yet again during the gospel, had nudged him sharply and told him to listen to what the priest was saying.

Francis had always used his weekly trip to mass as an opportunity to catch up on his daydreaming – Would England win the World Cup again in Mexico this year? His collection of Esso World Cup coins was almost complete. Only Brian Labone and Ian Storey-Moore to go. Which member of Pan's People was he most in love with? Cherry, Dee Dee or Babs?

This morning, though, he was listening to the liturgy, the absurdity of which he found rather disturbing.

"We believe in one God, the Father, the Almighty, creator of Heaven and Earth of all things visible and invisible......"

"Lord I am not worthy to receive thee under my roof but only say the word and my soul will be healed........"

"Lamb of God, you take away the sins of the world......

Lamb of God? What on earth were these people talking about? What is the Lamb of God anyway? And since when could a lamb take away the sins of the world?

A few of the flock, – particularly those nearest the front – looked worried – very worried indeed. There was a lot of bead-jiggling and breast-beating going on. Mea Culpa, mea culpa, mea maxima culpa. Old Mrs. Dunne looked terrified.

What dreadful sins had she committed as a girl in Ireland? What could have made her so desperate for forgiveness? She was praying now – eyes closed, beads clutched – with the speed and delivery of an auctioneer –

"........hallowedbethynamethykingdomcomethywillbedoneonearthasitisinheaven......

As Francis then joined the queue to receive Holy Communion, the opening bars from a familiar hymn struck up with a mighty resonance from the organ loft at the back: "Praise My Soul, The King of Heaven" which, according to the hymnbook had been written by somebody called H.F. Lyte. "Praise Him, Praise Him" was the chorus and general gist of it. It was the gist of most hymns and Francis found the sentiments expressed by H.F and his ilk rather disquieting.

If God is up there now, his beady eye trained on Kilburn, what must he think of the grovelling musical tributes ringing out of Quex Road? Doesn't he find them horribly embarrassing? Having "Happy Birthday" sung to you was bad enough so how excruciating was this?

Surely he's not enjoying this cringing sycophancy. If he is then he's very conceited. If he's conceited, he's not perfect. If he's not perfect, he's not God.

Francis felt the familiar hot pang of Catholic guilt for even entertaining such thoughts. How could he even consider such evil, blasphemous ideas about Our Lord.? But wait a minute – he wasn't thinking anything bad about God. at all. On the contrary. He was assuming that God was a nice man, a modest man` a man who had no desire to be fawned upon in this way.

Having pulled off this neat feat of self-exculpation, Francis re-boarded this train of thought, which was now calling at all stations to Eternal Damnation.

What about all the other things he and his fellow parishioners were asked to do in the name of the Lord?

It all began with baptism. At Quex Road, they were very

proud of the fact that they had the highest rate of baptisms, the busiest conveyor belt of freshly minted Catholics in the country. More than 600 babies a year, apparently, most of them no more than a couple of weeks old. Baptisms were arranged in great haste to secure the infant's place in heaven. Any child tragically returned to The Manufacturer before making it to the font, would. regrettably, not be eligible for a place at His side. Condemned instead to float forever between Heaven and Hell in the land of Limbo – the place where innocent little babies go if death tightens its icy grip before the Catholic Church does.

And Francis Dempsey, along with every other Roman Catholic, was seriously expected to believe this.

His mind then turned to Holy Communion; now that was a good one. How could that tiny round wafer actually be a part of Christ's body? If you stuck enough of them together would you be able to make a long-haired bearded man in his thirties? And even if these little wafers really were tiny pieces of a man's body, why on earth would you want to eat them?

And how could that old bottle of Mosaic Cyprus Sherry possibly be Christ's blood? And again, even if it were, why would you want to drink it?

How about confession? What in the name of God was that all about? Kneeling inside a wardrobe and telling a strange man your innermost secrets. Francis tried to remember the justification for this most peculiar of sacraments. Oh yes, inside our bodies, we have a heart and soul. Funny that the latter had never once figured in Human Biology lessons. And as far as Francis was aware, no doctor had ever been called out to treat a suspected soul attack. Yet apparently, there it was – pure white but picking up little black marks every time its owner committed a sin.

So confession was a bit like a trip to the launderette with a packet of metaphysical Persil. Those emerging from the wardrobe with their sins absolved, their souls cleansed, were supposed to feel as though they were wearing clean white shirts inside their bodies as well as outside.

Francis looked up at Jesus, depicted high above the altar, nailed to a cross. Who said he looked like that anyway? A bit like George Harrison on the cover of Abbey Road? Not Matthew, not Mark, not Luke, not John. He'd caught that little snippet on a religious affairs programme. Not one of the gospels contains any reference to what Jesus actually looked like. All we know for certain was that he was Jewish. Well Gus Harvey who used to live next door, was Jewish. So that was how Francis always imagined the Son of God. It was Gus Harvey healing lepers, Gus Harvey turning water into wine. So two days after Gus died, Francis half-expected him to rise from the dead.

This remarkable trick, allegedly performed by Jesus, was something celebrated every Easter and Easter was just two weeks away. So today, the priest clad in rather fetching purple vestments. Purple for lent and advent, white for weddings and christenings, black for funerals and the standard green for any other time.

Francis felt a sense of dread as he anticipated Friday week – Good Friday, a misnomer if ever there was one, it being the most miserable day in the Catholic Calendar, the day Our Lord was supposedly crucified. Any display of happiness or cheer on Good Friday was strictly forbidden. The Dempsey household, like hundreds of others in Kilburn was subject to a blanket ban on all forms of pleasure. Watching TV, playing records in the front room or football in the park – forget it. Good Friday was a day devoted to solemnity or rather, mock-solemnity. It occurred to Francis that it was all a bit of a charade. Wasn't it a bit like an old Hollywood movie that was shown every year? Yes, there is a weepy bit where the hero gets nailed to a cross but we all know that he's not dead really and gets up to live happily ever after..

Easter Saturday was a bit odd too. If people are going to

pretend to miserable on the Friday because Christ is dead then surely they should still be grief-stricken on the Saturday. He's still dead, isn't he? And yet, every year, on Easter Saturday, smiles return to Catholic faces as they pile into Woolworth's on Kilburn High Road to buy each other Easter eggs.

All very strange. And yet, here he was at mass, surrounded by grown-up, intelligent people, all buying into this nonsense.. There was Jim O'Hagan over there, Mr & Mrs. Quinn, the Mackens, the Hennesseys, the McKennas. Surely these thoughts had occurred to them too. Did any one of them truly believe the stuff they espoused every Sunday?

Francis only really believed the things he had actually seen. Which is why he no longer believed in monsters, ghosts or Father Christmas. There was, of course, one ghost in whom he was still supposed to believe – the Holy Ghost, recently rebranded as the Holy Spirit, as if making him sound less like a ghoul and more like a bottle of whisky would give him any more credibility.

Francis believed John Shanahan was the toughest boy in the class because he had seen him beat up Richard Fisher in the playground. He believed that the E-Type Jaguar was the most beautiful car in the world because he had seen one parked on Brondesbury Road and had stood and gazed at it for ten minutes

But God? These people believed in him not because they had seen him but, paradoxically, because they hadn't.

Most baffling of all was the fact that missing mass on a Sunday was considered to be a mortal sin on a par with murder or armed robbery. Why? Almost on cue, Joe Brennan handed him the most likely explanation.

Joe was a friend of his father's – a good man, parish hero, a Knight of St.Columba. Big and burly, Joe was dressed in his Sunday best – blue suit, brown shoes, tiny crucifix half-buried in the cloth of his lapel. As he leaned towards Francis, the pores of skin emitted the faint whiff of last night's Jameson's and this morning's Old Spice.

Joe was leaning over to pass Francis the collection plate. Ah, so that was it. Receiving no money from the state, the Catholic Church is wholly dependent on the contents of that plate. Without these enforced attendances every Sunday, the health and wealth of the Church could be terminally affected. So why not just admit it? Why threaten everyone with the roaring fires of hell if they don't turn up? It was clear, even then, that Francis Dempsey and his fellow parishioners were not, as the old cliché goes, singing from the same hymn sheet.

It got worse. After mass, Francis noticed the titles of some of the Catholic Truth Society's pamphlets on sale in the repository. One was called "Wrestling With Christ". Wrestling with Christ? What was that all about? Did it feature pictures of Jesus grappling with Mick McManus or Jackie Pallo? Did Jesus form a tag team with the Holy Spirit? That would be some tag team – one invincible and the other invisible. Well, Jesus may have had had the rest of the congregation in a half-nelson but Francis was refusing to submit. He wandered behind his mother, father and two sisters into O'Brien's newsagents for the traditional after-mass treat. Whilst picking up the News of the World, the Sunday Press and forty Majors, his father would bestow a shilling upon each of the children to spend on various items of confectionery. They would always eke it out – Francis in particular. He'd fill the little paper bag with blackjacks, fruit salads little chewy Frother bars, spreading that shilling over at least a dozen items.

This Sunday he was in a different state of mind. Hang the expense; he was living dangerously now. He was going to blow the whole lot on something really sinful, something really decadent like a Tiffin, an Aztec or an Amazin' Raisin bar. He was breaking old habits and by the time they'd all walked back to their terraced house in Esmond Road, he'd decided to break the biggest habit of all. He'd made an important decision. A decision for life, something about which he would never change his mind. Francis Dempsey did not believe in God.

Odd then, that years later, he would return to Quex Road and, witnessed by hundreds of people, would appear to proclaim the very opposite.

II

There are generally two routes to emigrate from Ireland to London. It's either Dun Laighoire to Holyhead or Rosslaire to Fishguard. The Holyhead train comes into Euston; the Fishguard train into Paddington. Those arriving at Euston would tend to settle a couple of miles north in Camden or Holloway. Those arriving in Paddington would often head a few miles west to Shepherds Bush or Hammersmith. However, it was Kilburn, lying between the two termini and equally convenient for either, which attracted far more Irish settlers than any other area in Britain.

Eamonn Dempsey was one of thousands arriving at Euston in the mid-fifties to help re-build a nation still recovering from the Second World War. He headed up to Camden, the weight of his battered old suitcase blistering the skin from his fingers. Up and down he trudged, street after street before eventually finding a house which wasn't displaying the almost standard "No dogs, no blacks, no Irish" sign in its window. It was a huge, once grand Victorian villa in Gloucester Crescent, now in the depths of decay and carved up into a dozen damp and dismal "bedsits". Each contained an old and cripplingly uncomfortable bed and one dangerous looking gas ring, presumably provided for when the occupant inevitably decided to bring his miserable existence to a premature close. Very basic sanitation was shared with several other homesick and lonely immigrants in a freezing cold privy at the end of a corridor.

With only this to return to, was it any wonder that Eamonn preferred the warmth and conviviality of North London's many pubs?

The house was a short walk from Camden Town tube where Eamonn and scores of others would gather at 6.30 every morning when the building site foremen or "gangers" would come looking for casual labour.

It was like the feeling they'd all experienced at school, waiting to be picked for the football team but this was rather more important. If you didn't get picked, you didn't get paid. Which meant that you couldn't afford to eat. Or more importantly, you couldn't afford to drink.

This was the other route to gainful employment. You soon discovered which gangers drank where and for quite a few of them, it was Kilburn High Road. The Cock, the Old Bell and the Cooper's Arms could be particularly fruitful. Fortunately for Eamonn, aged twenty-two and already built like the brick walls he would soon be erecting, he was never short of work. Never left standing at Camden Town Station and never needing to give too much of his green and folding to the publicans of London, NW6.

Mary Heneghan had also arrived in London courtesy of the Holyhead train. She too dragged her suitcase up to Camden Town and was given a tiny room in Arlington Road by her sister Eileen whose husband John was a leading hand (whatever that was) at the Black Cat cigarette factory in Mornington Crescent.

Mary found work as an auxiliary nurse at the Whiitington Hospital in Archway and it was at a dance at the nearby Gresham Ballroom that she was swept of her feet by Eamonn Dempsey. Well, swung off her feet really. They were, after all, dancing the Siege of Ennis, a complex Irish reel involving dozens of participants which had long served as an informal mating ritual. Eamonn had grabbed hold of Mary and had never, ever let go.

Catholic courtships in those days were fairly brief and to the point. If there was a solid attraction between you, that was usually deemed good enough for Holy Matrimony. A physical attraction simply meant a visual attraction since sex before marriage was strictly taboo

The proposal, when it came, was fairly low-key. Eamonn did not fall to one knee (Only Our Lord was worthy of genuflection). He did not produce a big diamond ring and beseech Mary to marry him or his heart would surely break and his life become utterly worthless.

"Mary", he'd said over a quiet drink in the Archway Tavern, "Will we get married?"

And in response, Mary did not scream "Yes, yes, yes" and burst into tears of orgasmic delight. She just nodded and within a matter of weeks, they were in their first home together – a small flat in Kilburn. If, that is, the lower half of an unconverted house could be described as a flat. Mr & Mrs Dempsey lived at the bottom of the stairs, Mr & Mrs. Ward at the top.

Agnes Ward was from Leitrim and every Sunday morning she would clip-clop around the bare floorboards of the upstairs "flat" so that Eamonn and Mary, sleeping peacefully below would be startled from their slumbers in time for the eight o'clock mass.

They'd lived there for just over a year when Mr. Thompson, the landlord, suddenly gave them notice to leave. He was selling this and the various other dilapidated houses he owned around Kilburn and Kensal Rise and was retiring to the South Coast.

This was a pity. Despite Agnes Ward's stiletto-heeled reveille, Eamonn and Mary were very happy there. They didn't want to move and seemed no nearer the summit of the London Borough of Willesden's council house waiting list. They asked Mr. Thompson how much the house would cost to buy.

"Two thousand pounds", he replied, almost embarrassed by the certain knowledge that the sum was far more than this charming young couple could afford. He was right, it was but Eamonn and Mary asked him to give them a month before placing their home in the hands of the estate agents on Salusbury Road. He agreed and over the next four weeks, they hardly ate, they didn't go out drinking or dancing and shelved their hitherto immediate plans to start a family. They scraped together every pound, shilling and penny they could find plus many more borrowed from various members of their family to piece together the £200 required by the Allied Irish Bank as a deposit. They only ever managed £190 which meant that, ultimately, they would be £100 short of Mr. Thompson's asking price.

When the month was up, he came to see them.

"Will you accept nineteen hundred?" said Eamonn, expecting the answer no.

Mr. Thompson pushed some Old Holborn into the bowl of his pipe, lit up, took a couple of puffs, gazed quietly into the middle distance and considered the offer. Or at least, he pretended to. They were good tenants, they'd been no trouble. Never damaged his property, never been late with their rent. Such was his regard for them that he'd probably have let them have it for even less.

"Okay", he said, after what seemed like an eternity, "on one condition – that you can raise the money within, say, three weeks. I've got my eye on a nice little bungalow in Bournemouth and if I'm not quick, I'm going to miss it"

"Three weeks. That'll be fine" said Eamonn. He'd get the money within that time, even if it meant robbing the Allied Irish Bank to do it.

He held out his hand for Mr. Thompson to shake but in his excitement he'd alarmed his soon to be ex-landlord by spitting on it first.

III

On a fine August morning in 1977, Francis. now eighteen – tall, dark and almost handsome – was sitting in the box room of that very house in Esmond Road .

You could call it a box room for two reasons: Firstly because it was a little square bedroom, the smallest in the house. And secondly because it was filled with boxes – those long wooden ones which had once contained little bottles of Britvic orange juice but now housed Frank's huge and ever-increasing collection of seven-inch singles. He'd stopped answering to "Francis" years ago. It was too reminiscent of St. Francis of Assisi and, if he were going to be called Francis, he'd have to start wearing open-toed sandals and a sackcloth robe.

Old singles were his passion and his collection was now approaching four figures. He'd long ago made the sweeping generalisation that, with the noble exception of The Beatles, most tracks on most albums were crap. He couldn't bear the overblown pomposity of even the most revered examples – tracks like Supper's Ready by Genesis or Led Zeppelin's Stairway To Heaven.

How could this pretentious drivel ever compare to Levi Stubbs pouring raw emotion into every line of "Baby I Need Your Loving".

For Frank, it was the three minute single which best encapsulated what pop music was all about. He'd picked most of his older ones up for next to nothing in junk shops and jumble sales. For a few of the choicer items, he'd paid a little more at specialist outlets like Spinning Disc in Chiswick or

Rocks Off just behind Tottenham Court Road. These resided alongside the shiny new punk stuff, often on brightly coloured vinyl with picture sleeves.

Recently, Frank had been putting his collection to good use. Since passing his driving test a few months earlier, he'd been occasionally allowed to borrow his dad's old Corsair to embark upon a part-time career as a mobile DJ. He'd saved his Saturday job money from Riordan's Butchers in Kilburn High Road and invested in a rudimentary disco deck, a pair of bass bins and a set of flashing lights. He'd been playing records at parties for years. At each one, he'd tend to gravitate towards the music centre in the corner and would have a quick flick through the host's (or the host's parents') record collection. Then, almost like a good chef supplied with even the most unpromising ingredients, he could concoct a selection of tunes that could turn a bad party into a good one. He seemed to have the knack of finding the right track fat the right time.

Today, he was looking for the appropriate track to clatter on to one of his twin BSR turntables. It was one of his oldest singles, released in 1957 on the purple HMV label, the label on which you'd also find the very early Elvis singles. Frank had them all– All Shook Up, Paralysed, even the rarer than rare Mystery Train, all on purple HMV with the gold lettering. Now, in August 1977, with The King having just joined the queue at The Great Hamburger Joint In The Sky, the value of these waxings had increased a hundred fold.

He finally found it – The Banana Boat Song by Harry Belafonte. He wanted to hear that famous chorus "Day-o, day-o, daylight come and she wanna go home".
The record was surely made for this occasion.

Frank had just received his A level results – a D, an E and an O. DEO, DEO, daylight come and she wanna go home.

Well, Frank thought it was funny anyway. Though in reality, these grades were no laughing matter. Oh, they weren't disastrous – nothing to be ashamed of and considering how little effort had gone into them, they were remarkably good. They just weren't going to be very much use.

Harry Belafonte was faded out and replaced by a spinning blue Phillips label – Dusty Springfield singing the painfully apposite "I Just Don't Know What to Do With Myself

As he listened to Dusty's peerless vocals, soaked in hopeless self-pity, Frank couldn't help feeling the very same emotions seeping through him. It dawned on him then that there was no point in leaving school at eighteen.. No point at all. At sixteen, you could get started, as most of his Kilburn contemporaries already had, and begin your apprenticeship as brickie, chippie or spark. Or perhaps put your foot on the bottom rung of any of a number of clerical ladders in the City or the West End.

Alternatively. at 21, in your cap and gown, you can take your pick from the world's graduate appointments and set off on a sprint round life's inside track where the chairmanship of ICI awaits you as you breast the tape".

The primary purpose of A levels is to unlock the doors of universities but those latches will only unfasten if your grades are good. Frank had no real desire to go to university. He quite fancied Oxford or Cambridge but only in the same way as he quite fancied Farrah Fawcett-Majors. With his grades, he'd be lucky to loosen the locks of Doncaster Poly and the thought of spending the next three years sharing grotty digs up North and having to put his name on his yoghurt was wrist-slittingly bad

With a D and E and O, he'd fallen between two stools with only a limited number of places to land.

The Metropolitan Police, for instance. Now as much as Frank occasionally fantasised about being in the Sweeney, tearing round London's still derelict docklands before snapping the cuffs on a vicious team of armed robbers, he knew the reality would be rather more mundane: Ordering hapless motorists to produce their documents or strip- searching innocent Rastafarians at the Notting Hill Carnival.

No, a career in the Old Bill did not appeal. Neither did the thought of working all day on a building site and doing day release at Kilburn Tech in order to become a QS or Quantity Surveyor. Real progress for a lot of boys. One rung up from their bricklaying fathers.

The only career on which Frank had been vaguely keen was journalism. Unfortunately this budding enthusiasm was strangled at birth by the arrival at his school of a stulteyingly dull old hack from the local paper. He gave a talk explaining how rewarding it had been to spend thirty-six years as part of the local community.

"I've covered their weddings and I've covered their children's weddings" was the phrase that had Frank hanging the noose over the beam. He had imagined a life as a principled and crusading reporter working for one of the broadsheets. but the thought of thirty-six years at the Kilburn Gazette covering stories of the "Man Drops Bag Of Sugar In Supermarket – We Have Pictures" variety had turned him off forever.

He thought of becoming a full-time DJ but was forced to concede that this was not a "proper job". It was a hobby, something in which he loved to voluntarily immerse himself. Once that hobby became work, then he knew that the fun and the pleasure would be instantly removed.

So it was with heavy heart and dragging heels that he returned one last time to St.Michael's Roman Catholic Grammar School to see Mr. Bracewell, English teacher and head of Upper Sixth. Bracewell was the sort of teacher who doesn't exist anymore. He had leather patches on the elbows of his tweed jacket, he smoked a pipe, he voted Conservative. He also had that understated brand of sarcasm which takes at least thirty years to perfect. Never was it more evident than today when he opened his one-off "surgery" to dispense advice to pupils whose only choice of career was "Dunno, sir".

"Come" he drawled in response to Frank's tentative tap on the door.

"Ah, Dempsey", he said through an expression that was neither smile nor frown. " A D, an E and an O".

Bracewell's expression said it all. Neither smile nor frown. – these grades weren't really worthy of either. Frank sat down for a perfunctory trawl through all those dull career options for which they both knew he would be completely unsuitable. Having got those out of the way, Bracewell leaned back in his chair and made a ridiculous one-word suggestion:

""Oxford".

"Oxford Poly?"

"No, Dempsey, Oxford University"

Frank went to speak but no words came out. He tried again. Nothing.

Bracewell was either smiling benignly or sneering cruelly, Frank couldn't work out which. The world had turned temporarily surreal.

"Well, Dempsey, you – lost for words. This is a sight I'd have made good money to see".

"But, well, sir......er.....Oxford.....you know.....Peter Staunton" was the best Frank could manage.

Peter Staunton was the class swot. Top every year, he gave the impression of having emerged from his mother's womb spotty and bespectacled, already reciting the formula for solving quadratic equations.

"Yes, Dempsey you're quite right, Staunton has achieved three A's and is going up to Balliol to read Physics. He is a brilliant scholar who has earned his place on merit"

He paused, almost conspiratorially, and lowered his voice

"But there are other ways". he winked, of getting in".

Frank was confused. There were only two "ways of getting in" which sprang to mind. A sports scholarship. Like most of his mates, Frank had turned his back on any form of competitive sport at the age of fourteen when he discovered cigarettes, alcohol and the girls from St.Angela's Convent across the road.. The other way was a music scholarship but unless you counted being able to play "Land of Hope And Glory" or "We Hate Nottingham Forest", as it was better known, n the paper and comb, the doors to the world's most prestigious university seemed Banham-locked and bolted.

Bracewell enlightened him "At all colleges, Dempsey, there are certain – how can I put it – not so popular subjects – which can sometimes be under-subscribed. Those departments are naturally very keen to keep themselves going and can therefore be rather more lenient with their entry requirements".

"But even so, sir, a D, an E and an O"

Bracewell arched an eyebrow, "Well you never know."

He paused.

"Though I have to say the only subject unpopular enough to accept you, Dempsey would be....."

He paused again.

"Theology"

Theology?? That was it. Frank was certain now – Bracewell was having a laugh, wreaking a slow, satisfying revenge for that incident all those years ago with the blackboard duster. Even now, Frank was having to suppress a smirk as it flashed back into his mind. The way he had removed the tiny red heads of those Swan Vesta matches – the ones that strike on anything – and carefully inserted them inside the folds of the duster. When Bracewell then went to wipe the blackboard clean, he nearly set the school on fire.

But surely, he'd paid his debt to society for that one. Six swift strokes of the cane, delivered with pitiless ferocity across the seat of his pants.. So much worse than across the palm of your hand. With a cane across the hand, your hand was numbed after the first three. You could take another twenty without any further pain. What's more, you could always run your hand under one of the cold taps in the boys' loos.. Try doing that with your backside.

One question was gnawing away at the back of Frank's mind. Why would Bracewell want to help him into Oxford? This was the man who had written on his report "Not content with wasting his own time, he comes to school and wastes everyone else's". However, just in case the old goat was serious, Frank decided to play along.

"But theology, sir? I don't know the first thing about it".

"Nobody does, Dempsey, nobody does. Not even, I suspect, those who teach it. From what I understand, much of it involves eternal questions about life and death. You know – what's it all about? Why are we here? That sort of thing. You can't really get it wrong . Just so long as you can assemble a fairly cogent argument to substantiate your theories. Something, if I remember rightly, Dempsey, you've displayed quite a talent for"

"Me, sir?"

"Yes, you, sir. Last year when we were studying Waiting For Godot, I remember you suggesting that Estragon and Vladimir were Beckett's personification of fish and chips".

"And I remember you, sir, dismissing that theory as utter rubbish".

"Utter rubbish for a student of English Literature, Dempsey, but for a student of theology.........quite brilliant".

Now he really was having a laugh.

Bracewell continued, "Now it just so happens that Professor Gerald Crosby is a very old friend of mine. He runs the Theology department at Christ Church. If you like, I could give him a call this afternoon and arrange for you to go up and see him.".

By now, Frank was beginning to suspect that "Professor Crosby" would turn out to be Peter Dulay, long-time host of "Candid Camera". There would be a secret camera hidden in "The Professor's" study and their meeting would be filmed. Then, when the whole nation had finished laughing at Frank Dempsey's lame attempt to get into Oxford, Bracewell would appear on screen, wagging his finger in a stern warning for Britain's recalcitrant schoolboys:

"So, think very carefully before you insert Swan Vestas into your teacher's blackboard duster".

Blinking back into reality, he realised that Bracewell's expression, accentuated by the half-moon spectacles perched on the bridge of his nose, was deadly serious.

"Er......well......um...yes.....if you...er....wouldn't mind, sir, that'd be....er.....great like".

Bracewell gave a tight smile, "Good because I've already spoken to him and he's expecting your call,"

"Did you tell him about my grades, sir/"

"Yes, a D, an E and an O. Deo. He thought that was rather amusing".

Bracewell chuckled and Frank shared the joke.

"Yes, sir. , The Banana Boat Song – Harry Belafonte".

Bracewell's chuckle receded, replaced by a quizzical expression.

"No, no I was thinking of the Latin, Dempsey, the Latin"

It was Frank's turn to look quizzical

"Deo", he explained, "With God".

IV

It was a bit of a worry. Frank was making a serious application to Oxford University and he'd never read a book in his life. Ever. His A level in English Literature had been acquired without ever reading any of the books on the syllabus.

He'd simply invested in a copy of Brodie's Notes for each one and familiarised himself with the plot and the main characters. He would then skim through copies of Brodie's Notes on other books, for example, by Shakespeare or Hardy and then compare them.

"Hamlet", he'd write, "*unlike Macbeth*" or maybe "Tess of the d'Urbevilles, *unlike Jude the Obscure*" to give the impression he'd broadened his reading to encompass the author's other great works when, in reality, he hadn't read any of them

But reading – that's what people did at university. Those bearded contestants on University Challenge were always *reading* history or *reading* engineering. Wasn't it time he started reading something?

As he stood perusing the Literature section of the Kilburn Bookshop, one particular volume caught his eye – Animal Farm by George Orwell. This book had two things going for it. One, it was a famous piece of English literature. Two, it was very thin – little more than a leaflet.. Excellent. At least, if he didn't understand it, it wouldn't take him very long to not understand it.

However, he did understand it. And he enjoyed it. Right, that was the reading cracked, now on to the clothes.

In 1977, most London boys between the ages of fifteen and

twenty could be roughly divided into three categories:. The Teds, the Punks and the Erics. Despite his huge collection of fifties rock 'n' roll, despite his burning desire to drive a '57 Chevy or at least a PA Cresta to the Chelsea Bridge Cruise, Frank couldn't be bothered to be a Ted. It was too much like hard work. Having to schlep out to Harrow to have your drape suits made by Jack Geach. And all those hours in front of the mirror with Brylcreem and comb getting the DA and quiff just right. Oh, forget it. Anyway, Brylcreem always seemed to encourage acne and he'd only end up looking like his mate Vince Caruana, the teddy-boy son of a Maltese pimp (a devout Catholic pimp, mind you) who had the complexion of a cheese and ham pizza.

Looking vaguely punk was a lot easier. The Oxfam shop seemed to have a limitless line of old narrow-lapelled suits. A spiky haircut and a smattering of safety pins and you could pass for the bass guitarist of any one of a hundred new wave bands.

"Erics", were soulboys They who took their name from Tall Eric a vicious but sartorially sharp Chelsea hooligan. Eschewing the number one crop and steel toecaps, Eric preferred pleated trousers known as pegs, pointed shoes and mohair sweaters

Frank could make the journey to Oxford as a punk or as an Eric but unfortunately not as a happy, clappy Christian. What he really needed was to borrow the contents of Peter Staunton's wardrobe. Failing that, he'd have to suffer the indignity of buying some Staunton-esque clothes for himself.

But where? Kilburn High Road was out of the question – he was bound to meet someone he knew. Oxford Street? Absolutely not. Along the busiest shopping street in the world, he was more likely to bump into someone there than anywhere else in the world.

The trip to Christ Church was a secret known only to

Frank, Mr. Bracewell and Professor Crosby, who had surprisingly turned out to be a real person.

Frank hadn't told his friends and he hadn't told his family. He felt he stood less chance of getting into Oxford than he did of getting into Mandy Wheeler, the most gorgeous girl in North West London. And since the entry requirements for Mandy Wheeler included a brick-thick wad of cash and a set of car keys, Frank's chances were slim, if not anorexic.

What would his mates say? Theology at Oxford? Are you queer, Dempsey, or what? What's wrong with working on the sites, becoming a QS, meeting a nice girl at a St.Patrick's Night dance and settling in a semi in Sudbury?

His parents would probably find it even harder to understand. Their reaction, even if he got in, would probably be a little pinch of pride and a big dollop of dismay. With some justification, they regarded their son as a rather idle student who had "messed around at school" for long enough They would now expect him to find a job. And since he had A levels, a job where he wore a suit. At eighteen, it was now his filial duty to weigh in with some housekeeping money.

So it was in secret that he boarded the number 36 bus, hopping off at the corner of Westbourne Grove and Queensway. After a quick double-check to make sure nobody was watching, he darted in to Whiteley's of Queensway., a gargantuan old-fashioned department store in a most incongruous setting. It was the size of Selfridge's., only without the customers.

Stepping inside was like stepping into a time-warp, into a scene from "Are You Being Served". By the late seventies it was on its last legs, surely costing more to run for a week than it could possibly take in a year. He certainly wouldn't meet anyone he knew in Whiteley's. It would be a miracle if he met anyone at all.

As he passed the perfumery, he cast a furtive glance at the heavily made-up assistants behind the counter. His mother had once whispered that underneath the four inches of pan-stick, they were hookers. Happy to work there for nothing because of the lucrative contacts they could make with wealthy Arab clients.

Frank had always thought this was a ridiculous story, but probably no more ridiculous than Jesus throwing a dinner party for five thousand with just five loaves and three fishes.

He made his way through to the menswear department. It was practically deserted. Perfect. And the shelves and racks were filled with exactly the kind of apparel that he was looking for. He found a white shirt and a vomit-inducing brown knitted tie to be worn beneath a green lambswool V-neck sweater, lovat slacks and a pair of those Clarks Polyveldt shoes, the ones that looked like Cornish pasties. Even he thought that open-toed sandals would be taking this ghastly charade a little too far.

As the crusty old assistant, tape measure around his neck, folded the goods and placed them in a Whiteley's of Queensway carrier bags, Frank was wondering, since the interview was a secret, where on earth he was going to hide them? While most of his mates were worrying about where to hide their secret supplies of fags, dope and porno mags, here he was panicking about where to hide a lambswool sweater and a pair of crimplene slacks. He had an idea. The train to Oxford went from Paddington Station, which was only a few minutes' walk from Whiteley's.

"Um.......I was wondering", he asked the assistant, "Could you keep these for me? I'll pay for them now but can you keep them until next Wednesday? I'll come back and pick them up then. It's a long story".

The following Wednesday, Frank returned and fortunately, the same assistant, tape measure around his neck, was on duty. He remembered Frank possibly because he hadn't had another customer to serve since Frank's last visit. Frank took his purchases, returned to the changing room and put them on. He then put his Ramones T-shirt, ripped Wranglers and black suede creepers in the Whiteley's carrier bags and went back out to the assistant.

"Um....sorry to be a pain but would you mind keeping these for me. I'm going for an interview and I'll be back later on today. What time do you close?"

"Five-thirty, sir".

"Fine. I'll...er......see you later then, thanks"

He left the store and, as he strode up towards Paddington station, he couldn't help but concede how comfortable those slacks and Polyveldt shoes were. By the time he got there, he was totally in character, having even paused to buy a copy of the Catholic Herald to read on the train. As he crossed the station concourse, however, he heard a sound that made his blood run cold.

"Frank?"

The upward inflection suggested that the owner of this teasingly sexy voice couldn't believe what she was seeing.

"Oh my God", he thought, "It's Mandy Wheeler, the most gorgeous girl in North-West London. Never mind, I'll just ignore her and pretend I'm not me and......"

"Frank?". She was touching his arm now. He had no choice but to turn and face his tormentor. Mandy Wheeler. the zenith of his desires, the girl in front of whom he had always tried to cultivate an air of nihilistic chic,. Now she's finally engaged him in conversation and he's dressed like a paedophile..

"Oh......er......Mandy, hi......er......didn't recognise you there......er"

"Well, I almost didn't recognise you", she giggled, taking a little piece of the green lambswool sweater between her thumb and forefinger, "What's with the clobber?"

"Er....fancy dress party......part....part......."

Hang on, something was coming through on the wire, could be a plausible excuse

"......part....part....I'm actually auditioning for a part in a West End play. Only a small part.....er.........a Christian youth club leader".

Very good, well done and look, Mandy's expression seemed to be turning into one of genuine admiration.

"I didn't know you were an actor"

"Well, I'm not. I just....you know....thought it was something I might like to try....and.....well, you've heard of method acting. I thought that wearing these clothes might help so that by the time I get there, I'll be....you know.....in character and I'll stand a much better chance".

She wasn't giggling now but Frank couldn't now be sure whether that expression was one of admiration or pity.

"Anyway, better go" he spluttered,. I'm late already".

"All that time spent preparing, I suppose".

"Yeah,. Yeah, exactly.".

"Well let me know how you get on".

Admiration. Definitely admiration.

"What? How?"

"Ring me".

With a coy but knowing smile, Mandy pulled a pen from her bag and scribbled her number on Frank's newspaper. As she finished, she noticed that it was the Catholic Herald and she looked at him again. Pity. Definitely pity.

V

As the train wobbled into Oxford, Frank realised that the lie, which had elicited Mandy Wheeler's phone number, wasn't too far from the truth. He, Frank, irreligious Punk/Eric hybrid from Kilburn was about to audition for the part of Francis, earnest young Christ Church theology student.

This was how he'd got through his driving test. Mr. Lynch from the Brondesbury School of Motoring had told him to treat it as an acting audition. Prove to the examiner that you can act in a certain way for about twenty minutes, remembering your actions and remembering your lines and he'll grant you licence to then act however you like.

Today's audition was a little more tricky. At least with the driving test, he knew exactly what he was supposed to do. Today, however, he was about to undergo that most difficult of appraisals – the "informal chat".. No real rights, no real wrongs, no real way of determining success from failure.

Frank had never ever been to Oxford but imagined it to be full of scarf-wearing nerds on bicycles.

It seemed very different today, very quiet. Early September, term not yet begun, the whole city an almost empty playground for American tourists, carrying in front of them the twin protuberances of huge stomachs and zoom lenses. Not a nerd in sight. Except for one, of course, strolling down St.Aldates in his lambswool sweeter and Polyveldt shoes.

Christ Church is easily the most impressive and imposing of all Oxford Colleges. Architecturally stunning, it was founded in 1525 by Cardinal Wolsey who fell from grace before it was completed. It was re-founded in 1546 by Henry VIII and many of its magnificent buildings date back to then. Frank arrived at the gates, told an officious looking porter that he had an appointment with Professor Crosby and was directed across Tom Quad to the Professor's study.

As Frank, he would have found this hugely intimidating but as Francis, he took it all in his crimplene -slacked stride and gave a polite knock on the Professor's door.

Professor Crosby was as thin as his luxuriant shock of snow-white hair was thick. Surely well past retirement age, he looked very frail, except for his sharp darting blue eyes which were ablaze with curiosity.

"You must be Francis Dempsey" he said with an ice-breaking smile, "John Bracewell has told me a lot about you".

"Shall I leave now then?" asked Frank, breaking it still further,

"Good heavens, no", he chuckled, "It is extremely rare for old Braces to recommend one of his students to me. He must think a great deal of you".

"Well, he's got a funny way of showing it", said Frank with a smile. The ice now liquid, the pleasantries complete, Professor Crosby turned to the matter in hand.

"So, Francis Dempsey, tell me about Francis Dempsey".

It was an old interviewing technique. If a candidate couldn't interest you with a little light chat about himself, he was hardly going to keep you riveted with a twenty-page discourse on the Later Philosophy of Wittgenstein.

Frank talked about Kilburn, Catholicism and about his great passion for popular music. How he preferred singles to albums (for Professor Crosby's benefit, he called them LP's), how he loved the way so much history, geography and philosophy could be distilled into three minutes. How music had the power to move him, to evoke memories: sights, sounds and smells. The Professor, whose musical knowledge didn't really extend beyond the classical cloisters of Radio 3, found this fascinating. He moved on

"So what brings you here? Why would you want to spend three years studying theology at Christ Church?"

Frank could have been brutally honest – "Well, professor, my A Level grades are about as much use as an ashtray on a motorbike. I have no prospects and bugger all else to do" but he spoke instead of his fascination with the power of religion and his failure thus far to comprehend it.. How he'd had stood so many times in that church in Quex Road, completely nonplussed. How all these people – people he knew, liked and respected – all seemed to possess this certainty of faith that somehow eluded him

"So you think that these hundreds of devout Catholics in your parish are all party to some divine truth, all part of some exalted club, the door of which is closed to you?" asked the professor.

"Well, I don't think the door is closed", replied Frank, "it's actually wide open. I just don't feel that I've got sufficient belief to....to.....

"Cross the threshold?" suggested the Professor, "But you think everyone else in that church has"

"Well, I'm not sure. I don't see how they can have. A moment's thought can throw up all sorts of doubts. I sometimes think they're just scared of not getting into Heaven. That perhaps these "good Catholics" who seem so holy and virtuous are simply looking after number one. You can almost see them clutching imaginary Green Shield Stamp books in their hands. Every time they go to mass, they collect another stamp so that sooner or later, they'll have enough to get them into Heaven"

"So you often think", said the Professor, immediately identifying Frank's suspicions, "that despite their apparent altruism, it's really just their own souls they're seeking to save"..

"Exactly", said Frank and Professor nodded sagely. Old Braces had been right. Francis was an unusual and interesting boy, out of whom great potential could be drawn. He gently led Frank to another tack, just to see what his answers would be.

"But again, why theology? Why not more mainstream subjects as History or English which some might argue would be more use to you?"

They both knew the answer to this. History and English were extremely popular subjects. The country's finest triple A students would be competing for places and Frank would stand about as much chance as a one-legged man in an arse-kicking contest.. The opportunity, however, to live and loaf rent-free for three years in such magnificent surroundings, was a very powerful incentive and now Frank was on a roll.

"Well, oddly enough, I think that Theology combines the best aspects of History and English".

"Really?", the Professor intoned, "Go on".

Making it up on the spot, in a way he didn't know he could, Frank took a deep breath,

"Well, much of Theology is history. The History of Christianity and other religions and the momentous effect they have had on the way we live our lives".

"Quite so", said the Professor, "but Theology including aspects of English literature? I'm afraid you've lost me there".

"Well, over the years, I've begun to suspect that many of the stories in the bible were simply made up. Adam and Eve, for instance, just a convenient and picturesque way to explain the creation of the world. with about as much basis in fact as, say, Lady Chatterley's Lover"

"So you and Darwin are agreed on that one".

" I suppose so. The thing about the bible, though, is that it's had a far greater impact than anything by Shakespeare or Chaucer, so I would regard studying it as lot more important".

Professor Crosby had to admire Frank's interesting, if rather superficial grasp of theological precepts. He nodded again.

"So do you, for instance, believe in life after death?"

"I don't know", replied Frank quite truthfully, " How can anyone? There's only one way to find out and that's to kill yourself".

The professor laughed, "And you're not prepared to do that in the name of theological research. Mind you, three years studying theology might be considered by some as a fate worse than death".

Frank laughed and the professor continued

"Some students come here with fundamental questions and they expect the study of Theology to provide the answers. Unfortunately, although they might discover one or two answers, they usually end up with a lot more questions. Can you cope with that?"

Frank nodded, "I'm not looking for answers, I'm just looking for......." The words "a good excuse to piss about for three years" were on the tip of his tongue but he managed to swallow them back down again "........stimulation – intellectual stimulation".

"Well, " smiled the Professor, "this is the right place and for that, Theology is an excellent subject. It's one of the University's best kept secrets".

So well kept, in fact, that if the Professor couldn't attract a few more students, it could find itself removed from the prospectus, replaced by something ghastly like Business Management or Computer Studies.

"I've been studying it now for more than fifty years and still find it endlessly fascinating and maddeningly inconclusive. Now, as for your application, well, I've thoroughly enjoyed our discussion and feel that theoretically, at least, you could be an excellent student. However, this alone is not enough. At Christ Church, we require proof of achievement as well as potential and you're A level results are....well.... not really up to scratch, are they? In fact, they're well below those of any other student here ".

To his surprise, Frank felt an enormous disappointment. My God, wasn't that the beginning of a lump in his throat and a hot, prickly sensation behind the eyes? All right, so his coming up to Oxford was always a bit of a joke. He'd come in fancy dress. for God's sake, with absolutely no expectation of being granted a place to study here The very notion was absurd.

And yet......and yet.....He'd really enjoyed his brief chat with the Professor. The wily and learned old man had encouraged him to form and articulate original thoughts and beliefs and hadn't ridiculed or dismissed any of them. For the first time. he realised that the feelings he'd first had as a small boy in Quex Road weren't necessarily blasphemous, wrong or invalid. He realised these elliptical views could have formed the basis of a happy and successful time at Oxford.

But Professor Crosby hadn't finished.

"Before I could seriously consider your application, I'd need you to demonstrate your ability to cope at a very high academic level"

His heart leapt. The lump in his throat started to soften and melt The game wasn't over. It was going to penalties.. The professor tottered over to his desk and handed Frank a small stack of theological text books..

"I want you to go away and learn to read"

Learn to read? What was he talking about?

The professor explained , "Everyone learns to read once in their life, at the age of five or six but the most fortunate people learn to read twice. For the more studious, it's a seamless progression as they graduate to more challenging and difficult books. Others can be shown as teenagers by a good

English teacher how to understand and appreciate fine literature. But a lot of people teach themselves to read again as adults, usually on holiday, where they have the time to acquire the necessary concentration. Now to appreciate these books, you'll need to learn to read very quickly. Don't try it at home – too many distractions, especially. I suspect for you with your compendious collection of gramophone records. The ideal environment is a long train journey. Have you ever been to the Lake District?"

Frank, shook his head which seemed to genuinely delight the professor.

"Oh, I do envy you", he said, the blue eyes shining brighter than ever, "Catching sight of Windermere or Ullswater for the very first time – a glorious image that will stay with you forever.. Now, I suggest you get the train up to Kendal and start reading, the journey takes at least four hours. Book into a cheap bed and breakfast and stay overnight. Read all evening if you have to, making notes as you go. And remember to read those notes just before you go to sleep. That way they'll still be fresh when you wake up. Carry on reading all the way back to London but when you get there, don't go home. Go straight to your local library, sit down and write those two essays and send them back to me. I'll need them one week from today. And one week after that, you'll be informed as to whether or not your application has been successful".

Frank nodded gratefully as Professor Crosby rose and showed him to the door. He placed an avuncular hand on Frank's shoulder and told him not to worry.

"If I thought this little task were beyond you, I wouldn't even bother lending you the books. Now, good luck, Francis, I do hope we'll be meeting again soon"..

As Frank made his way back to the station, he was very thankful for the simple route he was being offered into Christ Church. At the same time, however, he was more than a little daunted by the prospect of having to write an essay on the Development of Early Christian Doctrine to 451 AD..

Returning to London, Frank made it into Whiteley's just before the 5.30 deadline. He retrieved his old clothes, changed back into them, changing back from Francis to Frank as he did so. He then donated his outfit, appropriately enough, to the Christian Aid shop. All except the green lambswool sweater. His father would be unwrapping that on Christmas morning.

VI

Frank never made it as far as the Lake District. For a number of reasons. Firstly, they'd be too much explaining to do. He was eighteen, his parents didn't mind where he went or what time he came home but if he didn't come home at all, they'd want to know why. Not in a strict or forbidding way, just out of concern and curiosity. And since his application to Oxford was currently sitting at Number One in his Top Ten of Deepest, Darkest secrets, parental curiosity was the one thing he didn't want to arouse.

What's more, if Windermere and Ullswater were as beautiful as Professor Crosby said they were, he'd prefer to experience that heart-stopping splendour under different circumstances. With a gorgeous girl, for instance, instead of a bag full of dreary theological textbooks. That night, he felt sure, after an evening spent in a pub where all the locals had gone silent when he walked in, where he'd only had "Christian Life And Thought In Europe 1789–1914" for company, he would have gone straight back to his horrible little B&B and hung himself.

So he spent the day roaming around the country on British Rail's rolling stock, passing through places like Coventry, Kidderminster, Leicester and Crewe. Places he had no desire to visit, places where he wouldn't be tempted to get off.

He'd made his way from Kilburn High Road to Euston station and, with half an hour to kill before his train departed, he was driven half-mad by the temptations that lurked on the shelves of John Menzies: Melody Maker, Sounds, the NME, Record Mirror. The Sun, The Express, the

Daily Mail. Even titles like Jackie , Fab 208 and Good Housekeeping had never looked so appealing. However, to buy and read any one of them would be to close forever the back door to Oxford University, which had been left so tantalisingly ajar.

As the guard whistled the 9.32 to Manchester Piccadilly out of Euston, Frank played that peculiar game he always played on train journeys in the London area – namely the "Coo, doesn't it all look different" game. This involves passing through familiar places but, as you are passing them from an unfamiliar angle, you think to yourself "Coo, doesn't it all look different". Houses, streets, shops, schools, viewed from the back rather than the front, huge depots and vast expanses of track that you'd never realised were there, the back end of the big white Wrigley's Chewing Gum factory – coo, doesn't it all look different?

The train gathered speed as it swept through the suburbs of North West London and the names of the places began to take on a rhythm redolent of Betjeman.

"Camden and Kilburn, Willesden and Wembley, Hatch End and Harrow, Carpenders Park".

Then out beyond Watford into the green hinterlands of Hertfordshire. Place names that were vaguely familiar – Garston, Kings Langley, Hemel Hempstead, Leighton Buzzard. Places were some Londoners moved to get more for their money, never to be seen again.

But enough of this idle daydreaming. There were books to be read, essays to be written and the time to start was now. He opened the first book – Chapter One.....

"Kant in the Prolegomena began by asking himself the question: How, in the light of Hume's scepticism is metaphysics possible?"

Fuck me! That was the first line. And it didn't get any easier.

"Dualism is of course a somewhat discredited and unfashionable philosophy today. More satisfying intellectually, however, are the various forms of Monism".

Frank sank deeply into his seat. He felt so inadequate, his clothes suddenly felt about five sizes too big What was he going to do? How would he ever digest and understand such difficult and impenetrable prose. If he'd bought those copies of Fab 208 and Good Housekeeping, he'd have given up there and then,

However, an imaginary Jiminy Cricket type figure suddenly hopped on to his shoulder and barked out a shrill admonishment into his ear.

"Come on, what's the matter with you? It can't be that difficult, you can do it. Professor Crosby thinks you can. Think of Oxford, the dreaming spires, loafing around there for a few years, all those girls. Come on, start again. I want you to have a handle on this one before we get to Birmingham."

With Jiminy's help, Frank slowly began to take it all in. It was a bit like talking to Tom Sheehan's dad. Sheehan Senior was a Kerryman with the broadest, most unintelligible Irish accent you were ever likely to hear. For years, Frank couldn't understand a single word he said, just nodding or shaking his head at what he guessed were appropriate junctures. Then one day, something clicked. The scales, if you like, just fell from his ears. They were suddenly attuned to all the foibles and vagaries of the Kerry native dialect. Suddenly, it was all very clear – perfect English just spoken with a very lyrical lilt.

And so it was with this weighty theological tome. Suddenly, just beyond Coventry, Frank could hear what the author was trying to say. His underlying contention was that religion was wholly necessary to bring man's fundamental goodness to the fore.. Man needed blind faith. He needed belief, however scientifically unsteady, in something other than proven fact. He needed to feel that his goodness would one day be rewarded or, more to the point, his badness would one day be punished.

In other words, all goodness is subtly underwritten by selfishness. Frank's feelings exactly.

On the return journey south, he was ready to tackle the Old Testament, silently comparing its writers to contemporary tabloid hacks. Goliath being "nine feet and nine inches tall" simply wasn't true. And as for Samson deriving superhuman strength from the length of his locks, enough strength to push down the two supporting pillars of a huge temple – well, if that appeared on the front page of The Sun, the Press Complaints Authority would come down on them like a ton of bricks. Or perhaps like the several hundred tons of bricks from which the temple had been built in the first place..

And yet, whole religions, involving millions of people had their roots in this rubbish. Frank's essay on the Old Testament would question the morality and ethics of this.

Further volumes were absorbed the following day between Paddington and Penzance. And yet more between Penzance and Paddington.

The next morning was spent at Kilburn Library. Frank only had a limited time to transport what he had read from his brain down though his right arm to his Papermate ball point before it was erased forever. He'd have to scribble it all down while it was still fresh and scribblable. He didn't want his brain cluttered up with questions of moral philosophy. He needed all his spare brain capacity for other, far important questions.

Who had a number one hit in 1966 with "Out Of Time"?

Who won the FA Cup in 1954?.

Who's the black private dick who's a sex machine to all the chicks?

These were the sort of items that took up the room in Frank's head. There was no space for theological theories and arguments. And yet some of things he wrote that morning had been floating around the outskirts – the Garstons and Hemel Hempsteads – of his mind for years. Acknowledging them and writing them down had formed them into fully-fledged thoughts. They had been promoted and moved to a cerebral Soho where they were destined to reside forever.

VII

They're the words every parent dreads.

"Mum, Dad – I've got something to tell you."

When Frank, uncharacteristically solemn, uttered these words, Eamonn and Mary feared the worst.

"I'm gay..... I've got my girlfriend pregnant..... I've smashed up the car.......I'm joining the Moonies..... I'm joining a Loyalist Paramilitary group."

So the words "I'm going to University" came as a something of a relief.

"Er....that's grand, son. Which one?", said Eamonn sipping his tea,.

The word "Oxford" made him splutter it back out again.

"Oxford? Do you not have to be clever to go there?".

"Obviously not" said Frank, a little wounded

"No, no" came the ameliorating lilt of his mother, "Your father didn't mean it like that. But do you not have to have, like, three grade A's from your A-levels".

"Well, obviously not" he said with a light smile that belied a cauldron of passionate pride..

His parents were dumbstruck, cups of tea frozen half-way to their lips. They just stared the stare of silent incredulity

"Well, since you ask", .said Frank, breaking the silence, "I'll be reading theology".

"Theology?", said Mary, inhaling air as she spoke, in that way that only Irish women do, "Eamonn, it's a miracle".

"It certainly is, Mary, it certainly is".

They were now looking at their son as though he were Our Lady appearing at Lourdes.

"God moves in mysterious ways" said Mary with a smile.

"God? God?" thought Frank "for the first time in my life I achieve something truly impressive with no real help from anyone and Our Bloody Lord gets the credit for it".

The astonishment of Frank's family, however, couldn't compare with his own. His parents hadn't been up to Christ Church and felt the intimidating weight of intellectual brilliance. They hadn't witnessed the majesty of Tom Quad, the towering splendour of Christ Church Cathedral or that magnificent 18th Century library. He had never thought for a moment that his application would be successful.

When he'd posted it off, he felt much as he did every Wednesday, when he posted his father's pools coupons. The chances of either Eamonn becoming a millionaire or his son becoming an Oxford undergraduate were so slim that Frank, once he'd left the letterbox, had given no further thought to either.

The fact that Eamonn had never won the pools, had never earned a great deal of money and was a very long way from being a millionaire now worked in Frank's favour. This was 1977 – there were no student loans, just generous grants. Extremely generous if your family's income happened to be as low as the Dempseys'.

So, if Frank's parents believed it was all down to divine intervention, his mates were rather more prosaic.

"Oxford? You jammy bastard. God, what I wouldn't give to go there?"

Paul Frost was delivering his verdict from underneath a Mark II Cortina.

"Frostie" and Frank had been friends from the age of five and the former had now been working for two years as a mechanic. He may have left school without so much as a CSE but he was as sensitive to the moving parts of a car as a neurosurgeon is to the moving parts of the brain and now he spent every spare moment customising cars.

According to Frostie, Oxford was the easy option. " A degree from there, mate and the world's your fucking lobster. Me? All right, so I love motors an' that but I'm looking at, what, fifty years' hard graft. And how many millionaire mechanics do you know?"

How many millionaire theologians do you know? thought Frank but said nothing, basking instead in the warmth of his friend's enthusiasm.

"Anyway", he asked, "How's the van coming on?"

Frostie had recently acquired a bright yellow Ford Escort Van into which he was going to drop a Lotus engine, a Jag rear end and all manner of other accessories.

"I'm going to flog it"

"You what? You've only had it a fortnight"

"Yeah, well. Bloke I know wants to sell his old Ford Pop, 1951, sit up and beg. Now that's what you call a project. Put a V6 lump in that, 18 inch Wolfies on the back, Recaro seats, Mountney wheel – it'll be the bollocks, the absolute bollocks. I'm going to spray it metalflake red. I gave four hundred for the van, should be able to get six for it. It's as clean as a whistle."

Indeed it was as "clean as a whistle" and when Frank saw it, he saw the ideal mode of transport for anyone making frequent trips between Kilburn and Oxford with his records, books, bass bins and bicycle.

The ensuing transaction could only be described as "Catholic Haggling", for it could only practised by people brought up with a healthy disregard for all things financial. People brought up to give their pocket money to Cafod or the Crusade of Rescue, people who would feel guilty about profiteering. How many ruthless Catholic tycoons do you hear of? How often does the word "Catholic" crop up in the same breath as "business acumen"?

Frank offered Frostie six hundred the van. Frostie refused, insisting he would only accept four, since that how much he'd paid for it. It was worth more, said Frank, how about five. Frostie was adamant – not a penny more than four hundred. Four fifty, said Frank and that was his final offer. He wouldn't consider paying a penny less.. Frostie finally agreed to four twenty- five because "Three years on a student grant, Dempsey, you're going to need every fucking cent".

VIII

"I've got a motor now" thought Frank " I qualify" and so he dialled Mandy Wheeler's number.

"Mandy?"

"Yeah?"/

"Hi, it's Frank – Frank Dempsey"

"Oh, hiya Frankie".

"I just wanted you to know, I passed that audition. I got the part and....well.....I wondered if you fancied coming out to celebrate".

"Yeah, great", she gushed, "Any night you like"

Frank almost passed out but managed to recover enough of his senses to make an arrangement for eight o'clock the following Thursday. By five-thirty that evening, he was already in the bath. Naked this time, without the Levi's 501's that he had pre-shrunk for just such an occasion.

Of course, they weren't known as 501's then. This was ten years before a hugely successful advertising campaign would make them fashionable, desirable and ubiquitous. They were then simply known as Red Tags. There were three types of Levi's – White Tags, Orange Tags and Red Tags. The White tags were the cheap ones, the naff ones, the not much better than British Home Stores ones. Orange tags were the normal ones, the standard Levi's, but Red Tags? Connoisseurs and fashion victims only. Very few places sold them because very few people bought them. They did not come soft and ready to wear like other jeans. They were stiff, hard and unforgiving and, as the proud owner of a new pair, (one size too big, of course), Frank had put them on and baptised them in a bath full of warm water.

Nothing could have prepared him for the flood of deep indigo dye that was immediately released into the water. Within a minute he seemed to be sitting in a tub full of navy blue Quink and the longer he sat there, the worse it got. But he had to sit and wait until the button-flied Levi's felt sufficiently shrunk and softened.

When they finally did, he'd stood up in the bath rather too quickly, slipped down again and sent a Hawaii Five –O style tidal wave of inky blue water all over the tiny bathroom.

Was it worth it? Did anyone notice that the little tag on the back pocket was red and not orange? Well, that's not the point, is it?

Now for the hair. Walk into any bar in Manchester, Melbourne or Massachusetts and how would you identify the Irish patrons? The hair. The Irish hair. Thick, coarse and uncontrollable (the hair, that is), it will immediately confirm the person beneath it to be a true son of Erin.

Nowadays, you often hear the phrase "bad hair day". Well, these people have a bad hair life and, with his frizzy dark thatch, Frank was a classic example. From an early age, he'd wanted long hair like Rick Wakeman or Robert Plant but any attempt to grow it soon had him looking like one of the Jackson Five. He was all right for a while in the mid-seventies when Kevin Keegan perms were all the rage but since the advent of punk that was no longer the case. His only option now was to keep it short. Sometimes, Nick the Greek on Kilburn High Road would get a little too keen with the clippers and Frank would emerge looking like he'd just had a brain scan and was waiting for the results of the tests

When Nick's assistant, Theo had once enquired whether Frank would like "something for the weekend", Frank bought a tube of KY jelly, thinking it was hair gel. And although he now knew how to put it to better use, he still found its clear, odourless consistency far more effective than either his father's Brylcreem or his sister's Shockwaves by Wella.

Just the after shave to go then After shave? Before Shave would be more appropriate. About Two Years Before Shave since, for most adolescent boys, the discovery of Brut 33 always pre-dates the discovery of the Gillette disposable razor by at least that long. Today it was a toss-up between Blue Stratos and new West by Faberge. Having taken a good sniff of each, Frank went for the West on account of its funky brown bottle and big square cork lid.

Finally, he was ready to go. Crisp white T-shirt, Shrink to fit Levi Red Tags, new Dr.Marten's boots – black eight hole, yellow stitching , nicely worn in biker's jacket from Lewis Leathers in Great Portland Street, good splash of Faberge West, all topped off with a dab of KY jelly, belying the old assumption that girls spend more time getting ready than boys.

Frank climbed into the yellow Escort van for its maiden voyage to Neasden to pick up North-West London's most gorgeous girl. The air-cushioned soles on his new Dr.Marten's felt particularly springy so when he bounced up the pathway of the neat terraced house in Warren Road, he felt like Tigger from Winnie the Pooh. He rang the doorbell and was greeted by a frowning bald man whose name just had to be Norman.

"Er.....hello", said Frank, "Is Mandy in?"

Norman, his frown firmly fixed, just grunted and Frank suddenly felt sorry for him. What a terrible thing it must be to be the father of North West London's most gorgeous girl. For years, his face must have been a permanent smile because his little girl was the prettiest in the class, the one whose sweet and captivating features shone out in every school photo. And then, his face must have clouded over – the smile supplanted by the frown – as that sweet little girl developed into North West London's most horny looking bitch with every bloke within a ten-mile radius desperate to give her one.

Poor old Norman.

At this moment, Mandy came sashaying down the stairs and the intoxicating smell of Charlie eclipsed Frank's Faberge West. Tight black mini-dress, long bare lightly tanned legs and cascading blonde locks. Oh God, the thought of her naked caused an immediate stirring inside Frank's Red Tags and had to be hastily replaced by the thought of Norman naked which was grisly enough to ensure that his sap shrank like a salted snail.

"Dad, this is Frank", said Mandy, her glossed lips parting in a big smile, "Frank, this is my Dad".

Frank held out his hand but again. Norman just grunted.

"Well...er.....see you later then", he tried again.

Another grunt.

As they drove off, Frank could almost read Norman's mind. – "Oh my God, this one's brought his own van".

They headed for the acme of local sophistication – a Chinese restaurant in Wembley with a silly name.

Despite trying hard to affect a relaxed and cocksure manner, Frank was even more nervous now than he had been in Professor Crosby's office. Shit, this was Mandy Wheeler – the most gorgeous girl in North West London – sitting opposite him. He knew that he was punching well above his weight. Mandy Wheeler was, aesthetically at least, way out of his league. He'd have to try to compensate somehow. How? Humour was always touted as the most successful way. What was that phrase? The one that sounded like an owl hooting? Oh yeah, – the wit to woo. Make sure you've got the wit to woo. If you can make a girl laugh, you're...well....laughing. You don't have to be gorgeous. Christ, look at Woody Allen.

The wit to woo, the wit to woo – as they sat down, Frank

nervously tried a little observational comedy. He looked at the name of the restaurant, there at the top of the menu.

"Why do so many Chinese restaurants have daft names?" he wondered out loud "The Happy Garden" "The Diamond Cottage" What's this one called? "New Golden World". Who thought that one up? " Yes...er...I think I've got it – New Golden World" Perfect – captures the very essence of Peking cuisine, don't you think?"

Mandy had never really thought about it and wasn't particularly interested. Frank's little routine had gone to waste. Instead of Woody Allen unfeasibly squiring a beautiful woman, he felt more like Norman Wisdom, pitifully rebuffed and singing "Don't Laugh At Me 'Cause I'm a Fool"

"So tell me about that part", said Mandy, thinking she was dating a soon to be famous film star.

"Well, I'm going to be playing the part of Francis, an Oxford theology student. I'll be doing it for three years. And I'll be doing it for real".

Mandy's beautiful, bluey-grey eyes stared blankly at him. Frank was going to have to spell it out.

"I was going for an interview at Oxford University so, to increase my chances I decided to dress like a geeky student. It worked. I start in October".

She was disappointed. He was not going to be a famous actor. His face would not be adorning the cover of the TV Times. She would not be able to tell her friends that she'd been out with him.

"So you're not an actor then?" she asked, her tone heavy with disappointment.

"Well, no", said Frank, "Mind you, after that performance, who knows? I could soon be doing Hamlet at the Old Vic".

Mandy clearly thought that "doing Hamlet" meant smoking a small cigar and that the Old Vic was a pub because not so much as a polite smile flickered across those luscious lips.

Fortunately, the food arrived and Frank asked for a fork.

"I could never get the hang of chopsticks", he smiled. "What's the point of them anyway? Look at this fork – isn't it far better suited to the job? I wonder if these people go out and dig their gardens with a pair of giant snooker cues?"

Mandy, however, thought chopsticks were "classy". The evening was not going well. It occurred to Frank that Mandy, being the most gorgeous girl in North West London had never had to develop a personality. Beautiful people were often like this – irritatingly passive, accustomed to letting everything come to them. Seldom were they amusing or riveting company. Or maybe Mandy had simply inherited Norman's sense of humour. People with no sense of humour aren't necessarily miserable, they're often very smiley, very jolly but they simply "don't get it".

Trying to establish a rapport, a little light raillery with someone who "doesn't get it" can be like trying to swim through porridge. Frank looked at his watch – eight thirty. Four hours later he looked at it again – eight thirty-five. He was beginning to regret asking for that fork. At least his attempts to use chopsticks may have leant some comedic value to the evening. Instead, it was as flat as the two cold pancakes that are always left after you've eaten all the crispy duck.

According to an old maxim, a truly witty person is one who inspires wit in others. Mandy Wheeler just inspired long, awkward silences in Frank. His many valiant attempts to open conversation seldom made it over the net. When they did, her returns rarely made it back.. By nine o'clock, the most gorgeous girl in North West London made become plain, and unattractive. By a quarter to ten, she'd grown a beard.

During the silent drive home, he didn't bother to slot in the Al Green/Teddy Pendergrass smoochy soul tape he'd spent hours making. He didn't even attempt to kiss her. Each promised to give the other a ring. Each knew they were lying. Each knew the other one was too. As he headed back to Kilburn, Frank couldn't believe that the date he'd dreamed about for years could have been such a monumental anti-climax. Norman needn't have worried..

"Fuck me", he muttered to himself over the strains of "Love TKO", "if I can't find Mandy Wheeler attractive, I might as well jack it all in now. I might as well become a priest".

What a ridiculous thought.

IX

Measured literally, it's just 55 miles from Kilburn to Oxford. Measured metaphorically, it's about a million.

Now this was more like it – exactly how Frank had imagined it. The coachloads of American tourists had been replaced by students. Students, students, students. Bicycles, bicycles, bicycles Yet, looking at the people riding them, Frank was surprised how few of them fulfilled his Staunton-esque expectations. Very few duffle coats, even fewer college scarves but more than a smattering of punks. Actually, this was no surprise at all. There had always been something very middle-class about punk – music with a message, music as a vehicle for social and political comment. The Clash releasing a triple-album dedicated to the Sandinistas. Even Mr. Lydon himself is said to have modelled "Johnny Rotten" on Richard III.

Punk wasn't as raw and hedonistic as it liked to think it was. It was not Boogie Nights, Baby Love or Be-Bop-a Lula.. Frank found just one quiff which belonged to a man in his forties who probably wasn't an undergraduate. Just come in from Cowley to do a bit of shopping. And, obviously not an Eric in sight.

Oxford's one and only Eric drove slowly down towards Christ Church wondering how previous freshers had felt on their very first day. Albert Einstein, for instance, WH Auden, Lewis Carroll or any one of thirteen British Prime Ministers.

One thing was certain – none of them would have arrived in a bright yellow Ford Escort van and not one of them would have been told by a stern bowler-hatted warden that he couldn't park here – round the back of Tom Quad – before having a sudden change of mind

"Oh, I'm sorry, sir– you must be the plumber. Park there then go in and ask for Professor Routh"

As the warden waved him in, Frank didn't know whether to feel relieved or insulted.

"Mr Dempsey" was shown to his accommodation – a classically proportioned set of rooms overlooking Christ Church meadow beyond which was a glorious unimpeded view of the Cherwell. The fresh air outside carried the heavenly scent of gillyflowers in through the open window. He was so happy, he almost started believing in God again.

However, just before the Almighty could re-capture another prisoner, there was a rat-tat-tat on the door. Without being invited , a tall student with an expression of permanent disdain on his long aristocratic features, wearing an ancient Harris tweed sports jacket, cravat, elephant cords and brogues, breezed in and presented his credentials.

"How do you do?" he smiled through a wreath of cigarette smoke, "I'm your next door neighbour – Charles Morgan. Big M, small organ".

"Frank Dempsey"..

"So what are you in for?", said Morgan, shaking Frank's hand firmly "Something clever? History? English? PPE?"

"Er.....theology", said Frank, a little sheepishly.

Morgan's face broke out into a huge grin, "Excellent!", he cried "Another dimbo. Me too. Isn't it the most wonderful scam?"

"Scam?"

"Theology" he chuckled, "They'll take anyone. Fucking desperate for students. Good job too. Any other subject and I wouldn't have had a prayer. Ha, ha, prayer! Do you like that?"

"Oh", said Frank, "very good".

"So what grades did you get?" said Morgan with alarming directness.

"D, E, O" said Frank.

"My God, you're a fucking genius. I got E, E, F and they still let me in. Mind you, the old man was here, so was my elder brother, awful swot, worked his arse off and got a First. Completely wasted his time here in my book. Anyway, promise me, you won't show me up. Just do the bare minimum, there's a good chap. Do you know many people here?"

"Just one. Bloke called Peter Staunton. He's doing physics at Balliol"

"What's he like?"

"Bit like your brother by the sounds of it"

"Oh God. And you don't know anyone else?

"Not a soul"

"Do you know, I rather envy you", said Charles, "Half my fucking school are here".

"Which school?", said Frank. He knew the answer.

"Slough Comprehensive", He just didn't know its nickname.

X

At Christ Church, you are told that students are welcomed from all backgrounds, all walks of life, inner-city state schools, anywhere.

What you're not told is how many. Or rather, how few. The number of "ordinary students" like Frank was minuscule. For the vast majority, it was simply an extension of Eton, Harrow or Winchester. – a place where the brighter pupils went to prepare to rule the world. Many gave the impression of merely dropping in at Christ Church on their way to take up seats in the House of Lords

Frank's room contained just his books, his GEC music centre, his records and his clothes. Charles Morgan and his ilk, however, had arrived with a variety of other accoutrements: Teacups, port glasses and decanters, shooting sticks, trilbies, and umbrella stands. Charles even had a pig's head on his mantelpiece.

Frank had never encountered their kind before – ex-public schoolboys who, seemed to be carrying almost illegal levels of self-confidence

Every fibre of Frank's being told him he should despise them and yet, oddly enough, he didn't.

He found them, for the most part, intelligent, charming and endearingly eccentric. They were here at Oxford principally for a laugh. Drinks parties, tea parties, getting "seriously pissed" in The Bear, The Kings Arms or The Turf, staging mixed doubles wheelbarrow races down The Cornmarket – rowing, playing rugger, beagling with the Christ Church pack – all ranked far higher than actually doing any work.

Self-doubt was an alien concept to them so they were neither pushy nor ambitious. Well, what did they have to prove? What's more, despite their often very high spirits, they were never looking for a fight.

For the first time in his life, Frank wasn't surrounded by blokes, full of beer-bellied belligerence, starting trouble, for any number of reasons, the most popular of which was "What you fuckin' looking at?".

The relief of not having to contend with this every Saturday night, not having to constantly watch his public bar behaviour or risk getting a glass in his face was more of a relief than he could ever have imagined.

The Old Etonians' general attitudes, if not their specific activities, were identical to his own, so at Christ Church, Frank found himself surprisingly at home. Even if the words "At Home", when he first saw them in raised italics on a drinks party invitation, were something of a mystery to him.

The mantelpiece in Frank's room was never without at least three such invitations or "stiffies" as they were commonly known, probably because their recipient never once tried to emulate the people with whom he now associated. Nobody liked the pushy, middle-class parvenus from places like Godalming and Harrogate, desperately trying to be something they weren't. These college hacks, these social mountaineers, simply couldn't understand why Frank Dempsey was invited to all the smartest parties and they weren't.

And these parties were fantastic. Frank was used to a hundred people crammed into a council flat, all getting obnoxious on Strongbow or Party Seven where the highlight might be the chance to get lucky in the spare bedroom with some drunken slapper on a pile of coats. At Oxford, it was just a little more civilised – ball gowns and black tie. Frank loved the whole spectacle, even if, in his Oxfam dinner jacket, he looked like he should be on the door of the Hammersmith Palais.

He seldom left these parties alone because, apart from their mothers, their sisters and Matron, most of Frank's fellow freshers had barely ever seen a woman before. Let alone touched one. They were woefully inexperienced. This left him with a pretty clear field and it was one sort of popularity with the girls that ensured his gaining another sort of popularity with the boys. In London, of course, his prowess was nothing exceptional, but here they thought he was Warren Beatty.. For a budding Beatty, circumstances could hardly have been more ideal. It was 1977, post-pill and pre-Aids and in the first week – the "settling in" week- it was just party after party after party.

The week began with the Freshers' Fair where all the societies, clubs and special interest groups lay out their wares and try to press-gang callow newcomers into joining. There were hundreds. From the dull and straightforward like the Oxford University Conservative Association, to the rather more bizarre like the Association for People Afraid of Meringues.

Dead Poets, perennially popular, had a number of societies devoted to them. Best avoided, apparently, was The Algernon Swinburne Society whose members concerned themselves less with the great man's work and more with his predilection for having his bare bottom whipped after a good dousing in eau de cologne.

Though far worse was the Robert Lowell Society whose members really did concern themselves with the great man's work.

The only one Frank was even slightly tempted to join was SAFC or the Society For the Appreciation of Fabric Conditioner who met once a month in a launderette and compared the olfactory merits of Stergene, Comfort and Lenor.

Towards the end of his twenty-third party that week, Frank found himself slow-dancing in the Undercroft with a fresher from St. Hilda's called Anna.

"Have you ever noticed", he said opening up one of his tried and trusted "comedic observations", " that slow dances are always clockwise"

"I have, yeah". she replied, "but have you ever wondered whether, in the Southern Hemisphere, slow dances are anti-clockwise"

Whoa! That wasn't in the script. She was supposed to giggle girlishly and say "Aren't you funny?" or "Aren't you clever?" You wouldn't have got that sort of rapid riposte from Mandy Wheeler. Anna went further,

"Do you want to come back to my room for coffee?"

"Er....yeah", said Frank, "yeah, great", his hopes rapidly rising.

"But it's strictly coffee", she warned and his rapidly sank again.

"Well, yeah, of course".

Never mind, he thought, knowing he could hardly duck out now.

She invited him in, and had barely closed the door behind her before ripping off her clothes and his too. Frank, used to taking the lead in these situations, was rather taken aback.

"Er....I thought you said it was strictly coffee/" he managed to say, as she tugged at the buckle of his belt.

"Just testing", she giggled, "just testing to see if you'd still come".

Anna, it turned out, was reading Psychology and, as Frank later discovered, her nickname was Spanner. Apparently, because she undid anything with nuts..

XI

For all his outward bravado, Frank was not without his own crises of confidence. Most people, from fairly humble beginnings who do well in life, do well gradually. As they ascend the pole of their chosen career, they slowly acclimatise to the finer things in life. Top Man is gently eased out by Paul Smith, the Berni Inn falls victim to Alastair Little.

For someone suddenly transferred from Kilburn to Christ Church, the effect can be terrifying. Dinner, for instance, was now lunch and tea was now dinner. At that first formal Christ Church dinner, gowns, tutors and the Dean were compulsory and it comprised several courses and a bewildering array of cutlery. Charles Morgan was quick enough to spot that Frank was about to flounder, like a child without armbands in the twelve foot six.

"Start at the outside", he whispered, "and work your way in".

Sighing with relief, Frank whispered back, "Wasn't that what I told you to do with that blonde girl from Somerville?"

And so began a tacit, reciprocal arrangement between them. Tips on matters social were exchanged for tips on matters sexual.

Academically, Frank coped reasonably well, tugged gently along by the patience and perspicacity of his tutor, Dr, Mike Grady. Dr. Grady, who had seen Frank's type many times before, had very gradually – gram by gram- increased the weight of his workload. Frank still only did the bare minimum but even this was considerably more than he'd ever done before.

Like all students, Frank, would tell you that he'd spent his entire time at college getting pissed and having sex , but this wasn't strictly true.. He may have had more sex than most of his Christ Church contemporaries. He may have had more sex than he would have done had he remained at home in a strict Catholic household, but he still did a fair amount of work. All students do. No-one has ever acquired the suffix "BA" or "BSc" without working reasonably hard, even if all that effort and application does tend to become lost in a mist of rose-tinted hindsight.

Learning Ancient Greek had been a bit of a grind but Frank completed the journey from Alpha to Omega by telling himself that this was a small price to pay for the fun he was having. He was now able to read and understand the New Testament in its original form without having to rely on the linguistic whims of generations of translators. He was now able to see first-hand what a load of far-fetched old nonsense it almost certainly was.

Still, all these millions of Christians surely couldn't be wrong so it was now that Frank started trying to find God. Not in a floaty, ethereal, religious sort of way,. No, he was expecting something a little more concrete. He wasn't expecting His Elusive Omnipotence to appear like Our Lady at Fatima but to perhaps just give a little clue to his existence, just peep over the parapet in a way only a serious student of theology would see and understand. If Frank could be Randall and God would just play Hopkirk, he would start to see the benefit of all this tiresome toil.

But, no. Nothing. As all Catholics were always told, if God were to just turn up every now again, that would be proof rather than faith. It would all be too easy, everyone would know. There would be no conflicting religions, no conflicting theories to study and appraise, so Theology course at Oxford through which Frank Dempsey could have the time of his life at the taxpayers' expense.

It was this fundamental flippancy which kept him afloat. Oxford was the most fun he'd ever had but it hadn't changed him a bit. When he looked in the mirror, he saw the same person grinning back at him. The mirror, of course, was a liar.

Of course, he'd changed. The yellow van, for instance. He'd bought it originally so he could escape back to London and join the lads on a Friday night for a pub crawl along Kilburn High Road. For the first couple of months, this is exactly what he did but after a while, its purpose was reversed and he used it now so he could escape back to Oxford. Each trip home was a little more uncomfortable. He loved his family and friends and was always delighted to see them, However, once the brief euphoria of salutation had worn off, he began to see the once vast tracts of common ground between them disappearing like the Amazonian rain forests.

He now did the old pub crawl along Kilburn High Road more as a tourist than a native. He did it almost in irony. Standing at the bar, pint in hand at Biddy Mulligan's, ostensibly having the crack with the lads before all piling down to the Kilburn Tandoori, or Tony's Steak House – "*Tony's Steaks Are The Best Value In Town*", his mind would wander wistfully Westwards and he'd find himself dreaming of spire and quad, cursing the surfeit of Guinness in his bloodstream which prevented him from jumping into the van and heading straight back there at once.

So, for his next trip down, Frank went teetotal. Told the lads he'd caught a dose and was on anti-biotics till it cleared up.

"Thought you had a regular bird up there" said Frostie.

"I have", said Frank, pulling a guilty face, "And I'm having to avoid her. Why do you think I'm here?".

They all laughed uproariously and Frostie went up and got the beers in.

"Phew" though Frank, "Got away with it". The drinking of lemonade could have lost him a serious quantity of face but, luckily, the mendacious story about having the clap had sent his stock soaring.

Many of Frank's college friends were fascinated by his life in Kilburn, probably because he'd told them dozens of highly embellished stories about what he and the lads got up to. They were desperate for him to take them down there one weekend but this was something he would never, ever do. Charles Morgan and his chums would be appalled and disappointed at just how dreary a Friday night in Kilburn could be. His mates, nice as they fundamentally were, all still lived at home, had very limited horizons and were quite content just to et paralytic every Friday night. Very often, once the drink took hold, the atmosphere would turn a bit nasty and it could all go off for any reason. The sight of a couple of Old Etonians, for instance, having the fucking cheek to be standing there minding their own business.

The longer Frank was at Christ Church. The more mannerisms he seemed to absorb from those around him It was most noticeable in his speech patterns. His North London accent remained unchanged but his tone and inflections now contained an almost aristocratic confidence and certainty. Vocally, he seemed to have leap-frogged the bourgeoisie entirely. – going from "Eh?" to "Sorry?" without ever pausing at "Pardon?"

This dual identity should have been a blessing. After all, he was equally at ease with his old schoolmates in Kilburn as he was with his new college mates at Oxford. The trouble was, he was equally ill at ease too. The dual identity was more of a curse. Instead of fitting in anywhere, he fitted in nowhere. He knew the loneliness and discomfort of being in a "class of his own". He'd never be upper-class, wouldn't want to be, but at the same time, he could never be an ordinary working class boy again. This awkward disaffection extended into his relationship with girls.. Frank had lost count of the number he'd slept with. His room at Christ Church may as well have been fitted with a revolving door. However, although he was attractive to and attracted by girls from either end of the social spectrum, the attraction seldom lasted. He had no shortage of admirers but never really found one with whom he shared enough common ground to build a lasting relationship.

Anyway, that wasn't the reason he'd come to Oxford – to find a long-term girlfriend. Quite the opposite, he had years to do that. At the moment, he was just doing enough work not to get sent down and have this great avenue of pleasure prematurely curtailed.

He worked his way through New Testament Greek and Biblical Hebrew, Pauline Christology and the theories of Kant and Troeltsch, all the time expecting to find something, just a tiny shred of tangible evidence about the validity of the teachings of the Catholic Church. Yet the more he looked, the less he saw. It was simply a matter of faith, of suspending disbelief, something his study of theology had now rendered him completely incapable of doing.

The summer holidays were spent back in London, working on building sites. He could cope with this because he knew his ticket to the construction industry was a return one. He pitied those whose tickets were one-way. Physically, it was just so hard. He was now in awe of his father who had been doing this sort of work every day for more than thirty years. Having hauled bricks up and down ladders all day, Frank would get home exhausted. After a bath and a bite to eat, he had to decide whether to go straight to bed or stay up late and watch John Craven's Newsround..

Towards the end of each break, he would be itching for the new term to start until one day there were no more breaks and no more new terms. His time was up, it was all over. It ended as suddenly as it had begun. He sat his finals and when he completed the last paper on Early Syriac Christianity, that was it.

Game over .

What now?

Unlike most undergraduates, Frank hadn't gone up to Oxford to get himself qualified for a career. He'd gone there simply to postpone the day when he'd ever have to have one. Neither was he a man in so love with his subject that he'd be prepared devote further years to academic research.

Anyway, he felt his turn was over. He'd had a wonderful time but had no wish to become one of those eternal students, too lazy or frightened to emerge into the outside world. He didn't want to feel like a grown man still trying to play for the under-14's football team. Moreover, he felt that he would no longer fit in. Since the lavish TV adaptation of Brideshead Revisited, Christ Church had become awash with a new breed of undergraduate. Fey, foppish fogeys with smug, punchable faces, they wandered around Tom Quad and punted on the Cherwell, dressed in 1920's clothing, carrying their battered teddy bears The trend would probably pass but Frank had no desire to see his beloved college being turned into an Evelyn Waugh theme park.

More worrying was the fact that many of these young fops professed, like Waugh, to be Anglo-Catholics, seduced by the pomp and pageantry of High Mass. That posed the real danger of Theology becoming a fashionable subject, taken up by people who were actually interested in it, rather than just a tradesmen's entrance to Oxford for the likes of himself and Charles Morgan.

So the question remained, what now?

It slowly dawned on him that he was the only one who had no future plans, nowhere to go, nothing to do. The only one who really had only gone to Oxford just for a laugh. His drunken contemporaries had suddenly sobered up. Christ

Church had been a hoot but now it was time to follow the time-honoured path into banking, the law or the City. They were quite earnestly taking their places behind old oak desks at Kleinwort Benson or Grieveson Grant. Others were heading for the new, very eighties option of management consultancy – "We came, we saw, we invoiced".

Even Charles Morgan, the laziest and most crapulent of them all, was following his father's footsteps into the Foreign Office, inevitably ending up as a diplomat.

"It'll be fucking great", he told Frank, "I'll be able to park in the middle of Selfridge's Food Hall".

Some, having served their time in the Oxford Union , were destined to be politicians. Maybe not immediately but almost certainly in the future. Frank had been increasingly courted by both sides of the debating chamber. The Left saw him as that very rare thing – an articulate Oxford undergraduate from a genuine proletarian background. The newly emerging Thatcherite Right saw him as the very emblem of meritocracy. A working class boy who, through his own grit and industry, had propelled himself to Christ Church. Since arriving at Oxford, and witnessing many debates in the Union, Frank had adhered firmly to the old maxim that politics was just "showbusiness for ugly people" and avoided both factions like the plague.

But now he couldn't bear the thought of the dismal drudgery of everyday life which seemed to await him. As an Oxford graduate, there were now many doors open to him that would otherwise have been closed.. But behind those doors, Frank suspected were just de luxe versions of the same unappealing things. The things that awaited him at sixteen, the things that awaited him at eighteen and the things that would still await him if he remained in full -time education until he was thirty. Commuting every day to a job he detested – marriage, mortgage, misery.

And so, blinking like a pit pony, Frank re-emerged into the

real world. In a bit of a daze, he and his yellow Escort van drifted back down the A40. He unloaded it at the other end,, put his records back in the box room, sat on his bed and moped.

Moped and moped and moped.. Not so much about having no job, not so much about having no money, not so much about having no future, but about the dismal prospect of having no fun. This feeling of utter despondency was worsened by the fact that his family and friends were so thrilled to see him again. To have him back where he belonged. He'd be expected down the pub every Friday night to drink a skinful of Guinness before throwing up either on the pavement outside or on the dancefloor of the National Ballroom. He simply couldn't face it. His mother fussed around him "What time will you be home?" "What'll you have for your dinner?" It was all he could do to stop himself screaming at her,

"Pleeeease!!! For Christ's sake, will you just leave me alone!!"

But he knew that she was only being kind and concerned and he would hate himself forever if he did. Worst of all was the prospect of Sunday mass. He could have a stand –up row with his parents "I'm a grown man, I don't have to go to mass if I don't want to...etc, etc"

But why bother? Why fall out with the people he loved over something about which that they cared very deeply and he cared very little. He was living under their roof, to abide by their rules wouldn't kill him. Yet.

So once again, he found himself heading for the eleven o'clock mass at Quex Road. He'd been embarrassed enough about doing this when he was eleven but now at almost twice that age, walking between his parents to the big church, he felt like a patient from a mental hospital who had been released back into the community.

He was welcomed back by the O'Hagans, the Quinns, the

Mackens, the Hennesseys and all the other Quex Road regulars. Maybe he was imagining it but they seemed to treat his time at Oxford as a bout of temporary insanity. Perhaps it was. After all, wasn't this home? Even at Oxford, wasn't there always a piece of elastic with one end tied round his waist and the other anchored firmly in Kilburn?

Still, the question gnawed away at him. How could he escape? He had to escape before he became used to it again and, heaven forbid, began to enjoy it. He reckoned that he could probably put up with Kilburn life for a maximum of six weeks. By then, the tunnel would need to be dug and the light clearly visible at the end of it. Otherwise, he feared the whole Oxford experience would be completely erased and he'd find himself, three years behind everyone else, training to be a quantity surveyor. So, how could he prevent this from happening?

Once again, he thought he'd contact God and see if the Almighty had any suggestions.

Nothing.

"Come on", he pleaded, "I'm in church, I'm on my knees. I need a bit of help here".

Silence.

Frank sat back on his pew and watched Father Rogan deliver the sermon. Although he was paying no attention to the content, he found himself transfixed by the concept. What other career offered the sermon – a weekly opportunity to get up and say whatever you liked to a captive audience of several hundred people who then felt duty-bound to go off and do as you tell them? Where else could you make such a difference to people's lives? In what other walk of life were you automatically assumed to be virtuous, even saintly?

No, no, surely not. He couldn't even consider it. This was the most fatuous idea he'd had since applying to Christ Church. Fatuous or not, what else was he going to do?

XII

The priesthood. The more he thought about it, the more it appealed.

As a DJ, he'd had unwittingly begun to develop some of the qualities of a really good priest. He'd shown a flair for bringing people together, making them happy, controlling their emotions. His records, his decks, his speakers and lights had all been agents for the forces of good. During his three years at Oxford, the charity balls at which he'd performed had raised thousands for people in need. Even the sobriquet "MC" which was used by a lot of black American DJ's had a sort of priestly parallel. Mass was a ceremony, the priest was its master and the 11 o'clock mass, heaving with punters must be, in DJ speak, a great gig to be playing.

One tiny hitch, though. He didn't believe in God. But then,, do barristers really believe in the innocence of their bank-robbing clients?

Far more worrying was the vow of celibacy. No marriage, no sex. Ever. Or in Frank's case, ever again. Frank had no desire to get married anyway. Although he had loved many girls, the concept of being "in love" was something he felt would always elude him. He doubted whether he could ever love for life, possess that depth of adoration that would carry him through to his dotage. He worried that, as youth ripened into middle age and rotted into old age, he would cease to love his partner and more to the point, she would cease to love him. In short, he was not the marrying kind.

Nor did he want to feel, in his forties and fifties, the deprecating gaze of suspicion which invariably falls upon the "senior bachelor". Nothing wrong with homosexuality, he just didn't want to be falsely suspected of it. Any more than anyone wants to be falsely suspected of anything. Wouldn't it be far better to go into a job where bachelorhood was compulsory?

What about sex? Frank reconciled this impending self-denial by inventing a quota system. Everybody, he decided, is allowed to have a certain amount sex in his or her lifetime. A finite quota. Frank, unfortunately, had used up his entire quota at Oxford. He could hardly complain if he was forbidden to have any more.

How about children? He loved them, he'd always been very good with them but viewed them in much the same way as he viewed heroin addiction. From the moment they're born, you fall hopelessly in love with them and you're a prisoner to your feelings forever. Yes, they bring immense pride and pleasure but also worry – the most horrible, gut-wrenching worry. And there's no re-hab programme either. You can't kick children the way you can kick smack. Best not to get hooked in the first place. Anyway, his sister Bernie was pregnant, his sister Maria wouldn't be far behind. He'd content himself by being Uncle Frank.

Finally, money. This was something that had never really concerned him., didn't really motivate him. What would he spend it on anyway? No wife, no children. Accommodation, food and clothing already taken care of. He'd always have Christmas and birthdays to provide him with the occasional treat, so money? What would he need it for?

His mind, always so quick to make itself up, was made up again. He was opting out of real life. Father Dempsey – it had rather a nice ring to it. Father Frank even had an additional alliterative quality. He would apply to Allen Hall, the diocesan seminary. Allen Hall was in Chelsea and that was the other thing. Kilburn or Chelsea? Where would you rather live?

XIII

Father Denis Vaughan was vocations director for Allen Hall, charged with task of attracting suitable candidates for the priesthood. Fewer and fewer young men were volunteering for what they felt could be a lonely and ascetic life, so the sight of Frank Dempsey in his office, appearing more than willing to sign up, was like manna from heaven.

He was just the sort of candidate whom the priesthood always claimed to attract but never actually did. Father Vaughan was only too aware of the social and intellectual shortcomings of many of those he was asked to consider. Yet here was a handsome, intelligent and articulate young man presenting his application. He was a London boy from a good Irish Catholic background, he had a degree from Oxford and, Holy Mary Mother of God, it was a degree in theology. Father Vaughan, who was himself starting to doubt Our Lord's existence, suddenly began to re-believe.

Nonetheless, he was a little suspicious. Why would a young man who could surely choose any career he wanted. pick the priesthood? What was wrong with him?

Like all applicants, Frank had to face a strict selection committee whose job it was to identify anything "wrong". To unmask any weird or unhealthy motives. Father Vaughan wondered whether such a seemingly kind young man had had his heart broken by a girl and was using Allen Hall the way others had used the French Foreign Legion. However, Frank's impressive performance before the committee, his plausible mix of truth and lies carried him through with flying colours.

He told them that he had always been fascinated by the Catholic faith. Truth.

That his study of theology and now given him a greater understanding of it. Truth.

That he now realised that it was the one true faith. Lie.

That he'd felt a calling from God to go out and preach the gospel. Lie.

That he had a genuine desire to help those in his pastoral care. Truth.

That the best way to achieve fulfilment from his life was to become a Roman Catholic priest. Half-truth.

The best way to for Frank to get what he wanted out of life was to become a *parish priest* and there is a very big difference

The parish priest is in charge of the parish and in some of the larger ones, may have four or five priests below him. As an ordinary priest, your parish priest is very much your boss. You may silently oppose his beliefs about everything from the story of Adam & Eve to the way the tombola is run at the Christmas Fete but yours is not to question why. You just do as you're told. You help him run the parish the way he wants it run until such time as you're trusted with a parish of your own, then you can do as you please. That was what Frank was aiming for. He was happy to learn, to comply, to obey until he had his own parish and the chance to put some of his idiosyncratic ideas into practice.

XIV

Frank didn't really explain his decision to anyone. He knew he didn't have to. The taking of Holy Orders was seen as such a laudable thing to do that its wisdom and merit were accepted without question. His parents were very proud. It was as though God would be particularly pleased with Eamonn and Mary Dempsey because they were donating their son to the Church, almost like he was a bag of old clothes dropped off outside the Sue Ryder shop.. Neither ever could, or ever would admit it to the other but each felt a tiny twinge of disappointment. Good looks, charm, intelligence – they were rather hoping their son might have chosen something a little more lucrative. Never mind, they were lucky, they were blessed, this is what God had called him to do.

Oddly enough, his mates had no difficulty at all in accepting his new vocation. They were far more accustomed to priests than they were to poncey Oxford intellectuals. They rather liked it, he was one of them again. Having a mate who was going to be a priest was quite cool. It gave them what they felt was an inside track on the Almighty.

Only his sisters, who probably knew him best, betrayed signs of cynicism. They admitted to each other, though not to Frank or to their parents, that although his motives were probably sound and that he'd no doubt make a wonderful priest, he was only doing it because, despite countless girlfriends, he simply hadn't met the right one. God help him if, once ordained, he actually did and – to quote the saddest words in the English language – it was "too late".

Frank took up residence in the former convent in Beaufort Street. His room was cold and spartan and had none of that lovely faded grandeur that seemed woven into the very fabric of his rooms at Christ Church. Still, it could have been worse and until fairly recently, it was. These small, single rooms had only been introduced in the last few years. Before that, Frank would have shared a long draughty dormitory with several other seminarians. Strict curfews had now been replaced by keys so, as long as lectures were attended and duties performed, Frank and the others were reasonably free to come and go as they pleased.

Frank knew that one day, as soon as possible, he would achieve his ambition of becoming a parish priest. He was sure that he would love it just as he was sure he would loathe the training period, which unfortunately was the only route that would get him there. To his own astonishment he liked it. Probably because he was good at it. Really good at it. Perhaps the most promising pupil Allen Hall had ever had. For the first time in his life, he knew how it felt to be the best at something. And it was a feeling which convinced him that he was doing the right thing

There was a lot of studying – Kiekegaard, ancient Hebrew, bereavement counselling but unlike the purely theoretical nature of his work at Oxford, this had a more practical purpose. Much of it he had covered before, so in general he found his studies relatively easy.

Special privileges were extended to the one pupil who already had a degree in theology and therefore needed to spend less time in the classroom. For most newcomers, the academic timetable was quite demanding but for one who'd done so much so recently, it was a doddle. Almost like being an international striker asked to turn out for a Sunday pub team. Frank was therefore allowed to spend more time assisting the priests at any one of over two hundred parishes in and around London.

All he really missed were his records, though he did manage to play them every Friday night. Saturday was a day off for the students at Allen Hall. When the week's final lecture finished at about 4.30 on a Friday afternoon, they were free until 7.15 mass on Sunday morning. Frank headed straight back to Kilburn, loaded a few crates of records into the Escort van and took up his Friday night residency as a DJ at Crackers nightclub in Wardour Street..

No-one at Allen Hall knew about this.. Father Vaughan was hardly likely to turn up at a West End nightclub and even if he did, who'd have the most explaining to do? Similarly, no-one on the London club circuit knew he was training to be a priest.. He told people he was a student, reading philosophy at London University. This was perfectly true, since the course at Allen Hall was linked to Heythrop College.

The years seemed to fly by and after the requisite six, Frank Dempsey was now considered ready for ordination.

If the diocese of Westminster were a firm, Bishop Thomas Hayes was one of its four area managers, responsible for North London, the biggest chunk. He officiated at a quite spectacular ceremony which saw Quex Road church full to capacity. The local boy was being ordained. As a trainee, Frank had helped out at dozens of parishes, so well-wishers flocked in from all over the diocese. From Watford and Ilford, from Croydon and Kew. The pews were packed with family and friends, some of whom still couldn't quite believe that this most irreligious of creatures really was becoming a priest.

Frank did not enjoy the experience. Perhaps he was subconsciously ashamed of what he was doing, perhaps he thought it was uncool. There was an awful lot of fuss. These people would not have turned up in their hundreds to see him welcomed into the world of quantity surveying or chartered accountancy. This was more like a wedding. He therefore wished he could have been ordained in a registry office with just a couple of passers-by as witnesses, but then realised that this would rather defeat the object. He didn't want them all there, gazing and gawping and congratulating him. He felt like a phoney, a fraud, and consoled himself with the thought that perhaps every ordainee felt the same way. Perhaps the moment when he officially became a priest would be a truly seminal one.

When this moment came , that split second when Francis Dempsey became Father Dempsey, he braced himself and thought "This is it, this is where I become a member of the magic circle. This is the moment when God finally reveals himself. This is the moment when I am inducted, where a two-thousand year old secret is whispered into my ear. This is how far you have to go before that privilege is granted to you. Now I am about to find out.........."

Nothing.

Perhaps it was being whispered but the agnostic priest was just too sceptical to hear it.

He listened again. Nothing, absolutely nothing.

"Oh God", he murmured, "What have I done?"

And God, true to form, didn't answer him.

PART TWO

ONE

Frank's early times as a priest passed largely without incident. That was the way he wanted it. He was lying low, perfecting his craft, keeping his powder dry It was all just a dress rehearsal for his appointment as a parish priest. His turn would come. Bishop Hayes was following his progress and had always noted how good his young protege was with people, how they seemed drawn to him, how inventive and original his sermons were and how well he put them across.

He'd make a marvellous parish priest. But not yet, Not just yet.

Frank was particularly good at weddings, even though Holy Matrimony was just another sacrament in which he didn't believe.

"Love and marriage, love and marriage", he'd sometimes sing in the sacristy as he prepared for the ceremony, "Go together like a horse and water-skis"

Nonetheless, he was more than happy to officiate. Throughout his late twenties and early thirties, Frank spent most summers marrying his Catholic contemporaries, people he'd grown up with, including one or two ex-girlfriends. On these occasions when he had to ask the congregation the standard question, "If anybody here today knows of any reason why these two people should not be joined together in Holy Matrimony, please speak now", he had to stop himself putting his own hand up and shouting out to the groom

"Don't marry her – she's a fucking nightmare".

The priesthood had proved a marvellous boon to his record collection because at every parish he always volunteered himself for the same task; organising the record stall at the Parish Jumble Sale. He'd put a little note in the newsletter, asking his flock to dig out any unwanted old singles and albums which he and the Escort van would call round to collect over the next couple of weeks.

He'd duly arrive like the rag and bone man and the parishioners, only too keen to contribute and smooth their own paths into heaven, would hand over vanloads of vinyl.

He would then spend hours alone in his room, sorting through the plunder, keeping the records he wanted and only those he didn't would make it as far as the stall at the fete. This little scam had, over the years augmented his collection by thousands. Some items rare and sought after. Three original absolutely mint US 45's for instance, Johnny Restivo's "The Shape I'm In" on RCA, Barrett Strong's "Money" on Tamla and Warren Smith's "Red Cadillac And a Black Moustache" on Sun, all in the same haul. . Frank remembered this fondly as his "haul of fame" but it wasn't always like that. The records donated weren't usually gems, just everyday Top Ten hits from the previous twenty-odd years, the bread and butter of any collection and Frank was always more than happy to steal them.

Each time he moved parish, the back axle on the Escort van was put under a little extra strain until one day, just after its twenty-first birthday, after two engines and 160,000 miles, it could take the strain no longer. It was taken away for scrap and replaced by a second hand Suzuki motorbike

As Frank watched his beloved van from the window being winched on to the breakers' tow truck for its final journey, he stood to attention and placed Jim Reeves's "Adios Amigo" on the turntable. Then, realising that he was more upset at this particular requiem than he ever seemed at parishioners' funerals. He sniffed back his tears and pulled himself together.

TWO

Funerals were, in fact, Frank's speciality. He was brilliant at them. He did death very well. He was genuinely unafraid of it and it was from this attitude that bereaved parishioners seemed to draw comfort and confidence.

If that nice Father Dempsey, a Roman Catholic priest – a man who knew about these things – was not afraid, then there really was nothing to fear. Of course, Frank knew absolutely nothing about "these things", he hadn't a clue about what happened to people once they'd checked into the Wooden Waldorf . Though, many years ago, he'd narrowed it down to two scenarios.

Scenario One: There is no God. Death is the full stop to end all full stops. Utterly final, Utterly silent. The end. Well, what's so what's so frightening about that? You're finished, you are no more, no harm can ever come to you because there's no you for any harm to come to.

Scenario Two: There is a God. Whether he tuns out to be Allah, Buddha or Jesus Christ, he is all powerful but more importantly, all merciful, so he's hardly going to condemn you to hell for the venial sins you committed during your life time. Hell was a place strictly reserved for the likes of Hitler, Pol Pot and Paul Daniels.

You see? Absolutely nothing to worry about.

In Frank's experience, although deaths were very sad. very few were truly tragic. The funeral of a child, for instance, with the sobbing father carrying a tiny white coffin into the church wondering how God could possibly allow this to happen, the deep and bitter grief that no amount of condolences could assuage. These occasions were mercifully rare.

Frank's funerals, for the most part, had been for those whose hearts had finally succumbed to a lifetime of fags, booze and unsaturated fats. He tried to make them joyous rather than sorrowful occasions. If the family wanted their loved one dispatched to the strains of "Return To Sender" rather than "The Lord's My Shepherd", then that was absolutely fine. Frank truly believed that the deceased was heading for a better place. How could Heaven be worse than Harlow?

It was in this unappealing Essex new town that Frank was wearing the black vestments for possibly the last time before taking up his new post as a Parish priest.. He was up on the altar of a stupendously ugly concrete edifice known as All Saints Church

You could almost imagine the scene in the mid-sixties when the church was built and none of the saints wanting anything to do with it, refusing to put their names on the door. Even the virtually unheard of St. Plachelm, who had been waiting for nearly twelve hundred years to have a church named after him, even he didn't want this one. In the end, God calls a big meeting and tells them that he understands their aesthetic aversion to this revolting 1960's architecture but the hideous building had to have a name and it was to be called All Saints. Firstly so as none of them has to take sole responsibility for it and secondly so that, in thirty years' time the good people of Essex will think it was named after a pop group.

Anyway, the dearly beloved were gathered in All Saints Church there to say goodbye to Bill Waites, a London cabbie and one of Frank's favourite parishioners. As handkerchiefs all around the church were snuffled into, Frank went into his "mild bewilderment whilst still acknowledging the pain of bereavement" routine

"Let me ask you a question?" he began, "Or let me ask you to ask yourselves a question: Why are you crying? You're not crying for Bill. And if you are, you shouldn't be. Out of all of us, isn't he was the lucky one? He was a good man. Our Lord won't be turning him away. He's, just about to embark on an eternity of unfettered happiness and joy. He's finally found a place with no traffic jams, no speed bumps, no Japanese tourists with nothing smaller than a fifty-pound note and you're crying for him? But you're not, are you? You're actually crying for yourselves and that's understandable. He was a lovely man, you're all going to miss him, I'm going to miss him but remember, our separation from him is only temporary. The fact is, that unless anyone here has led a lifetime of irredeemable evil, we'll all be joining him sooner or later. It's going to be one long party. Really long, it's never ever going to end. It's just that Bill has arrived at that party a little earlier than we have."

The snuffling seemed to stop Brave smiles started to flicker across tear-stained cheeks and the atmosphere of dark tragedy gradually lightened into one of acceptance, almost happiness.

Even at the graveside, whilst going through the perfunctory prayers and procedure, Frank was mindful of the common horror of seeing a loved one lowered into the ground or conveyor belted behind a curtain to be burnt to a frazzle.

He paused.

"Try not to be distressed. Try to remember that it isn't Bill inside that coffin. It's just his body. And our bodies are just things we wear during our time on Earth, like clothes. Bill is in heaven. All we're really burying are his clothes".

Irene, Bill's widow, invited everyone back to the house and as Frank stood chatting and nibbling a cheese and tomato sandwich, she drew him aside.

"Bill thought a lot of you, Father, and towards the end, he decided to leave you something in his will. It's something you might find useful, Come into the other room for a minute , let me show you.

THREE

"Bingo", yelled Sarah Marshall in the middle of a client meeting. She would have startled everyone in the room had she not yelled it silently to herself

Until her recent introduction to the game of "Buzzword Bingo", Sarah's working life owas becoming insufferable. After university, she'd opted for a career in advertising, carried along like so many before her, on a white-water raft of excitement and optimism. The industry itself hovered on the fringes of big business and show business, of politics and sport and she went in confident of enjoying the big salary, the company car, the lunches at London's most chic and expensive restaurants, the glamorous shoots in exotic locations, the sheer pizzazz of it all.

However, by the time she'd made it to the fashionably stark offices of Collins Davies and Pearce, one of London's top agencies, she felt as though she'd arrived at a party long past its peak. As heads older than hers would confirm, the fun and the funds seemed to have gone from the industry and it was all a lot more sensible, a lot more professional, a lot less attractive.

And least attractive of all was Mike Babcock – "the client", sitting there across the table from her. Mike, 36 – wife two children, Barratt house with carport for Vauxhall Vectra on new estate just outside Basingstoke – had one redeeming feature of which he was blissfully unaware. If you wanted to play "Buzzword Bingo, Mike was your man. The rules of the game were very simple. There were thirty irritating "buzzwords" or phrases, which to Sarah were like fingernails scratching a blackboard. They had an increasing tendency to crop up in meetings, invariably from the lips of the client.

You know the sort of thing – "basically" "bottom line" "core business" "at the end of the day" "ball park" "pro active". Players had to tick off six on their imaginary score-card before crying "Bingo". To themselves, of course.

An hour with Mike Babcock and you could usually complete half a dozen full houses. Sarah still smiled at the memory of "Buzzword Bonanza" – the day when she cried "bingo" at the end of his opening sentence.

"*Basically*", he began, "*At the end of the day*, we're hopefully looking at *a win win situation. The bottom line* is, we need to *think outside the box* if we're going *to put this one to bed*".

Buzzword Bingo had brought a little welcome amusement into Sarah's life. Instead of dreading the total banality, the predictable boredom, the drivel dressed as marketing analysis of everything Mike said, she found herself hanging on his every word.

The elusive sixth buzzword had been a long time coming, but once Mike had expressed his intention to "go the full nine yards", Sarah congratulated herself on another full house.

Whilst listening, she looked at him with disdain – Top Man suit, Duty Free tie and all too visible cufflinks. She reflected on how conventional wisdom would assume that those who worked in flash London ad agencies would be more ostentatious, more status-conscious, more money-driven than their provincial clients. Nothing could be further from the truth.

Every word Mike uttered was uttered to show what a razor-sharp guy he was. The way he shook your hand too firmly. His predilection for making intrusive and unwelcome eye contact whenever he spoke to you. His ever present little stack of business cards "Michael P. Babcock – Divisional

Marketing Manager" the unseemly pride he took in that title and in his Vectra SRI which had colour coded bumpers – so much more prestigious than his more junior colleagues' Vectra SR's which hadn't.

Mike was currently – or as he would incorrectly put it – presently very excited about his latest top-level project. He was "heading up a team" involved in the marketing of Slattery's, a chain of truly awful faux-Irish pubs which Mike assured Sarah would have "representation" in very major town centre within a "timescale" of three to five years.

It had been Sarah's unenviable task to visit some of these establishments and she was horrified. If you had a drop of Irish blood in your veins, you'd have every right to find them patronising, insulting and barely the right side of racist. With their outsides painted a lurid shade of green, their identikit "Oirish" interiors and accoutrements, their diddley-dee music and their inflated prices for badly poured Guinness, they were a greedy, ignorant, multi-national brewing chain's attempt to cash in on the vogue for Celtic culture.

Sarah had visited the genuine article in Kerry, in Wexford, in Cork. Wonderful places, often comprising little more than the landlord's front room. Focal points for small, friendly communities where a lot more than alcohol was dispensed.. To see this marvellous tradition reduced to a quick way to fill shareholders' pockets made her want to vomit. And the sites they'd chosen were usually in places with a big Irish community. Camden, for instance, where they'd converted a proper Irish pub, frequented by Irish people, into another branch of Slattery's. The Irish regulars naturally got up and took their custom elsewhere and were replaced by tourists and out of towners deluded into thinking they'd found a little slice of the Emerald Isle.

Sarah felt real guilt and shame about what she was now involved in. All right, so it was perfectly legal and technically not even wrong but debasing what she believed to be a noble and delightful culture left a taste in her mouth as nasty as Slattery's badly poured Guinness.

Only "Buzzword Babcock" unwittingly made it tolerable for her. Snapping his attaché case shut, he said goodbye and left the meeting room. To Sarah's intense disappointment, she was left one word short of her fifth full house. Just then, Mike turned back round. "Sarah, need to sit down and discuss the new research findings – *touch base* on Monday."

Bingo.

It was five to one, she was due to meet her friend Helen for a gossipy lunch in Clerkenwell in five minutes.

She ran out on to Golden Square, hailed a cab and jumped in. In her haste, she failed to notice two things. Firstly that this particular cab did not have a Metropolitan Police licence plate on the back. And secondly, that the man at the wheel was a priest.

FOUR

Frank had followed Irene Waites into the back room where she'd taken an envelope from the top drawer of an old teak sideboard. He opened it and inside was the Document of Registration for vehicle no G339 YMC – Bill Waites's taxi – his mode of transport, his place of work, his life.

"Towards the end", she explained, "Bill was quite relaxed. He knew he wasn't long for this world.. In fact, thanks to you, he was quite looking forward to it. He wasn't too worried about me, with his policies and whatnot, he's actually left me quite a tidy sum. He wasn't worried about the kids. I mean, they've grown up and made their own lives. But he was worried about you"

"Me?" Frank was simultaneously flattered, surprised and alarmed.

"You and that motorbike of yours. He said he'd seen you tearing around on it – nearly knocked you off once. He was worried that if you weren't more careful, you'd come a cropper".

Frank was close to tears at a deceased parishioner's touching concern for him but quickly managed to smile himself out of it.

"So just before he went, he had the idea of leaving you the taxi. Insisted, he did. A lot safer than that motorbike so it's yours. It's in very good nick. Well, black cabs have to be, the Old Bill are very hot on that. . Besides, he's been part -time really for the last few years so this one hasn't clocked up so many miles. I mean, you can sell it if you want".

"No, no. Absolutely not" said Frank, perishing the very

thought "I wouldn't dream of it. I'm....I'm .....I mean, I....no, no....I'd never sell it. What a wonderful way to get around. But I tell you what, I will sell the bike. Bill was right. And, much as I'm going to miss him, I'm not ready to meet up with him just yet".

Embracing her warmly, Frank thanked Irene again and rode his old Suzuki X7 back to the presbytery for the very last time. As a mark of respect to the late William Waites, he rode at twenty-nine miles per hour.

Within a few weeks came the moment Frank had been waiting for. The reason he hadn't even considered the other career options which could have been open to him after Oxford. The reason he had endured six years in the seminary and taken a vow of celibacy. The reason he served a further ten year apprenticeship as a priest in all those different parishes The moment he had been building up to for the past sixteen years – written confirmation of his appointment as a parish priest.

At 38, he was very young. The whole priestly process is painfully slow. It is not a career which offers any sort of fast track. Your own parish, however, at 38. That was about as fast as anyone had done it.

Frank knew he'd have to tread very carefully. He was only too aware of how reactionary some Roman Catholics could be in their outlook. Many still regarded Henry VIII as a cocky young upstart with trendy. new-fangled ideas about and divorce.. Any new parish priest would have to appraise his flock very carefully before attempting anything that may look unfamiliar or he could risk alienating them altogether.

Frank's new church was to be St. Thomas's in Wealdstone. Wealdstone is a drab North London suburb, not far from Wembley with a big Irish community. It is not to be confused with Willesden, a drab North London suburb not far from Wembley with a big Irish community.

All Frank knew about Wealdstone was the Railway Hotel which had been for The Who what the Cavern Club had been for The Beatles. Somewhere amongst the thousands of records in the back of his taxi was an old copy of The Who's Meaty Beaty Big & Bouncy which featured an old shot of the Railway Hotel in the middle of its gatefold sleeve.

With its scruffy old factories and Coronation Street terraces, Wealdstone has always looked like a little chunk of the North of England, transported to the North of London. When the Irish arrived looking for work, they found plenty. Whitefriars Glass, Hamilton's Brushes, Winsor & Newton and Kodak all had sizeable plants in the area and as Frank drove his taxi full of records to what was to be his new home, the atmosphere seemed to be doing its utmost to dampen his excitement. The acrid, asbestos-filled smoke belched up from Winsor & Newton into a slate-grey January sky and the rain fell on a High Street which boasted branches of both Kwik-Save and Cash Converters, both sure signs that house prices in the area are not about to soar. The Evening Standard's Property Section had never touted Wealdstone as an up and coming area, concluding that it had too far to up and come.

Never mind, St. Thomas's church was beautiful, if a little run down, as was the priests' house, set just behind it. Frank knocked on the door and was "welcomed aboard" by his two assistants, the semi- retired Father Lynam, almost seventy and for whom the duties of Parish Priest had become a little too onerous and the recently-ordained Father Conlon. It seemed absurd to call a baby-faced youth of twenty-six "Father" but Liam Conlon – gentle, Irish and wholesome -, could never been anything other than a priest.

Frank was struck by the aura of real goodness, almost holiness which seemed to emanate from both men. This was something he really envied, something he himself had never managed to acquire. There was no side, no scepticism, just undemanding goodness. These two were like the priests from Central Casting and standing between them, their new boss was going to look like the devil incarnate.

Both were genuinely delighted to see him. Father Lynam had been desperate to relinquish the reins to a younger man for years but such was the paucity of suitable candidates that he'd had to hang on far longer than he'd intended. Father Conlon had heard so much about Frank. This charismatic Oxford theology graduate with his Suzuki X7 and his legendary sermons. Here was a man from whom he could learn. A man already at the helm of a big and challenging parish long before his fortieth birthday.

"Er....Father Dempsey" he said nervously, "the....er.... taxi still appears to be outside... You want me to go out and pay it?"

Frank chuckled, "No, no....er.....the taxi is actually mine. It was left to be by someone at my old parish who just died.. Far more fun than a motorbike. Anywhere you want to go, just let me know. Do you drive?"

"Well, I've passed my test", said Father Conlon" but I've never actually owned a car. Hardly ever driven one".

"Well, you can drive this one", said Frank, "I'll get you insured".

Father Conlon flushed with pleasure. Friend for life.

The house was fairly basic though it seemed to have been freshly decorated inside. Magnolia woodchip and cheap brown carpet throughout. Anything more lavish would be decadent, almost sinful. However, thanks to Mrs. Ruane, the housekeeper, immaculately clean and tidy. Frank wasn't bothered either way. He' wouldn't be spending much time there.

FIVE

Sarah Marshall clambered into the back of the taxi on the West Side of Golden Square.

"Farringdon Road, please".

Instead off driving off, the driver turned round.

"Before I take you", he said, as he had said a hundred times before, "you ought to know I am not a licensed taxi driver. I am Father Frank Dempsey, parish priest of St. Thomas's in Wealdstone. I'm happy to take you to Farringdon if you wouldn't mind leaving a small donation in the box there".

Sarah then noticed that there was no meter inside the cab. The driver was gesturing instead towards a collection box, where the meter would normally be, bolted securely to floor.

"Because your donation is strictly voluntary" he told her, "You are fully insured. If you want to get out and hail a proper taxi, I quite understand".

Sarah didn't get out. Nobody ever did. It crossed her mind for a moment that "Father Dempsey" could be a serial rapist but then so could anyone.

"No", she said, "If you can get me to Farringdon Road in ten minutes, I don't care if you're the Archbishop of Canterbury".

Frank smiled and headed out on to Regent Street. Sarah simply stared at him. People always did. A priest driving a taxi – well you would stare, wouldn't you? But Sarah was staring for a different reason.

"God, what a handsome man", she was thinking, "And what a terrible waste. Why the hell is he a priest? Look at him – tall, square-shouldered, with his short dark hair and navy blue eyes. God, what a waste"

He reminded Sarah of pictures she'd seen of Dean Martin in his Rat Pack heyday, standing outside the Sands Hotel in Las Vegas.. She carried on staring, angling her head in an attempt to get a better view of his face..

"Look, I know everyone must ask you this but....well.... this taxi...er....why? How come?"

"The taxi was left to me by a parishioner. I couldn't bear to sell it so I thought I'd put it to good use. I have to come down to Westminster two or three times a week on diocesan business, so on my way home, I do a little bit of fund-raising".

"Only when you come down to Westminster?".

"Depends. Sometimes on my day off, or if I'm a bit quiet, I just get in the cab and put the light on. It's a fantastic way of raising money"

"So what do you do with it?

"Well, the church and the parish cost an awful lot to maintain and rather than organise endless coffee mornings and bring & buy sales, it's quicker and easier to just go out cabbing".

Frank had given this schtick hundreds of times before, often to beautiful female passengers,. literally without turning a hair, but this time was different, He found himself feeling deliciously queasy, as though a little demon was pumping red hot lead into his stomach. He felt the way an excited five-year old feels, jumping into bed on Christmas Eve. Something strange was happening. That magical conspiracy of factors that just sometimes all combine at the right moment to produce a hole in one, a 30 yard free kick straight into the top corner or, in this case, a perfect right hook delivered with stunning force and accuracy right on the point of his jaw. He was reeling, dazed, flat out on the canvas, taking the mandatory eight.

"God help me", he thought and he meant it.

God ignored him, leaving the poor wretch to experience the ache of desire in a way he had never experienced it before. Of course, priests are only human and their vows of celibacy can never entirely eradicate the natural desires of an ordinary man. But over the years, it becomes easier to keep these desires in check. You get used to celibacy. After all, nobody put a gun to your head and forced you to forego these pleasures. It was your choice. You must have thought you could do it.

And anyway, one of the human male's great secrets is that his sexual appetite is not as great as he pretends it is. A lot of men can't admit this, not even to themselves. They're pre-programmed, almost duty bound, at the sight of a good-looking woman to react accordingly

"Phwoarr!! Look at the tits on that, wouldn't mind giving her one, etc, etc".

They don't even mean it. And, as most priests will tell you, once the decision has been made to live a life of chastity, it's not as difficult as you'd think. Human beings simply don't have sex as often as they claim to. When surveys are conducted, people just lie. Couples all claim to have sex seven nights a week because they think everyone else does. If a man says he's slept with 92 women, his mate will say he's slept with 93. No-one can ever prove otherwise, If Homo Sapien's physical desires were as consistently great as he says they are, nobody could ever become a priest or a nun and if they did, those vows would be broken on a daily basis.

In every parish Frank had ever worked, there'd been attractive women, Some seemed to be planted like landmines to test the strength of his vows. One or two of members of the Young Wives Guild had been particularly hard to resist. – devout Catholics ostensibly, but quite taken with the idea of seducing a handsome young priest.

But for Frank, today was different. Very, very different.

His desires – or desires of this potency, anyway – had been sealed and buried for years like dangerous radio-active waste. But, oh God, the canister hadn't been sealed as firmly as he thought. He adjusted his rear-view mirror to get a good look at his passenger without appearing to gawp. Sarah would tell you that she had "footballer's legs", that her nose was too big and her boobs were too small. She'd like her bum to be half its size and her mouth to take up just a little less room on her face. However, it would be almost impossible to find a man with a pulse who'd agree with her. Frank was a man with a racing pulse and, from where he was sitting, Sarah Marshall looked vow-breakingly gorgeous. Her wide, generous mouth occupied centre stage in the rear-view mirror and it was still asking him questions.

"So, you're not like a minicab firm, you don't take telephone bookings".

Frank didn't, never had, but suddenly decided to institute a dramatic change in company policy.

"Yeah, sometimes", he lied, "Why?"

"Well", said Sarah, "I've got to fly up to Edinburgh next week – only for the day – and I've got to be at Heathrow for 7.15. So I was wondering, you know, I'd rather give the money to your church than to some dodgy cab firm...".

"Okay", said Frank, "Where do you live?"

"Fulham,".

Fulham? Oh God, it could hardly be further from Wealdstone.

"Fine"

"What day?"

"Wednesday".

"Okay, give me your address and I'll pick you up, say, half-six on Wednesday morning. Take my mobile number in case there's a change of plan".

Sarah pulled a tenner from her purse, folded it and slotted it into the St. Thomas's of Wealdstone donation box, flashed a slightly awkward, slightly coy and more than slightly sexy smile that almost gave the poor priest a cardiac arrest. She hurried into the fashionable Clerkenwell eaterie, with the words "Helen, Helen – I've just had the most surreal taxi ride" all ready to tumble from the tip of her tongue..

SIX

It was all right for Sarah. She could tell Helen. She could tell anyone. For Frank, however, it was like he'd eaten a huge, delicious steak but he'd eaten it on Good Friday. Who he was he going to tell? Father Lynam? Father Conlon?

He turned the taxi round and headed up towards Islington and tried to expunge Sarah Marshall from his mind He thought instead of the ten pound note she had dropped into the box. That was about twice what she would have paid for an ordinary cab ride form Soho to Clerkenwell. His passengers always overpaid. He was reminded of that French restaurant on the Finchley Road where no prices are displayed on the menu. Diners are just told to leave what they thought the meal was worth. You'd have thought that this would be open house for the mean and greedy and the place would be besieged every night by freeloaders ordering four-course meals with wine, coffee and liqueurs and only leaving a fiver. But apparently not. When interviewed, the owner said that this had never happened. If anything, most customers tended to overpay. And so they did in Frank's taxi. Once they knew they were donating to a registered charity, they felt noble and virtuous paying £20 for a £6 ride.

He immersed himself in the busy London traffic. Driving a taxi did have its advantages. He could whizz up and down the bus lanes for a start, though he always felt rather guilty about doing this. Not because his vehicle wasn't a bona fide black cab and he was therefore breaking the law. He just felt that bus lanes were intrinsically wrong – horribly undemocratic, monstrously unfair to the vast majority of road users.

At least 90% of them were ordinary car drivers and yet, at the busiest times of the day, their road space was suddenly sliced in half, leaving them sitting there fuming, squashed up and stationary while the bus lanes lay largely empty.

Still Sarah could not be removed from his thoughts. This really wasn't working at all.

He turned his thoughts instead to the speed bumps which had appeared like a malignant growth all over London. The height of most of them was illegal. On most roads, you had a perfect right to proceed at thirty miles and hour yet on many highly humped highways, you'd lose your sump and half your exhaust if you ever attempted to do that. When the idea, surely, was to keep traffic flowing as freely as possible, speed bumps had precisely the opposite effect. Ah, but according to the unctuous arguments of some, absolutely essential because they save lives.

If anything, the reverse is true. Ask any fire-fighters or ambulance crews how many lives these bumps have actually cost? How many ambulances have been delayed in reaching patients or hospitals because of them? How many fire engines could have been at blazing houses those vital minutes earlier had the bumps not slowed their urgent progress to a crawl?

And the money, the money! Millions and millions of pounds had been spent on these "traffic-calming" though not exactly "motorist calming" measures. The good that St. Thomas's or any other charity could have done with that money. The good that London Transport could have done. The fantastic improvements they could have made to the tube, How much happier everyone would have been.

Within a nanosecond, Sarah's sultry smile had resumed its residence at the front of his mind, until he forced himself to fantasise about something else instead. That something was the punishments that should be meted out to those who had vandalised our streets in this way..

At this point in his private rant, the face of Kevin Stott usually flashed through Frank's mind. Kevin Srott had been in Frank's class at St. Michael's. Kevin Stott, dull and uninspiring, was never the brightest star in the firmament. Kevin Stott, and thousands like him were deemed too dull for most careers and, being almost unemployable, would up working for the local council, usually in the Highways Department. Suddenly, with real power and seemingly bottomless budgets, the Kevin Stotts of this world get creative and introduce ludicrous and unworkable traffic schemes designed to make motorists miserable. All over the country, ordinary people's lives were being blighted by Kevin Stotts Trouble was, this time Kevin Stott was nowhere to be seen. His ugly face had fought and lost the battle for Frank's attention with Sarah Marshall's altogether more appealing features. And no amount of righteous railing about bus lanes, no fabulous fantasies of speed bumps being flattened or the Secretary of State for Transport being publicly flogged on the steps of the Houses of Parliament could do anything to dislodge her.

SEVEN

Back at St. Thomas's, the parishioners were becoming accustomed to their new parish priest and his rather unusual ideas.

One if the first things he did was to be re-institute the old Latin mass. Only one mass a week, but it was the eleven o'clock – the most heavily attended, the one that the Parish Priest almost always said himself. Mass in Latin seemed somehow more spiritual, more holy, more mysteriously ritualistic. Latin put the "Roman" back into Roman Catholic .

This bold step brought him instant favour with the older, more traditional members of his flock, though his reasons for taking it had nothing to do with seeking their approval. Frank could trace the recent decline in the fortunes of the Catholic Church to the day they began saying mass in English. Had they stuck with Latin, most people would have been quite unaware of the ludicrous things they were saying.. Once the Liturgy was spelled out to them in plain English, they could see immediate flaws in its veracity and logic. They would start to question it, just as he had done as a small boy in Quex Road. They would stop believing, stop attending mass and, most significantly, stop putting money in the collection plate

The sermons, of course, were in English and these were Frank's trump cards of which he seemed to have a never-ending pack. He was a wonderful communicator with a natural knack of sensing his congregation's mood, choosing his words accordingly and timing them brilliantly.

As a DJ, he'd had that same knack of sensing the mood on the dancefloor, choosing his tracks accordingly and timing them brilliantly. His sermons could begin anywhere – Rice Krispies, boxer shorts, Arsenal's chances in the Champions' League, hang-gliding, tube drivers, carpet warehouses. His audience would listen, often wondering how on earth such an unconnected subject could, in the course of a relatively short sermon, be brought round to God. Yet he did it every time, using the verbal equivalent of sleight of hand. It was done skilfully, subtly, almost imperceptibly. Although the congregation were listening to every word, they would never spot the join. They'd never know how or when it was coming but come it always did, usually with an honest and open appeal to make the collection plate a little heavier.

This was Frank's greatest talent – parting people from their cash..

When he first started, he had very little competition but as time went on and Sunday trading laws were relaxed, there were more and more places open and ready to take the congregation's money. Frank was going to have to ensure that every Sunday they gave it to St. Thomas's rather than St. Tesco's

On his first day, he had been shown the old church hall round the back. It was huge, sad and hadn't been used for years. The wood on the doors and windowsills had gone soft and chewy and what paint still remained on them was now suffering from a severe form of leprosy. Inside it was cold, damp and musty. The air inside was heavy with that horrible stench which takes decades of decay to acquire.

As he strode gingerly around the hall, taking great care not to fall through a loose or rotting floorboard, Frank decided to make this place the subject of his first sermon.

The following Sunday, he concluded his reading from the gospel according to Mark.

"This is the word of the Lord",

"Praise to you Lord Jesus Christ", replied five hundred voices on automatic pilot.

Then Frank said nothing. Absolutely nothing. From his vantage point on the altar, he calmly surveyed the people in front of him. It was a full house. All keen to catch a glimpse of the new parish priest. They thought they were sizing him up. They didn't yet realise that it was the other way round. Still he said nothing. Oh, the power of silence.

Then he spoke. Not commenting on the gospel, not mentioning anything remotely biblical, spiritual or holy. He opened with three simple words.

"I want money".

Before they'd had a chance to be shocked by this, he went on.

"Your money. Together, we're going to build a parish centre. Your parish centre. Your money. I would apologise for such a direct approach but there's nothing to apologise for. I need your money. Every penny will be put to good use and how else am I going to get it? Asking for cash is nothing new. Read St.Paul's letters to the Corinthians. Full of appeals, begging letters, mail shots, whatever you want to call them. The message was very simple – he wanted money, I want money and I'm going to tell you why."

They were already spellbound. He left a beat before continuing

"We're lucky. Very, very lucky. Right here, we have an enormous church hall. We have the land, we have the building. Structurally, I'm told, it's very sound so we're half way there already but inside, as you know, it's in a terrible state. Because of...well... a lack of money, it has been left to rot, left to die. But the life of our parish centre is a life that can very easily be saved. Like Lazarus, it can be brought back from the dead and its life will become our life, the communal life of this parish. When I look at the skill, when I look at the talent – the strength and the enthusiasm of the people in front of me, I realise that if we all work together, the job will be done in a matter of weeks. Our Lord created the world in six days so I'm sure we can do up an old church hall in six weeks. Hands up any bricklayers".

A few hands were tentatively raised.

"Plumbers?"

A few more.

Chippies, plasterers, electricians and roofers all rather nervously revealed themselves.

"Right, any totally useless impractical people who can't do anything at all?"

Frank raised his own hand and smiled.

"I'm nominating myself and Father Conlon as general labourers. Father Lynam can make the tea. We'll have a proper community centre. Bar, dancehall, anything you want, all suggestions welcome. But it's going to take a hell of a lot of cash. Hard cash. So you're going to have to dig deep and give as much as you can. Now, if you're really strapped and can't spare a penny – that's fine. As the old saying goes, time is money, so spare us your time. Obviously, it's a big project so we're going to need a foreman and I'm sure you'll agree, there's only one man for the job. Ladies and gentlemen, Mr. Danny Power........."

Danny Power, the life and soul of the parish, stood up and took a bow. The congregation had never heard a sermon like this and, fired up by the rhetorical skill of their Parish Priest, found themselves bursting into spontaneous applause.

EIGHT

Frank had first met Danny Power the day before when doing the rounds of prominent parishioners on whom Father Lynam had suggested he call. The door had been answered by Mrs. Power, slim, blonde and a dead ringer for Clodagh Rogers.

"Mrs. Power?"

"Yes"

"I'm Father Dempsey. – n w parish priest. Just thought I'd pop round and introduce myself".

Rose Power smiled warmly, "Ah, come in, Father. I'm just after putting the kettle on".

It was a huge house in Harrow Weald, detached and unashamedly vulgar. The front door was flanked by Neo-Grecian pillars and in the huge, crazy-paved driveway stood a Land Rover Freelander, a Mercedes S-Class and a green Transit van with POWER emblazoned on the side.

As Mrs. Power ushered him in and Frank was immediately touched by an atmosphere of happiness, of fun and of devil may care vulgarity.

He followed her through to an enormous kitchen/ diner which led out on to a huge square patio and a gigantic garden where at least a dozen children were playing, squeals of laughter pealing out from all directions.

"Blimey", said Frank, forgetting that priests weren't supposed to say God Blind Me, "Are they all yours?"

"God, no", she laughed, forgetting that she wasn't supposed to take the Lord's name in vain in front of a priest, "Just five of them. Mind you, this place is always full of kids.

Saturday nights, I don't know how many I'll be cooking for".

It was easy to see why. Any child would be drawn like a magnet to Chez Power. The big garden had more attractions than Alton Towers. Swings, see-saws, climbing frames, a wendy-house bigger than the average semi, a paddling pool which could comfortably accommodate the next world synchronised swimming championships and in the distance he could see a carrot-topped child bouncing dangerously high on a trampoline the size of Belgium.

As Frank's eyes were just trying to take in the sheer magnitude of the industrial sized barbecue in the corner, he heard the flush of the downstairs loo and a huge, dark haired ruddy-faced man in his late forties emerged completely unabashed by two unusual things.

One – he wasn't wearing any trousers and two – he was eating a Big Mac

Danny Power, in his socks, vest and underpants was about six foot two and although he neither knew nor cared, well over twenty stone.

"Danny", said his wife, "this is Father Dempsey".

The big Irish face broke into a huge friendly smile,

"Ah, Father". he said between mouthfuls, McDonald's special sauce running down his chin, "Nice to meet you". Can I get you a beer?"

" Danny, I've just put the kettle on"

With a dismissive wave of one enormous, hand, Danny strode instead towards a gigantic American fridge which would have been more at home in a morgue. As the door swung open, all you could see was beer. Cans upon bottles upon cans upon bottles crammed in from top to bottom with scarcely an inch to spare.

"What would you like, Father? Lager? Bitter? Guinness?"

Frank, wondering if he should alert social services to the fact that the Power children were seemingly fed nothing but beer, couldn't take his eyes of the contents of that fridge.

"Er...lager, please, that'd be great"

"Stella, Carling, Heineken, 4X, Fosters, Bud, Bud Ice, Bud Lite, Becks, Schlitz, Rolling Rock......."

"Er... Bud. Yeah, nice cold Bud",

"Coming up", said Danny with a smile and pulled out two red and white cans and handed one to Frank who tore open the top and drank it straight from the can. Danny nodded to himself approvingly. This was his kind of priest.

"Cheers, Father", he said, that big smile again, "Welcome to Wealdstone".

"Cheers, Danny", said Frank, "Father Lynam has told me a lot about you".

He had as well. Frank knew all about Danny. Big, crude, crass and happy, Danny Power was a plasterer by trade. As any DIY enthusiast wandering around B&Q on a Sunday morning will tell you, plastering is the one thing they could never crack. Carpentry, plumbing, electrics can eventually be mastered with a lot of patience and step by step instructions but plastering? Forget it. You've either got "the touch" or you haven't and Danny Power's "touch" was heaven sent. To see him in action would be like seeing Mozart, Michelangelo or Maradona. The speed and artistry of his work had made him a fortune, most of which he had either drunk, smoked or eaten. As a natural leader and organiser, he was now a very successful "subbie" or sub-contractor, able to put together gangs of men to do any sort of building work.

Perfect.

"Come on, Father, shall we sit in the other room?"

Frank followed his host into the sitting room which, along with everything in it, was enormous. Enormous sofas, enormous mirror above an enormous fireplace, enormous "home cinema" style TV and hi-fi, enormous bar complete with optics and pineapple ice-bucket in the corner and enormous man in enormous underpants standing behind it serving himself a whiskey chaser.

"Something a little stronger to go with that, Father? Scotch, Irish, vodka, gin......"

"No, the beer's fine, Danny thanks".

Danny was the first to hear of Frank's grand plans for the church hall.

"Brilliant idea, brilliant. Sort of thing they should have done years ago. I mean, Father Lynam, he's a good man, God love him, but this is a big parish, the poor fella has had so much to do and he's not getting any younger. And it's the money, I've not been in there for a long time and the place was in a sorry enough state then. God knows what it's like now".

"Pretty bad", said Frank ruefully.

"Well, it'll cost a fortune just for the materials".

"Money", Frank assured him with an even confidence. "will not be a problem".

Danny raised an eyebrow, wondering where that sort of sum would come from. The Sunday Times Rich List had never featured anyone from Wealdstone.

"Well, labour won't be a problem", he said. "I can tell you now, Father, everyone you need will be at the eleven o'clock mass on Sunday. I could round them all up for you, but personally, I think it'd be better coming from you. More effective, like. They'll find it much harder to say no to a priest".

Danny was right. Frank had the best builders in the parish all volunteering their services for nothing. Everybody else in the congregation seemed to be falling over themselves to stuff fivers and tenners in the collection boxes and within a couple of weeks, Frank had dozens of men and thousands of pounds to put his plans to work. Danny was stunned by the amount of cash Frank's single appeal had raised.

Unbeknown to the priest, there was an another reason why those men, all of whom had worked for Danny at some time or other, were so keen. Their gaffer had assured them that if they didn't turn up and "work their fucking bollocks off" on the parish centre for nothing, he wouldn't be giving them any more work ever again.

NINE

Sarah had a terrible fear of cats. Not cats per se but actually owning one. In her mind, once a woman had a cat she was all but admitting that she had given up. She had failed to find a partner, a soul mate, someone to love and cherish her and the cat had taken the place of a man.

These little tragedies were always well-disguised. Sarah had heard many a cat owner tell her happy and fulfilled she was. Really clued-up women, most of them, usually prone to opining that "all men are bastards". Not quite clued-up enough, though, to realise that the cat is the biggest bastard of them all. Sly, cold, cruel and selfish, the cat embodies all the faults which its owner tries to ascribe to men. The cat gives nothing and takes everything. Sarah had watched the owner become accustomed to this bastard/victim relationship and then attract blokes who would her in exactly the same way. And then, all men really are bastards.

Sarah may have been single but she was still a long way from the litter tray and was fairly upbeat when she met her friend Helen for lunch that day. Between taxi and table, she'd decided not to tell Helen about Frank. That brief journey from Golden Square had been one of the most weird and wonderful events in her life. She wasn't quite sure how she felt or what she felt and until she'd worked that out, all she'd be able to tell Helen about it would be "djxplkqqwxrtlphbvcxzzpl"

Still, she'd booked a repeat performance from Fulham to Heathrow on Wednesday, after which she might be able to say something a little more intelligible.

Anyway, these girlie lunches with Helen weren't as much

fun as they used to be. Not since Helen had met Graham. Now that Helen was one seemingly happy half of "an item" and Sarah was steadfastly single, the former now considered herself qualified to dispense unwanted advice on how to "get a man".

Sarah was more than capable of "getting a man", she just had no desire to "get a man" like Graham. Oh, he was all right – nothing wrong with him, just a bit dull. And as Helen approached her thirtieth birthday, Sarah couldn't help feeling that her best friend was making a big mistake. Choosing contentment over happiness.

Graham was an accountant but, as Helen always insisted, "he's not like an accountant". Oh yes he fucking is. When he left college he thought "I know what I'll do – accountancy. I'll train for years and spend all my working life wearing a suit and ...er... accounting".

And the self-consciously wacky behaviour, – the oh so humorous signs on the desk – "You don't have to be mad to work here – but it helps" and what's that other one? "The impossible we do at once, miracles take a little longer" the consumption, with tie undone, of gallons of lager in the Pizza Hut on a Friday night , the hilarious paintballing weekends in Kent will never, ever alter this

Graham and his safe and dependable ilk hover for years like birds of prey. They wait for women like Helen to become frustrated with attractive, interesting but unreliable men. After a while, the Helens of this world start to worry. They're acutely aware of the ticking of their biological clocks, they don't want to be left on the shelf, they set their sights a little lower than they otherwise would and that's when the accountants get lucky. At any other time in their lives, the women who become their wives wouldn't have even looked at them. Helen had now become a little sachet of de-hydrated matrimony and there was Graham, more than willing to "just add water".

Tragic really, but Sarah wasn't about to follow her into soporific suburban stability. Not yet anyway. She still refused to believe that it was a straight choice between a cat and an accountant. There had to be another option. Over a bottle of Chablis, however, Helen decided to go through all the options that Sarah had already foregone.

"James", she began, "What was wrong with him?"

"Too posh"

"Too posh?"

"Fundamentally cold"

"Peter?"

"Too ambitious"

"Well, that's not a bad thing. Graham's ambitious."

"Not like Peter. I hope not anyway.. He always put himself first. On a plane he'd immediately recline his seat right back no matter how cramped that made the poor person behind . At the gym, he'd stand at the water fountain filling this great big two litre bottle while a queue of people were waiting behind him gasping for a drink Hard to feel much affection for someone like that."

"Ian?"

"Not ambitious enough".

Helen gave an almost cruel chuckle, "You can't have it both ways"

"Oh, he was lovely. Really sweet, really good person but what's that old saying? When poverty knocks on the door ......love flies out the window. And after a while a man of thirty-four living in a squat in Deptford waiting for his giro becomes a bit of a turn off.

"How about Michael?" said Helen dreamily, "He was gorgeous."

Sarah laughed "Well, he certainly thought so. I had to queue for twenty minutes to use my own hairdryer. And all the lotions and potions he used to use. He couldn't pass a mirror without gazing lovingly into it. No-one could ever love him as much as he loved himself."

Sarah took a gulp of wine.

"And by the way, his mother was not Italian. He just spent a fortune on sunbeds"

Helen recalled another of Sarah's ex's. "Andy?

"Mean."

"As in tight?"

"As a gnat's arse. He was the sort of bloke who'd turn the gas off when he turned the bacon over. Wouldn't expect it, would you? For some reason you think good-looking people are going to be generous but not him. Never went overdrawn, all his money sensibly invested" explained Sarah, suddenly realising that Graham was probably another one knee-deep in PEPs and TESSAs, "And with mean people, money is just the tip of the iceberg. They're mean with their time, they're mean with their love, they're the sort of people who 'don't see why they should'. When I moved out, his main concern was getting a flatmate to help pay the mortgage."

"Ah", said Helen, placing her hand on the back of Sarah's with genuine sympathy and affection but a hint of condescension, "You've been really unlucky, haven't you?"

Not as unlucky as you, thought Sarah, hitched up to a twat like Graham.

"Well, not really", said Sarah, "I've only mentioned the bad times with those blokes. The reasons why things didn't work out in the end. There were plenty of good times too".

"Oh, I'm sure there were", said Helen, "but there's this guy that Graham and I really want you to meet"

Graham and I? Graham and I?? Oh, no. Sarah's heart filled with dread.. She knew her friend was only trying to be kind but the alarm bells were going off and she thought about making a dash for the fire exit.

"He works at Graham's office. Real character".

"Works at Graham's office?" asked Sarah slowly, "So he's...er....he's an accountant?"

"Yeah, but he's not like an accountant".

At that moment, Sarah just wanted to bury her head in her wild mushroom risotto and scream and scream and scream.

TEN

Builders, generally, have a dreadful reputation and, in most cases, it's richly deserved. Whole ITV programmes with imaginative titles like "Builders From Hell" have been dedicated to their laziness, incompetence and dishonesty.

Britain lives in dread of cowboy builders and the reason why the whole nation seems obsessed with DIY is that people truly believe that even they couldn't make a worse bodge of it than the builders they employed last time.

To redress the balance, ITV should have sent a film crew down to Wealdstone to cover the renovation of St. Thomas" church hall. They could have called it "Builders From Heaven" or more accurately "Builders Terrified Of Not Getting Into Heaven". because Father Frank Dempsey had shrewdly and subtly put the fear of God into them.

He'd cleverly implied that by carrying out this work quickly and thoroughly honestly, they were working for God. Working their passage to the kingdom of Heaven. The inference being, of course, that if they didn't, then eternal damnation would surely await them and they really would end up as Builders From Hell.

The place was in a far worse state than had been apparent to Frank's cursory and untrained eye. Rising damp, dry rot, wet rot, leaking roof, timbers crawling with woodworm, you name it. Ginger Tom, the electrician could scarcely believe what he saw,

"This wiring, I mean, it's got to be pre-war. Any minute, any bloody minute, this place could have gone up like a tinder box".

His brother, Ginger Ken, the plumber, was similarly appalled,

"The pipes under here, they've nearly all rotted. I've never seen anything like it, any minute, any bloody minute, this place could have been flooded".

Frank couldn't help thinking that everything would have been all right then. The ancient wiring would have caused a big fire and the flood from the dodgy plumbing would have put it out.

Danny Power marshalled his troops like a sergeant major, his huge voice soaring above the cacophony of hammers, drills and Capital Gold to make its orders heard.

In his hands were the architect's plans from John Toomey & Partners. John was known to everyone as "Socket" – Socket Toomey – and had no ambitions to be Norman Foster or Richard Rogers. He was far happier helping ordinary people realise their dreams. Loft conversions, kitchen extensions, new conservatories. He was only too pleased to help Frank realise his. Naturally, he wasn't being paid a penny.

The whole place was re-wired, re-plumbed, it had new central heating, new joists and floorboards, a whole new roof. Danny ensured that Socket's plans were followed to the letter. Footings were dug, an extension on the back was built, stud partitions, RSJ's and catnick lintels were all heaved into place, parquet flooring was laid for the dancefloor.

The scene was now set, the canvas blank for the maestro. Satisfied with the standard of all the work that had been carried out, Danny Power waddled in with his plaster and trowel and set about his task like a whirling dervish. A big, fat sweaty one. He had toyed with the idea of letting someone else to the plastering but had opted to do the whole place himself. He would do it more quickly, he would do it more skilfully and it was a lovely big area to plaster, he could really go to town. And, most importantly, the back of his mind had not been immune to what Frank had implied. If he did the whole job himself, wouldn't that put a few bonus points on his celestial loyalty card? Wouldn't it make him less likely to finish up as one of Satan's Subterranean Slaves?

At the end of his mammoth task, Danny had pains across his chest and arms. Not surprising really but he had done a magnificent job. Everybody had. The centre was sectioned off into two areas. The "Big Bar" was enormous. Socket had modelled it on one he'd seen as a child at Butlin's holiday camp in Filey, said to be the "the longest bar in Britain". This new one ran the whole length of the dancefloor and comprised a long line of draught taps backed up by serried ranks of optics. Then there was the "Small Bar" – which was in fact huge, square and accessible from all sides. Around it were chairs, sofas and four giant TV screens.

Frank had assiduously taken the names and addresses of every person who had helped renovate the parish centre so that he could throw a big opening night party just for them with a lavish buffet and free drinks all night. For the work that these people had done, this would be a very small price to pay.

ELEVEN

Anne Walsh (Mrs.)

Strange way to sign a letter but that was how she'd always done it – Anne Walsh (Mrs.). As opposed to what? Anne Walsh (Mr.)? Anne Walsh (Miss)?

Was that it? Did Mrs. Walsh want the world to know that she had received the sacrament of matrimony? That she was a good woman, a holy person, a proper, practising Catholic?

Anne Walsh was prim, proper, po-faced, pious. Anything beginning with P, really. Private, pragmatic, purse-lipped, prosaic, persistent, petty? All of these things.

How about pretty? Well, she certainly used to be but since at least half of her fifty-two years had been spent frowning, her features had set that way and it was now her natural expression. She frowned even if she liked you, frowned if she was pleased to meet you. Her smile could be an impressive and rather beautiful sight. Rather like Halley's Comet. And witnessed about as often.

Her wealth and status that existed largely within her own head had brought with it a reproving respectability, a cheap snobbery. She wasn't particularly wealthy but if you were one of nine children brought up in a crumbling tenement on the north side of Dublin, everything is relative. She was Annie O'Malley then and, at nineteen, had moved to London to improve her circumstances. If damp digs in Kilburn were an improvement, you can imagine what those circumstances must have been like.. She'd worked behind the bar in The Crown, a huge Irish pub in Cricklewood and it was on the Number 16 bus to work that she'd met Pat Walsh.

Pat was the conductor, a chirpy little man from Limerick, usually teamed with a big, meaty-chopped driver called Len. Together they piloted the Number 16 out of Cricklewood Garage and along the Edgware Road through Kilburn and Maida Vale, round Marble Arch, down Park Lane, round Hyde Park Corner all the way to Victoria.

It was a lively, interesting route, busily cutting a swathe right through the centre of town. Pat Walsh, standing on the running board, helping people on and off, greeting regulars and calling out "Hold tight" and "Fares please", was a very happy man. He was brilliant with figures and, on more than one occasion, Annie O'Malley had marvelled at his arithmetical wizardry, his enviable ability to add up complex combinations of fares in an instant, never making a mistake, never giving the wrong change.

One night, she found herself the sole passenger on the last bus home. It was freezing and, as the rain lashed down spitefully on Cricklewood. She got chatting to Pat. Not difficult, he'd chat to anyone, and he was concerned for the well-being of a girl on her own late at night in one of London's less salubrious areas.

"Where do you live?" he enquired.

"Kilburn"

"Whereabouts?"

"Victoria Road"

At the next stop, Pat ran out into the rain to have a quick word with Len, returning seconds later drenched but smiling. A little later, to Annie's astonishment, Len took a quick detour. The bus left its scheduled route along Kilburn High Road and turned right up Victoria Road, squeezing carefully between the twin lines of parked cars.

"Now what number?" said Pat with a smile,

"Er.......124, right up the other end".

"Okay, the driver's going nice and slow now, just ring the bell when we're there",

Annie rang the bell, thanked Pat and married him six months later.

However, she hadn't left Dublin, worked hard at The Crown and endured the miserable squalor of Victoria Road only to spend the rest of her life married to a bus conductor. She was convinced that Pat could do better than that. A lot better than that. Within a matter of weeks, she got behind her new husband and began to push. He seemed immovable at first but gradually Pat Walsh and his head for figures began to roll slowly towards a more lucrative career.

During the day, he conducted the Number 16, but three evenings a week, Pat was at nightschool studying to be an accountant. After a few years . he was able to say goodbye to the Number 16 bus voluntarily. Just as well, since the introduction of one-man buses a few months later would have made his valediction compulsory.

They moved out to a little terraced house in Wealdstone and shortly afterwards. PJ Walsh Associates opened in a tiny office in Harrow

His clients were almost all from the building trade. They valued Pat, they needed his help with their VAT returns and to guide them through various tax loopholes but he'd never be really accepted. His little soft hands had never done a day's hard, manual graft. He was prudent, he was sensible and wherever he went, his wife's huge thumbprint was clearly visible on the top of his head.

Still, when it came to money, he was the man. Practising Catholic, straight as a die and Father Frank Dempsey knew that pretty soon, he'd have more money than he'd know what to do with.

TWELVE

He was a big man in a small garden.

A man trying to get to grips with a hobby he had taken up to stop him going insane in retirement and yet, if insanity were ever diagnosed in Edward Dempsey, this new hobby would be its most likely cause.

Eddie was 66, a year into retirement, and having followed his brother Eamonn over from Connemara, spent forty years as one of West London's most colourful publicans. Notting Hill, or "Notting Dale" as it was known when Eddie first arrived from Ireland, was not the cosy, gentrified honeypot it would eventually start to become.. It was of the most volatile and dangerous areas in Britain and The Elgin, The Eagle and The Bramley Arms were three of its most volatile and dangerous pubs. Though, it has to be said, not when "Big Eddie" was behind the bar. He had earned and kept the respect of some of London's hardest hoodlums. Just the sight of the huge ex-Gaelic footballer was usually enough to stop a disturbance before it even started. And God help anyone who didn't stop when he told them to,

Even now, retired in the garden of his neat little semi in Perivale, he was still a formidable figure. Horticulture just didn't suit him. Deadheading the roses, weeding the flowerbeds, nurturing the pansies – it simply wasn't him. He'd tried but was becoming increasingly depressed and frustrated at the futility of it all. He could spend three or four hours toiling in that garden and then, a week later, there would be no evidence that he'd ever stepped out of the back door. And so he'd have to do it all over again. In the pub trade, every day had been different. In the garden, every day was the same. And so he became morose and when he became morose, he drank and the more he drank, the more morose he became.

The children came to visit, the little grandchildren too, but for Eddie the visits were too few and far between, No matter how long they stayed , it was never long enough to fill more than the occasional crevice in the huge, empty rockface of his life. Just as he was considering growing a few tomatoes in the far corner by the shed, the phone rang. It was a cordless phone and its constant presence out there in the garden made Eddie feel a little less lonely

"Hello?"

"Uncle Eddie? It's Frank."

"How are you, boy?", smiled the reluctant Alan Titchmarsh, "Settling in to the new job all right?"

"Great, thanks", said Frank, "It's going really well. Do you know where Wealdstone is?"

"Yeah", said Eddie a little puzzled, "It isn't far from here".

"Good" said Frank, "Can you meet me at the church in half an hour, I've got a little proposition for you".

Eddie needed no persuasion at all to fling down his rake and come out of retirement. He was immediately installed as the new manager of St.Thomas's Parish Centre on an annual salary of absolutely nothing.

Frank had decided to extend his original scheme, some might say scam, where nobody was paid a penny for working there. He viewed it as ethical collectivism (he knew those Oxford philosophy lectures would come in handy one day)- all working together for the common good and, to be fair, it was true, Bar staff, cleaners, maintenance men all donated their services and were more than happy to do so.

With Big Eddie at the helm, the place was an instant hit. He'd anticipated a lot of trouble persuading his long-suffering wife Nora to go along with the idea. She'd worked hard and waited patiently for the big publican to throw in the bar towel and just eleven months later, he was going back. Not only that but he wasn't even being paid. Eddie explained without going into too much detail that the extra-curricular activities in which any shrewd publican, especially one on first-name terms with most of West London's underworld, could get involved meant that they'd always have enough money to live on. What's more, this was real charity work, a chance to put something back.

To Eddie's surprise, his decision met with very little resistance. Auntie Nora adored Frank and could also see that her husband was far from happy and fulfilled in the garden. He was getting under her feet, he was starting to drink too much and she feared that he might soon begin to age and decline. Death, perhaps, by missing adventure.

With "St.Tom's" staffed entirely by voluntary workers, any cash coming in was pure profit. There were discos, dances, aerobics classes, on Monday night live Premiership football; there were nights, karaoke nights, bingo and most popular of all, Jimmy Flynn's Horse Racing nights. Jimmy would bring in videos of old races from the Sixties and Seventies, usually in black & white. People would line up with absolutely no knowledge of the horses, no odds, five pounds a punt and anyone who picked the winner would split the jackpot, minus a sizeable chunk each time that went straight into the parish coffers.

Frank wanted the money handled properly and efficiently, any surplus being distributed among various charities. It was Danny Power who told him, "there's no finer fella than Pat Walsh".

THIRTEEN

Frank called round. The house was on a new estate of almost identical properties, all aged up with rustic brick, half-timbering and leaded windows in a vain attempt to disguise the fact that eighteen months ago, these houses didn't even exist. There was a carriage lamp above the doorbell and the name of the house "Patanne" a hideous hybrid of the names of its inhabitants, was carved into a flat board made of artificial bark. Frank pressed the bell and was alarmed to hear the strains of Vivaldi's Four Seasons chiming out.

"Mrs. Walsh?". he smiled at the frowning face in front of him, "I'm Father Frank Dempsey, the new Parish priest."

Anne Walsh almost smiled and invited him in. Frank was lucky. If he hadn't been the new parish priest, she would have made him take his shoes off.

Muddy boots – fair enough. If she were Mrs. Daniel Power, this policy would have been understandable, But she was Mrs. Patrick Walsh. Her husband spent all day behind his desk in a clean, carpeted office. His shiny, black slip-ons were spotless. Yet every evening at the front door, those slip-ons had to be slipped off and replaced by a pair of burgundy backless slippers. You know the ones – leather and prone to making that horrible "plap, plap" sound when walked in.

Pat came plap-plapping from the kitchen, his little fat hand outstretched.

"Father", he beamed, "Good to meet you"

Pat was a man who didn't wear clothes,. He wore outfits. Colour co-ordinated outfits which no man would choose for himself. Today it was a lemon Pringle golfing sweater, with a thin grey stripe through it, to which his wife had matched a grey and lemon shirt and a pair of grey slacks. It was a fairly safe bet that between his feet and those backless slippers, you'd find a little pair of lemon socks.

"Little bird tells me, Father, that you're big into music"

"The little bird's right", said Frank.

"C'mere, let me show you something", he said, leading Frank into the sitting room or "through lounge" as his wife preferred to call it.. "What do you think?"

He was gesturing towards something of which he was clearly chest-puffingly proud.

"Takes 100 CD's".

The object of Pat's pride was a brand new replica of a Wurlitzer juke-box, delivered and installed that very morning.

"Reproduction of course. but, well who can be bothered with old singles nowadays? This is the digital age".

Pat's views were quite valid but, to Frank, he could hardly have said a worse thing.. He could have dismissed the whole notion of Catholicism, transubstantiation, Papal infallibility. Scoffed at the very idea of an Immaculate Conception and a virgin birth, declared all four gospels to be nothing but a pack of lies and propaganda, accused Jesus of a sordid affair with Mary Magdalene who, incidentally was a whore, and the priest would have found it very hard to disagree. But, decrying the sanctity of old vinyl? Nothing short of heresy. The little, fat accountant should be burned at the stake.

However, Frank said nothing, just nodded with a tight, polite smile. Pat was warming to his theme, delighted with his brand new acquisition,

"CD's transformed music", he went on, " the sound quality, no hisses, no scratches, no surface noise".

Frank nodded again, considering Pat's point.

"Though, don't you think", he said slowly, "that life has surface noise".

The conversation had taken a philosophical turn for which Pat wasn't quite prepared.

"Very profound, Father", was the best he could manage, "very profound." He strode over to the juke box and said "What would you like to hear, Father? I'm a Country & Western fan myself".

Well, what a surprise.

"Me too", This was a blatant lie. Frank had always loathed country music's inherent tragedy, its mawkish sentimentality, noble women standing by brutal men, crippled orphans dying in the snow. To the backing of Charlie Rich singing "Behind Closed Doors", Frank settled back into the Parker Knoll dralon armchair. The house was immaculate. Horribly tidy. Nothing out of place not a speck of dust anywhere. Frank could imagine Pat sitting on the sofa, with his legs permanently raised eighteen inches above the carpet so Anne could hoover underneath him. Everywhere Frank looked, he could see tasteless attempts to be tasteful The books on the shelf had been bought by the yard. Cheap unread leather bound volumes of Shakespeare and Dickens, Austen and Trollope, all delivered within 28 Days from the back page of the Sunday Express Magazine. At the double-glazed windows were pristine nets and enormous, swirly-patterned curtains which looked like great big baggy knickers.. The new Yorkstone fireplace contained one of those Gas Effect log fires which looked about as convincing as the Turin Shroud. The place was alive with coasters, doilies, antimacassars – you felt henpecked just walking in there.

The henpecker herself then entered from stage left in blue velveteen slippers pushing one of those little gilt Hostess tea trolleys. A tray on the top shelf had a dainty and flowery bone china tea service whilst on the bottom were a selection of biscuits from Fox's Vienna Assortment neatly arranged on a circular plate.

"Earl Grey all right for you, Father?"

"Yeah, lovely, Mrs. Walsh. Thank you"

Again, the not-quite smile as she poured the tea and proffered the biscuits. This whole persona was an elaborate affectation. At least, that's how it had started out. After affecting any sort of behaviour for long enough, that behaviour becomes real. We are our affectations. Anne Walsh now really was that respectable Catholic woman, that paragon of piety. She was what you might call a born again prude, folding her arms. pursing her lips, shaking her head at anything she regarded as vulgar or crude. It wasn't always so. There was nothing remotely prudish about the feisty young Annie O'Malley, barmaid at The Crown, Cricklewood. Even now, when riled, her eyes would flash with anger and her accent would become laced with its original Dublin coarseness. Oddly enough, this always gave Pat a brief frisson of sexual excitement as he caught a fleeting glimpse of the pretty girl he had fallen in love with on the Number 16 bus.

She wasn't a bad person. In many ways, quite the opposite She worked hard for the parish. Oversaw the cleaning and flower-arranging rotas, did voluntary work at the local hospital and was Parish secretary of the Association of the Propagation of the Faith. She'd certainly been a very kind and dutiful mother and both Kathleen and Geraldine Walsh, now in their twenties, had done very well. Kathleen was a radiologist at a private clinic in Edinburgh. Eileen, with her father's head for figures, worked as a broker for one of the big banks in the City. The city being Tokyo. They loved their mother but both felt that the best way to carry on loving her was to live as far away as possible.

Both girls had grown weary of Anne's desire to be holier than thou. More respectable than thou, more hard- done by than thou – the martyr in the Mini Metro. She'd liked to have been a martyr, like St. Agnes or St. Anastasia, feeling that the more she suffered (or pretended to suffer) in this life the greater would be her reward in the next. Hence the illnesses. It was never anything serious. It was never "I think I've got breast cancer" because a doctor could immediately say "Oh no you haven't". They were always minor but always painful and debilitating ailments, mentioned on a daily basis for which Pat just had to take her word.

"I've got a terrible headache, I've got an upset tummy. I've got a sore throat. I've really hurt my back, I've twisted my ankle,". Sometimes it was the all-purpose "I don't know what's the matter with me but I don't feel well at all"

Over the years, Pat had kept a mental list of at least fifty of these medical complaints and often felt like typing them up, printing them off and pinning them to the kitchen wall.. His wife could then just tick the appropriate number each morning and save a lot of time.

If Pat outlived his wife, he could imagine the inscription on her gravestone "Now Do You Believe Me?".

If Anne outlived Pat, she'd do what a lot of people do when they've been consistently unkind to a so-called loved one in life – she'd venerate and lionise him in death. A huge marble headstone would be erected , eulogising Patrick J. Walsh who "fell asleep" on such and such a date, sadly missed by his adoring wife and family. Every day, she'd be up that cemetery, tending the grave, depositing fresh flowers making sure it was tidier and better-kept than any of the neighbouring plots, tut-tutting reprovingly at the way theirs had become so straggly and unkempt.

All that grief, all that suffering, all that martyrdom. Surely that would ease her passage to Heaven. Anne Walsh (Mrs) would revel in being a widow. So much more "Catholic" than being a wife.

Over tea, Frank had outlined his plans to Pat for the Parish Centre, expressing his need for a "sound man" to take care of the money adding that Danny Power and "all the lads" spoke very highly of him. It was the approval from "the lads" that clinched it. It was what he still craved and yes, he would be delighted to financially direct the whole operation. And no, of course there would be No Charge (one of Pat's Country & Western favourites) for his services.

FOURTEEN

Frank woke up at 3.23. Then again at 4.07. Then again at 4.51. Finally at 5.18, he got up. The house shook, the windows rattled to the sound of Father Lynam's snoring and Frank tiptoed into the bathroom, his stomach somersaulting at the prospect of seeing Sarah Marshall again. In just over an hour, she'd once again be in the back of his cab. Oh, Jesus!

Why was he bothering to tiptoe? If Father Conlon could sleep through Father Lynam's inhuman snoring which sounded like a large herd of wildebeest rampaging through the house, then nothing short of a nuclear explosion would have any chance of waking him.

Bathed, shampooed, scrubbed and flossed, Frank put his clothes on, all fresh from the laundry basket, impregnated with the divine smell of fabric conditioner that he'd always found so appealing.

Black T-shirt, black jeans, black socks, black Dr. Marten's shoes and black quilted F1 flying jacket. Giving himself one final check in the mirror, Frank felt that, dressed like this, he should come crashing through Sarah's window with a box of Milk Tray.

At 3.23, Sarah was also lying awake, lying alone under a crisp white duvet in her big wrought-iron bed. How had she ended up here? Not that "here" was a bad place to have ended up – far from it – but nonetheless, how had she ended up here? She hadn't set out to have a successful career. She wasn't particularly ambitious. She certainly wasn't one of those awful "driven" people setting themselves goals and drawing up five year plans. All she'd done, initially, was pass her A levels. This led to the offer of a place to read English at Westfield College, London. What was she supposed to do? Turn it down?. Three years later, with her graduation photograph proudly perched on her parents' piano, she was offered a job as a trainee account executive at a top London ad agency. What was she supposed to do? Not take that either?. She proved herself to be bright, sassy and charming and so, within a relatively short space of time, she's suddenly earning quite a lot of money with a garden flat in a nice part of London and a brand new candy blue Beetle parked on a resident's permit outside.

She was alone in the flat tonight. Her flat mate – Vanessa or Nessie as she was known – was just perfect – kind, generous and hardly ever there. Nessie was one of those Fat Vegetarians who believe that not eating red meat gives them licence to consume just about every other comestible on the planet. Sarah could always tell whether she was there or not by the amount of food left in the fridge. Nessie was an opera singer. Not a big star, she seldom graced the stage at Covent Garden but she worked fairly regularly and was usually on tour. When she wasn't, she generally stayed with whoever happened to be her current beau. At the moment, it was a rather effete set designer called Robert who had a flat in Kentish Town . Sarah preferred it that way. There are few things in life as unpleasant as lying wide awake in bed listening to the couple next door having sex. Nessie had always been fairly unbridled in her lovemaking and she was, of course, an opera singer. At the moment of climax, you can just imagine what the noise was like. It was a miracle that Robert's flat still contained any unshattered glass.

Sarah stretched her legs diagonally across the big bed. Sometimes she wished there was someone in there with her, sometimes she didn't. Anyone invited under that crisp white duvet now would have to be "right" – whatever that meant.

There was a long list of applicants, an assortment of male friends, colleagues and clients, all standing in an invisible queue outside her bedroom door

So how would she know when she'd met the "right" person? Perhaps she'd met him already. Perhaps one of her ex-boyfriends was as "right" as she was ever going to get. Not one of them, however, had proved "right" enough. Her thoughts turned to her happily married parents, David and Valerie. How did they know? Did they realise at once? Were they just lucky, like two golfers scoring simultaneous holes in one or were people a lot more easily contented back in 1962? They were lovely people, kind, well-balanced and normal. Yet at 3.23 in the morning, their marital nirvana was the bane of Sarah's life. Children from happily married parents often feel like this. They have so much to live up to, such high expectations from any relationship they enter into and therefore such enormous scope for disappointment.

At 3.23 in the morning, Sarah's parents would no doubt be sleeping soundly and peacefully together, as they always had done. David and Valerie Marshall each came from a long line of perfectly normal people.

These are the people who are seldom mentioned, who don't generally appear in books or magazines and about whom documentaries are never made. Anyway, the moment "normal" people appear in documentaries, their normality is over forever. Not that the so-called "normal" people in documentaries are ever normal. The very act of agreeing to star in such programmes is in itself an abnormality.

It would be impossible to stress just how normal David and Valerie Marshall were. There was nothing remotely odd or sinister about either of them. No dark secrets lurked behind the privet hedge. Valerie was not a secret alcoholic any more than David was a weekend transvestite. They were not members of the local Satanic Society, David wasn't even a freemason. Friends and neighbours, though frequently entertained, were not expected to throw their keys in the fruitbowl.. Neither were they boring or dreary. Happy, well-balanced people generally aren't,

David had worked for the Midland Bank for thirty years, ended up as branch manager at Alderley Edge. As the bank manager in such a parochial and prosperous part of Cheshire, he was a well-known and respected figure, a pillar of the local community, on a par with the doctor, the solicitor and the local headmaster, on first name terms with everyone and genuinely concerned for their financial well-being.

Then suddenly, it all changed. Banking in this country underwent a massive upheaval. Branches disappeared like red squirrels, David's among them. Far more cost-effective to subsume his branch and countless others into one gargantuan call centre on an industrial estate just outside Cheadle.. David accepted a handsome redundancy settlement and that night, over a bottle of particularly good South African red, he and Valerie decided that it might be fun to sell the stuff as well as buy it. He took his own advice, applied for a small business loan and entered the wine trade. Now, at 61 and 59 respectively, David and Valerie were happier than ever, constantly off on little buying trips to California, Australia or the South of France.

Sarah suddenly remembered – they were off to Chile tomorrow – uncharted territory. She must phone and wish them good luck. If only her life was as exciting as theirs. Actually, at the moment it almost was. She was going to see that enigmatic and rather hunky priest. After twisting and turning a few more times, she decided to get up and get ready. After all, he'd be here in two hours.

Two hours later with the sun just lifting its head over a deserted A40, Frank's taxi sauntered along it towards Hammersmith and Fulham., its driver trying not to throw up from excitement. At 6.28, he pulled into a street of handsome Victorian terraced houses just off the Fulham Road.

"Hello?"

"Taxi for Marshall".

"Just coming"

Once again, she slid on to the back seat of G339 YMC and once again she brought with her that delicious smell of freshly- washed hair. Frank raised a friendly eyebrow into his rear-view mirror and received that brown-eyed, wide-mouthed smile in return.

Oh, God.

"Heathrow Airport, please, driver", she grinned, "Terminal 3".

Frank grinned back, nodded and pulled the cab out on to Munster Road. He then slid the inter-connecting window all the way along so that their conversation along the M4 wouldn't have to be conducted through a two-inch gap in the glass.

"So how are you?" he began.

"I've been better", she replied, " I can do without getting up at half five".

Sarah had, of course been up since half-four, desperate to look her best, for some inexplicable reason, to meet a Roman Catholic priest who drove a taxi. Hardly the most eligible of men. This pre-dawn effort had paid off. Frank thought she looked stunning, even sexier than last time. Masses of dark tumbling hair, very little make-up – just enough to accentuate the beauty of those eyes and lips, tailored black suit , little jacket, short skirt – when it came to positioning his rear-view mirror, Frank was spoilt for choice.

In his mind, he was trying to fend off the devil, mentally fumbling for a crucifix or a few cloves of garlic. The devil was winning hands down.

Back to the conversation – getting up early.

"Oh, I'm used to it", Frank said, "I sometimes take the cab down to Euston or Paddington around this time. Get a bit of money in the box before the real work starts. Anyway, look – you know all about me. Catholic priest, not married, no children,. Hobbies include pretending to be a cab driver. How about you? What do you do for a living?"

"I work in advertising. I'm what's known as an account director. I have to deal with the clients. When they need advertising, I have to advise them on the sort of ads they should be doing. Maybe press ads, posters or perhaps TV or radio commercials. Once they've decided, I have go back and brief the teams of writers and artists who actually create the ads. When they've done them, I go back to the clients with rough drawings or scripts and try and get them approved. I mean, obviously it's a lot more complicated than that but, well, that's basically it".

"So what are you doing ads for at the moment?"

Sarah's big brown eyes rolled up to heaven, "Oh, don't. ask A chain of fake Irish pubs called Slattery's – you must have seen them, they're everywhere., dreadful bright green places".

Frank had seen them. There was one up the road from the church and part of the reason he was so keen to open the parish centre was he couldn't bear the thought of his parishioners' money lining their shareholders' pockets.

"They're about to open a huge new one in Edinburgh and I've been asked to go up and have a look. I wouldn't mind but it'll be exactly the same as all the others. Horrible, patronising places. These people have no feel for Irish culture, no interest in it at all. Their only concern is how much money they can make.. If there was a similar craze for, say, Italian culture, Slattery's would suddenly be closed down, re-opened and re-named Luigi's. Never mind, it's a job, I suppose".

"Don't you enjoy it?"

"Well, generally, yes. It wasn't what I set out to do. Nobody thinks at university, I know what I'd like to be – an account director in an advertising agency. At least

I hope they don't. I just fell into it really after college".

"Me too", said Frank which surprised her, " I sort of fell into this".

"How can you fall into the priesthood?", she asked, "Aren't you supposed to get some sort of calling?"

"Well, yes", explained Frank "I did feel a calling but only in the way that everything you ever do is in response to some sort of calling. You get a calling to go to the shops, to have something to eat, to go to the loo. That's even described as a 'call of nature'"

Frank was trying not to think of the calling he was receiving right now but it certainly wasn't from God.

"It wasn't so much a call towards the priesthood", he went on, "It was more a call away from other careers like, I don't know......accountancy".

He'd hit the right button.

"Oh don't", said Sarah with an exasperated laugh, "My friend Helen – actually it was her I was meeting for lunch that day when you dropped me off – she's going out with this accountant, Graham. . Fits all the accountant stereotypes although he tries his best not to. Anyway, she only wants to fix me up with his friend , another accountant – Jonathan, likes to be known as JJ. I hate him already and I haven't even met him".

"Fix you up?" said Frank not sure whether he was delighted that she was single or panic-stricken at the thought of her being fixed up with someone. Why should he care? He's a priest. He could never go out with her anyway. He'd taken a vow of celibacy, for God's sake. Quite literally, for God's sake, – certainly not for anyone else's.

"Are you going to meet him?" he enquired, trying (and probably failing) to sound as though it didn't bother him one way or the other.

"I don't want to. Honestly, I'd sooner stay in and remove my own gall bladder-but...well.....Helen's been such a good friend, and she means well and.....you never know, JJ could be the man of my dreams".

"No! No! No!" Frank wanted to scream but just raised a nonchalant eyebrow. He really was giving an Oscar winning performance as a man who couldn't care less.

"Mind you," admitted Sarah "we both know he won't be, don't we?"

Behind his mask of casual insouciance, Frank now wanted to weep with relief. He couldn't speak. . Sarah, not suspecting his feelings for a moment, didn't notice and simply carried on.

"Got to go to supper over at Graham and Helen's. Blackheath, wherever that is. I've heard of it. Haven't got a clue where it is though".

"South East", replied Frank, "Near Lewisham".

"Oh God", sighed Sarah, "Near Lewisham? Helen said it was really nice. Really villagey"

"It is....sort of", said Frank, " It's a bit twee. People who live down there like to think it's South London's answer to Hampstead but it doesn't compare. It's just a little oasis among some pretty scuzzy areas".

"Of course", said Sarah, "You'd know, wouldn't you? Being a taxi driver"

"Well, a pretend one anyway", said Frank who was at that moment feeling like a pretend priest as well.

"Yeah but you still have to know where you're going. People must get into your taxi and expect you to know every street. Black cab drivers have to train for years, don't they?"

"They do and I haven't , said Frank, "but I don't come unstuck as often as I thought I would. I mean, I know where any general area is. If you say Clapham or Harlesden or Walthamstow, I can take you there but I probably wouldn't know the actual street. you wanted. Thing is, the passengers themselves usually know the place they're going. Most times they're either going home or back to the office or over to a friend's house so they can direct you. If not, I'll get them to the area, then look in the A-Z. and anyway, if the worst comes to the worst, I always tell them, as I told you, that I 'm not a qualified black cabbie and they might prefer to take a real taxi".

"I suppose you're right", said Sarah, thinking about it, "I knew where Farringdon Road was and I know where Heathrow Airport is. In fact, that'll be it over there".

Their journey was coming to an end.

"Oh, I've really enjoyed this", she said, and then, not joking, she added "I wish you could drive me to Edinburgh"

"Well, of course I'd love to" Frank replied, not joking either "But I'm off to a meeting of the Diocesan Financial Affairs Sub-Committee. Wouldn't miss it for the world"

"Anyway", he concluded with a most un-priestly wink, "Good luck with JJ. When is this Blackheath dinner party?"

"Tomorrow night", she sighed wearily.

"Well there's a coincidence", said Frank in an "Isn't it a small world?" sort of way.

"Coincidence?" said Sarah, "Don't tell me Graham's invited you too?".

"Sadly not", said Frank, " Though, of course, I'd love nothing more than dinner in Blackheath with a couple of wacky accountants. No, I've got to over to Greenwich tomorrow night. Got to visit Father Conway, my old parish priest .Retired now but does a couple of days a week down there.. I'm always promising to go and see him and I've had to keep blowing him out. Can't put him off again, he's such a lovely old boy".

"Oh, right" said Sarah, not sure where this was leading.

"So, what I was going to suggest was……"

"Yes?" she said, just a little too eagerly

"….that if this dinner party really is a nightmare and JJ really is a…."

"Tosser?" she suggested before blushing,

"Well,", said Frank , affecting a priestly manner, "not the man of your dreams anyway"

"Yes?"

"Well, I'll keep my mobile on. You've got the number and if I'm still in the vicinity, I'll swing by and help you escape".

"It's a deal", she said with the biggest, sexiest smile Frank had ever seen. This time it was a £20 note that was dropped into the box. Frank thanked her and she thanked him and, having dropped her at Domestic Departures, Frank headed back off towards the M4.

Sarah waved and watched him go. And then she waited. Then waited a bit more. Then, once she was sure – once she was absolutely sure – that he was safely out of sight, she hailed another cab to take her straight back to Fulham.

FIFTEEN

Frank had an aversion to hospitals. Not just hospitals but clinics, doctors' surgeries, dentists, osteopaths – anything remotely medical. He was in very good health but any contact with these places simply reminded him that he might not always be.

Not ideal, really, for the new chaplain of Queen Elizabeth's Hospital but he couldn't help it. He'd tried to adopt the more positive outlook, telling himself the hospitals were wonderful places where the sick were healed, new lives were started and old ones re-built. He had nothing but the greatest respect and admiration for the selfless souls who worked there but none of this made a blind bit of difference.. The moment he went through the main entrance, the moment that uniquely unpleasant "hospital smell" reached his nostrils, he became wreathed in a dull, fuggy depression.

The simple fact was that people were only there because of either illness or injury and, marvellous though it was that they often made a full recovery, wouldn't it have been far better if they had never needed to go to hospital in the first place? And what about those for whom the ending wasn't so happy? People cut down in the prime of life? Children desperately ill with leukaemia? These thoughts always brought his latent doubts about the existence of God rushing to the front of his mind. Doubts that crystallised into one tiny but perennially unanswerable question:

Why?

Devout Catholic patients, submerged in the depression that illness can bring, asked that very question of their chaplain.

"Why?"

Why does God allow these things to happen? Illness causes nothing but misery and anguish, stress and pain. It is to the benefit of nobody. Give any person an imaginary genie with the power to grant three wishes and number one is nearly always to abolish all forms of illness So why God, who allegedly does have this power, refuses to exercise it is something about which a lot of patients, or more usually, their loved ones become angry and cynical.

Sometimes they viewed Frank as God's representative at Queen Elizabeth's and almost blamed him for it. He had no reply to their "Why?s". He'd been asking the same question himself for years. It was a question that generations of theology students had pondered, pontificated, appraised and discussed but were no nearer an answer.

In his capacity as priest or chaplain, Frank generally preferred death to illness. With death, you could make it all up. Comes to us all, blah blah, blah. Going to a better place, blah blah,. End to their suffering, blah, blah, blah. With illness, none of these arguments stood up. He felt there was no good side and no justification for it all...

As a child, Frank had developed his own little theory to explain things. An all-purpose answer applicable to practically everything.

Since time began, he'd decided, there'd been a metaphysical tug of war between God and the Devil. All good things – love, happiness, the majestic beauty of nature- could be attributed to God. All bad things – war, famine, Manchester United winning the treble – could be attributed to Satan. Moreover, the personalities of each and every one of us were microcosms of this. Tiny, weeny tugs of war go on inside every one of us all the time between these two superpowers to determine which course of action we take and, in the final analysis, who wins custody of our souls.

A crass, puerile, over-simplistic explanation, of course,

completely lacking any analytical thought but Frank was yet to hear a better one?

On a more quotidian level, he was always saddened by the fact that Queen Elizabeth's, like most other NHS hospitals was pitifully under-resourced. And on this particular Wednesday, to make matters worse, he was confronted by the thing that irritated him more than any other aspect of his hospital chaplaincy – Colin Liddell. Colin was "programme director" of QEFM – the hospital radio station. Liddell was a small, bespectacled creature in his mid-forties One of those people who somehow managed to be skinny and fat at the same time with thin sloping shoulders which pointed down to a most unappealing little pot belly and bulbous bottom. He lived nearby in a small terraced house with Mrs. Liddell. Mrs. Liddell, of course, was his mother.

On seeing Colin standing there, rattling his bright yellow fund-raising can, Frank was half-tempted to wrench the wretched can from his grasp and pocket the contents. He'd be doing the world a favour. Hospital radio was an appalling waste of time and money . It was a most peculiar "charity" since, given the total lack of interest shown in it by patients, it would seem that its only beneficiaries are its presenters' egos. Presenters like Colin who, Frank was sure, was unlikely to have a rip-roaring social life so hospital radio was drafted in to compensate. Colin and his colleagues had somehow convinced themselves that what they were doing was good and worthwhile Yet would you find them doing real voluntary work, heaving geriatrics in and out of bed, or working in a shelter for the homeless, providing help where it was really needed? . The limit of their charitable capacity was saying "Yes indeedy" and playing Leo Sayer records to people who weren't even listening.

That was the point – no-one was listening. Nobody wanted an expensive radio station at Queen Elizabeth's Hospital. In Frank's short time there, he'd heard nothing but complaints about it. If patients wanted to listen to music, they'd tune in to the BBC or one of the commercial stations. More likely, they'd simply slot a tape into a Walkman. Nobody was remotely interested in the inane Colin Liddell trilling his sad little catchphrase "Cooey, it's QEFM".

Colin had once read that Noel Edmonds began his career on hospital radio and ever since then, has long been harbouring fond dreams of having a Crinkley Bottom of his own. But for every Noel there are a thousand no-ones and hospital radio is where you'll find them.

Frank was a millisecond too late in avoiding Colin's eye.

"Father Dempsey", he called over, displaying a most unattractive toothy grin

Oh, Christ.

"Colin", said Frank, fixing a false smile to his face", "How are you?"

"Mustn't grumble, I suppose". he smiled before introducing a sickening expression of grave sincerity, "Not when I think of the people in here, There's always someone worse off than you. Isn't that right, Father?"

Frank silently swore that if Colin trotted out, "There but for the grace of God......", he was going to nut him. Mercifully he didn't.

"There certainly is, Colin, there certainly is. Donations going all right?"

"Not bad, Father, not bad at all. We've actually done very well lately. Just re-fitted the studio. Why don't you pop down and have a look".

"That'd be great Colin, I'd love to", Frank herd himself saying.

The toothy grin made a repellent re-appearance. "Well, I'm going to knock off here about four. Got a very busy show to prepare. Say about 4.15?"

Oh, what the hell? If Frank didn't agree to it now, Colin

would never let him off the hook. Might as well get it over with.

"Fine. 4.15 then.".

Frank spent the next couple of hours chatting with patients. Nothing too heavy,. No theological finger-pointing . Ordinary people recovering from routine operations. Just after four he made his way down to the QEFM studios and couldn't believe what he saw.

A beautifully-appointed, air-conditioned studio which would be the envy of the BBC. Three professional CD players, two Technics turntables. Twin cassette decks, a new mini-disc player even digital editing equipment.

Frank was horrified. Queen Elizabeth's Hospital was crying out for kidney machines and laser scanners. Wards were under constant threat of closure, waiting lists for serious operations were getting longer and longer. Under these circumstances, the sight of such sophisticated studio equipment used only to help talent-free amateur "broadcasters" to pretend they were on national radio seemed nothing short of obscene.

Colin's toothy grin had become a permanent fixture as he proudly guided his guest around his little fiefdom.

"If you'll excuse me, Father", he concluded with a glance at his watch, "got to sort out my running order. Martin, my producer, won't be in this evening. Got to drive the show myself".

Running order? Producer? While Frank's mind was swimming with the insanity of it all, there was a little idea at the back of his mind which was just beginning to form.

SIXTEEN

Nothing could ruin Sarah's good mood. The 9.30 meeting with Mike Babcock had been particularly fruitful. His decision to take an idea then "run it up the flagpole and see who salutes" scored triple points in Buzzword Bingo because nobody actually says that in real life.

This was followed by a trip to Staines for a meeting with the Supershine shampoo client. New brief for some new TV commercials. Sarah needn't have bothered turning up. She knew exactly what they were going to say., exactly what they were going to ask for.

"It's all about women being in control", explained one of the nondescript faces across the table.

Women's liberation comes to Staines. Well, whoop dee-do!

"Yes", the face continued, "Women in control of their destiny. Smart women......."

Sarah, having heard this breathtakingly banal strategy about a thousand times before for everything from mobile phones to sanitary towels, decided to chime in and finish the sentence

".......who know where they're going, know what they want from life".

The face was impressed, "Exactly, Sarah, exactly. In fact, you're a prime example of our target market".

How dare you?

"Well," she said with mock-coyness, "I do use Supershine every Day".

This was true but only because she had boxes of the stuff

lying around in her office. She took home the Frequent Use formula which, she had to concede, was the cleverest product ever invented. It was just the regular Supershine watered down, yet it was just as expensive. Not only that but being "frequent use", you were told to use lots of it. Brilliant.

Another way through which shampoo manufacturers made a fortune was by the addition of one simple word on their bottles "Repeat".

Wet hair, apply shampoo, work in, rinse off and.............REPEAT".

Hey presto! Profits doubled overnight.

Without really listening to another word uttered by the phalanx of faceless haircare marketers, Sarah was able to drive back up the A30 knowing precisely what they wanted.

The commercial would begin with a gorgeous intelligent career women in her mid-twenties washing hair in shower. Microscopic close-ups of hair follicles allegedly being "nourished and protected".

We would then see the same girl , shoulder-padded and power-dressed, strolling confidently but femininely down busy city street, boinging and bouncing her fabulous head of hair in a completely unnatural way as though there were something wrong with her neck muscles and eliciting admiring glances from lots of handsome men.

The Supershine people would do their best to ensure that the commercial was so mindless and bland that any person in any country, would understand it. Therefore, they would only need to make one commercial, dub it in an assortment of languages and inflict it on people all over the world. Despite vain protestations of creative integrity, the people from Staines were primarily concerned with doing everything as cheaply as possible.

Sarah's name would be associated with this dross. This was what she currently did for a living. Still, not even this depressing though could do anything to dampen her mood. Just after four o'clock, she rang Helen.

"Hi. it's me", she said, "still on for tonight then?"

Helen could practically feel her friend's big smile through the telephone and found this unusual enthusiasm rather hard to fathom.

"Yeah"

"Brilliant. What time?"

"Oh, I dunno – seven-thirty for eight?"

"Okay. Now did you say 52 Blackheath Drive?"

"Yeah. Flat B. Are you driving?"

"Well, hardly. I do intend to have a drink".

"Well, get a cab. No, second thoughts, traffic's a nightmare. Just hop on the train at Charing Cross. You can always get a cab home".

"Brilliant idea".

Now Helen really was suspicious. Since when was getting a cab home a "brilliant idea". Oh God, I hope she's not pissed. It is five past four. I bet she's been out on one of those client lunches of hers.

"JJ's really looking forward to meeting you"

This almost burst the bubble of Sarah's excitement but the constant thought of the cab ride home just about kept it intact.

"Is he? Well I'm really looking forward to tonight as well", she gushed, not technically lying, "Seven thirty for eight then".

"Right. See you later, bye".

Helen replaced the receiver with a light, bewildered smile and a shake of the head. What was the matter with Sarah? She's normally quite aloof, almost cynical. Why is she so excited about meeting a friend of Graham's? And then she thought, perhaps a little too defensively, well why the hell shouldn't she be?

SEVENTEEN

"Coming Home, Baby" by Mel Torme – Great track – Frank pulled out the original single from '63 – black London label. A lot of tip American artists in the fifties and sixties who were signed to smaller labels in the States were released in the UK on London. Frank had dozens of old London singles – Fats Domino, Jerry Lee Lewis, The Drifters, Roy Orbison and this cracker by Mel Torme. Good but the title – "Coming Home Baby" – too obvious, too contrived.

The mood had to absolutely right. Relaxed, late-night drive home music. Pastoral duties were suspended for the afternoon, Father Dempsey had a tape to take.

Frank had been a bespoke tape maker since he first had a Harry Moss radio/cassette player fitted into his old Escort van. He had dozens, all hand-complied from old singles. Rock'n'Roll, Motown, Funk, Punk, Rap, Summer Tracks, Christmas tracks, slow tracks to help ease the pain of heavy traffic but this particular musical sub-section was something he'd never tried to assemble before., something he was unlikely to find in HMV or Virgin "Now That's What I Call Music That Hits The Right Note When Giving Lift Home to Girl You Fancy Like Mad Even Though You're Not Supposed To Because You're a Catholic Priest".

At last, he'd found his opening track – on the early yellow Epic label from '73 – The Isley Brothers' Highways Of My Life. Perfect – slow, soulful without being sexy. He could hardly close the cab door and hit her with Marvin Gaye's "Sexual Healing" or Billy Paul's "Let's Make A Baby".

Having found the first track, Frank could always "hear"

the second and it was another yellow Epic one from the same era – "Family Affair" – Sly & the Family Stone. Oh, he was in a groove now. This led to "The Ghetto" by Donny Hathaway, William De Vaughan's "Be Thankful For What You've Got" James Brown's "The Boss" and Clarence Carter's rather apposite "I Was In The Neighbourhood"

As he spliced together this fabulous opening set, he grooved pensively around the back office of the Parish Centre which was now his HQ, complete with 5000 boxed and shelved old singles and twin decks in the corner. He picked up the old Mel Torme single and was about to put it back in its original old London sleeve when he remembered that on the B side was the original jazzy version of "Right Now". Superb. He'd follow that with Sinatra's peerless "Witchcraft" which he had on an original purple Capitol 45 from 1958. This was shaping up into one hell of a tape.

It was then that he was struck by a terrible thought

"What if all this effort – this seamless smorgasbord of aural delight is a waste of time? What if she's a big fan of Simply Red ,Michael Bolton or the Lighthouse Family?"

No, she couldn't be. She just couldn't be.

Sarah, no fan of any of the aforementioned, was standing amidst a throng of commuters on the concourse at Charing Cross Station They were all gazing like zombies at the huge overhead departures board, waiting for the letters of their own destinations to clatter into place. Destinations whose names were like a foreign language to Sarah – Chislehurst, Dartford, Swanley, Erith. The people waiting to go there were far from foreign. Every face was white and pasty with eyes that continued their silent, submissive and collective gaze, just waiting for their cue to be cringingly grateful to Connex South Central for deigning to provide a train to take them home.

Helen had made it sound so easy, like an episode of Thomas the Tank engine. "Just hop on the train at Charing

Cross". She didn't mention the thirty-five minutes of mindless departure board gazing that had sent a dull heavy ache seeping down her neck, spine and the backs of her legs. Suddenly the doors to Platform Six were snapped open like a greyhound trap. Sarah was nearly knocked off her aching legs and only just managed to keep a grip on her bottle of Chateau Musar and bunch of flowers. The mad rush of Kent commuters were galloping towards the train.

Having spent the entire journey standing about an inch and half from a man who'd had garlic for lunch, Sarah was deposited at Blackheath along with a few dozen City types who'd got on at London Bridge. She seemed to be the only one walking out of Blackheath station who wasn't wearing a blue stripey shirt and a red spotted tie.

Presently, she arrived at Graham's flat, Straightening the now slightly crumpled bunch of flowers, she rang the bell. Helen answered it, kissed her friend on both cheeks, thanked her for the lovely flowers and bottle of Lebanese red and, with an excited and conspiratorial smile, ushered her through to the sitting room.

"Sarah", she gushed, "this is JJ".

EIGHTEEN

Frank sat in the back of his cab, parked up all alone by the river on Ballast Quay in Greenwich, reading GQ and sipping from a bottle of Purdey's. He hadn't been to see Father Conway because Father Conway didn't exist. But then, he thought, neither did St. Christopher. Not in the way he is always depicted anyway. The hero of a million medallions could not have carried baby Jesus across the water because "Saint" Christopher wasn't born until than three hundred years after Christ's death. It took the Holy See until 1969 to spot this little anomaly and confiscate his feast day. Frank often wondered how many other so-called saints were Christopher-esque charlatans too.

Still, this was no excuse for creating a fictive priest and a concomitant pack of lies about going down to Greenwich to visit him. It was a very plausible story but as nine-thirty became ten-thirty, Frank became tormented by the thought that JJ could have turned out to be that highly unlikely species – a handsome, charming and interesting accountant. Stranger things have happened, like a parish priest who doesn't believe in God.

At ten forty, the phone rang, Frank turned the ignition so that the unmistakable sound of a taxi's diesel engine would corroborate his story before picking up the phone. Wrong number.

At ten forty-five, it rang again. He started the engine fired up again, Right number.

"Father Dempsey?" enquired a sexy, slightly husky voice with an audible note of apprehension.

"Yes?", he replied mock-cautiously.

"Oh, thank God", she whispered. Exhaling with palpable relief, " Listen, I've got to whisper, I'm in the bathroom at the moment so no-one can hear me. Not that they could anyway. They've put on The Best of Thin Lizzy – can you hear it? And they're in the middle a drunken accountants' rendition of "The Boys are Back In Town". I've had one of the worst evenings of life, I told them all when I arrived that I was feeling a bit dicky – stomach bug, you know, just to make my early exit a little more plausible".

"I see", replied Frank, not knowing whether he was supposed to approve of this lie because of their shared loathing of accountants or disapprove because he was a priest and lying was a sin. Perhaps this was just a very unorthodox form of confession. Probably the first time ever that a priest had heard a confession in a taxi from a bathroom via a mobile phone.

"So....er.....where are you?" she enquired.

"Just left Father Conway's", lied Frank, "Heading up towards Tower Bridge. Lucky you caught me. Another ten minutes and I'd have been across the river and miles away"

He paused for effect before continuing, "So...er...well, still want rescuing?"

"Oh, please", she almost begged, "You're not too far away, are you".

"No", said Frank, telling the truth for once, "Not at this time of night. I can be with you in ten minutes", he said even though he could have been there in three, "But how are you going to get out?"

"Helen's just called me a cab. I'll only take it as far as Blackheath Station so could you meet me there at eleven?"

"Yeah, no problem", said Frank, heading off towards Maze Hill.

"See you there then".

"Okay, bye".

Frank was desperate to ask her why she wanted him and not Blackheath Mini-Cabs. to take her back to Fulham But, remembering the axiom that there's nothing as attractive as somebody finding you attractive, he hoped he knew the answer.

He found his way to Blackheath Station. And within a couple of minutes, he saw the sexiest sight he'd ever seen paying off the driver of a white Ford Mondeo . He'd never seen Sarah at night and nightfall lends a certain sexiness to anything, especially an assignation as wicked and clandestine as this one.

Again, she slid into the back. Again the lovely smell of Supershine shampoo, this time slightly tinged with cigarette smoke.

The door clunked, the taxi pulled away. Frank tried to be calm,

"So how was it?", he enquired with a grin.

Sarah, unable to find the words that would do justice the full horror of her evening, simply screamed and licked her gorgeous tanned legs in the air. Frank gripped the steering wheel hard, trying to get a grip on himself in the process.

"That good, eh?", he said, recovering enough to loosen a little colour into his tightly whitened knuckles.

"Well", she explained, settling back into her seat, "I suppose a lot of it was my fault. I went in with completely the wrong attitude"

"And how" asked Frank, "did this 'wrong attitude' manifest itself?"

"Well, this bloke – JJ – I kept calling him Jonathan and he clearly didn't like it"

"Oh dear. Regarded himself as far too wacky a character to have an ordinary name like Jonathan?".

"Exactly", said Sarah.

"So", asked Frank, asking the question he had been dying to ask, "What was he like?"

"Oh, dreadful", laughed Sarah.

A 21 gun salute, firework display and full fanfare followed by a celestial choir immediately went off in Frank's head. Yes ! Yes! Yes!!.

"So," he asked with a light nonchalant laugh, "Exactly how dreadful?"

"Well, he was one of those people who clearly considered himself to be a 'classic personality'. A real hoot, a bit zany...."

"The life and soul of the Christmas party"

"Oh, that'd be him. The office prankster. But he also had to demonstrate that he had a serious side. Not an intelligent, sensitive sort of serious side. More the "ruthless auditor" sort of serious side, a guy not afraid to ask tough questions."

"Mighty impressive, eh?" said Frank with a grin.

Well, luckily, I'd already lied about feeling sick but I needn't have bothered"

"Why not?"

"Well, after the first twenty minutes of being regaled by "JJ" and Graham's oh so hilarious rugger tour stories, I really did want to vomit".

"Don't let me stop you"", shrugged Frank "Why do you think taxi seats are always wipe-clean vinyl?".

"Oh, no", she said warmly, "I'm fine now. Anyway, how was your old parish priest?"

"St. Christopher?" is what Frank almost said before remembering that he'd called the non-existent cleric Father Conway. "Oh, he was on fine form. It was really good to see him. Now he's a proper old character, Drinks like a fish. I can't believe he's still alive

"But then", said Sarah. "alcohol is a preservative"

"Well, that would explain it. Before I knew him he was a chaplain to the Royal Navy. Apparently, when he went on board ship, they had to organise a rota of people to sit and drink with him. It would be too much for any one man. Even a hard-drinking sailor. One by one they would get up from the table, absolutely stocious, while old Father Conway would remain a sober as a judge. The Whiskey Priest, they used to call him".

Frank was both impressed and appalled at the ease with which he could fabulate these stories and decided that perhaps it was time to say something that was true.

"Doesn't Tower Bridge look fabulous at night?", he said trying not to gaze too dreamily at something else that looked fabulous at night.

Sarah agreed, "Tower and Albert", she nodded, "my two favourite bridges"

"Mine too", said Frank. "You know, at school, we had a sponsored walk over the bridges. We started by going south over Tower Bridge, then north over London, south over Southwark. north over Blackfriars and so on".

Sarah had an idea, "Can we do that now?"

"What? A sponsored walk?" Frank would have said yes.

"No, no", she laughed, "A sponsored cab ride – Tower Bridge to Putney Bridge. I have cash and it's all in a good cause, isn't it?"

Cash or no cash, it was all in a very good cause. Making a young parish priest, starved of the joy of female company, feel happy and human.

Together they crossed thirteen bridges: Tower, London, Southwark, Blackfriars, Waterloo, Westminster, Lambeth, Vauxhall, Chelsea, Albert, Battersea, Wandsworth and Putney and in that time, they hardly drew breath. Frank wondered why he'd bothered compiling that tape of exquisitely cool night music when neither of them were listening to it.

"You seem to London pretty well", Sarah had begun.

"Well, ".said Frank, "I've lived here all my life. Even the seminary I went to was in Chelsea. I'm what they call a diocesan priest, attached to Westminster so all the parishes I've worked in are in London".

"Do your parents still live here?"

"No, the old man retired about three years ago and they went back to Ireland. Really lucky. The house they bought in Kilburn for two grand they sold for three hundred. They only needed a fraction of that to buy a cottage in Connemara with about half an acre so they'll never have to work again. They really are living happily ever after".

"Ireland's a beautiful country", said Sarah wistfully recalling the business trips she'd taken out there,, the only pleasurable aspects of having to work on the Slattery's chain of bars.

"When it's not raining", said Frank, "but Connemara's fabulous – like a picture postcard. It's where they shot The Quiet Man".

"What quiet man?"

"The Quiet Man", said Frank with a chuckle, "The John Wayne film where he plays the ex-boxer who goes back to his Irish roots. Don't tell me you've never seen it?"

"No", shrugged Sarah.

"God, I think I spent most of my childhood watching The Quiet Man. That and Song Of Bernadette with Jennifer Jones".

"Do you like old films?"

"I love them. I really miss going to the cinema".

"Don't you ever go?"

"Not really", said Frank with a rueful shake of the head, "No-one to go with. . Can't go with a woman. Priests aren't supposed to do that. Can't go with another man, priests certainly aren't supposed to do that and I have a morbid fear of going to the pictures on my own.. Thank God for the video shop. I get them all for nothing"

"You get videos for nothing?"

"I get most things for nothing".

"How come?"

"Well", explained Frank, "Look at the seats in front of you".

Sarah looked and on each of the flap-down seats in the taxi was an ad, rather crudely printed – one on bright blue paper, one on bright yellow.

"Wealdstone Videos", proclaimed the yellow one, "Free membership. All the latest releases. Open seven days till 10pm".

She looked at the blue one.

"Jeanius", it promised her, "All makes of denim at discount prices".

"Probably not quite as sophisticated as the ads your agency would come up with but they serve a purpose".

"Which is?"

"Unlimited supplies of videos from one. T-shirts and jeans from the other. The less I have to filch from St. Thomas's for myself, the more we can give away. I change the posters every couple of weeks. Some shops pay in cash but most prefer to pay in kind"

The conversation lulled for a moment and Frank realised that he was as happy now as he'd ever been in his life. Heading north over Westminster Bridge, he could see the towering majesty of the London skyline set against a clear and perfect night. In front of him, the sky looked like black velvet and the stars like a shower of uncut diamonds casually scattered all over it. . As he weaved the cab skilfully around the streets he knew so well, he was finally able to exorcise the ghost of punting.

At Oxford, a pretty sure way of bedding a girl was to borrow one of the college punts and go punting along the Cherwell. Well, it was if you were any good at it. Unfortunately, Frank wasn't. Had punting been a matter of brute force, he'd have been fine, but it was a matter of grace and style and, try as he might, he could never get the hang of it. He'd always thrust down just a little too vigorously, embedding the end of the pole in the riverbed, lose his balance and composure and almost pitch face first into the river.

Tonight, he felt as though he were punting with ease and elegance. He was, after all, guiding a vehicle along a river with the sure touch of an expert and a beautiful girl lounging lazily behind him.

"What about you?" he asked, "Where did you grow up?"

"Just outside Manchester", she replied, "A place called Wilmslow".

"So you're a Northerner? You don't have an accent."

"We didn't move there till I was eleven. Before that we were in Twickenham, then I came back down here to university in London when I was eighteen. Anyway, Wilmslow isn't like 'Oop North" – very genteel, more like Surrey. Full of Coronation Street stars and Man United footballers".

As they talked and laughed their way back and forth across the Thames, the attraction between them grew more powerful and if it could be honed down to one just reason, it was that Sarah simply didn't treat Frank like a priest. Possibly because she'd never seen him being one. To her, he was a bloke. Kind, funny, intelligent and different, so very different from anyone she'd ever met. These feelings, though she didn't know it, were mutual. Since he'd become a priest, Sarah was the first woman – the first person who didn't treat him like one. She wasn't careful or self-censoring in what she said. She was open and friendly and regarded him as a normal person instead of some sort of freak. Most people treated him with unseemly deference or unwarranted suspicion. They would often assume he was either gay or a paedophile whereas if he hadn't been a priest, it would be perfectly clear that he was neither. He'd had to defend this wearisome accusation about men of the cloth so many times before. Yes, of course, there were sometimes clerics with unorthodox sexual proclivities but this was no more common among priests than among any other group of people.

Such priests were, however, exposed far more ruthlessly by the media because a randy homosexual priest makes a far better story than a randy homosexual hairdresser.

Sarah wasn't remotely suspicious about this aspect of his life. She just enjoyed talking to him, enjoyed being with him. She found herself clinging to the vain hope that this perilously attractive man wasn't a priest at all. She didn't want to know about his pastoral duties, never wanted to see him up on the altar, blessing the bread and wine, reading the gospel, delivering the sermon. If she ever saw that, she knew her hopes would be dashed, her heart broken and she'd once again become prey to the JJ's of this world. She was desperately trying to engineer another chance to see him. She couldn't invent another business trip to Edinburgh and anyway she didn't want him as a chauffeur, she no longer wanted to talk to the back of his head, she wanted to gaze longingly into those piercing blue eyes.

She thought perhaps they could go and see a film together since he said he had no-one to go with and the moment, neither did she. They could be purely platonic "picture pals". However, just as she was about to suggest this, he began to tell her how, before taking his vows, he'd always gone to the pictures with girls he didn't like because he didn't have to talk to them.

"What about girls you did like?" was her obvious question,

"Well, if you really like someone and just love being with them, it doesn't matter where you go, does it?

"Even a cab ride from Blackheath to Fulham?" she ventured boldly, making his heart beat so loudly that he took the precaution of turning the music up

"Yeah", came the dry-throated reply.

As they whizzed over Putney Bridge, and across the Thames for the thirteenth and final time, Sarah was now at a loss wondering how she'd ever see him again. She got out and stuffed three ten pound notes into the box. Frank smiled and nodded gratefully.

"Thanks for rescuing me", she said,

"No, thank you", said Frank, "I really enjoyed that. Much better than sitting at home watching a video".

There was a couple of seconds' pause during which Sarah tried and failed to think of an excuse for another secret rendezvous She needn't have worried. The excuse would come very soon from a most unlikely source.

NINETEEN

"Shit, Shit! Shit!! Where is it? What the fuck have I done with it?" Sarah, in a state of blind panic, had emptied the contents of her bag and purse all over the kitchen table. She was frantically scrutinising every item. A bottle of Clarins spray, a little pot of kiwi fruit lip balm, a hairbrush,, receipts from taxis, shops and restaurants, an appointment card from Toni & Guy,, a state of the art matt black Palm Pilot which she still had no idea how to use and six pounds fifty's worth of Sainsbury's Reward Card Vouchers. Shit, we would have happily swapped all of these plus all her cash, keys and credit cards for the one bit of paper she was looking for. That tiny scrap on which she'd scribbled Father Frank Dempsey's mobile number. . She'd tried several different configurations of numbers but had only succeeded in ringing an assortment of electricians and drug dealers

Her mind was completely colonised by taxis and priests. She found herself scrutinising every black cab she saw just in case the driver had a dog-collar.. She even took a secret trip over to Willesden one night, looking for St. Thomas's church, and was alarmed to discover that there was no such place.

So he wasn't a priest after all. She didn't know whether to be horrified that he was some sort of weirdo priest-impersonator or delighted because, in that case, he wouldn't have taken a vow of celibacy. She began to wonder whether he'd simply been a ghost or a figment of her imagination. She'd asked most of her friends – very casually of course, whether any of them had ever been picked up by a cab driver who was also a priest. Most stared at her as if she was either demented or experiencing some sort of flashback from dropping too many E's in the summer of '88.. Perhaps he was a ghost, perhaps she could syndicate her story to the National Enquirer about riding in the Phantom Taxi of Old London Town.

Oh, where was he? What had happened to him? Why isn't there a Directory Enquiries for mobiles?

She emerged one afternoon from a two -hour meeting with the faceless and interchangeable Supershine clients and realised that she couldn't remember a single thing about it. All she knew was that the words, "protect and nourish" "healthy shine" and "women in control" would have all featured heavily.

She found it difficult to concentrate on anything – work, Graham and Helen's rather alarming plans to move out to Chislehurst, the plotlines of Brookie and EastEnders .

Her reverie was suddenly disturbed by the shrill ring of the phone on her desk

"Sarah? Mike Babcock. Bit of a crisis. Need to sit down".

What had happened? Wife left him? Fallen two rungs on the company squash ladder? Carport collapsed on the Vauxhall Vectra? What?

"Mike, hi. What's the problem?"

"Well, don't know if you remember but about six months ago, we opened a big Slattery's unit in Wealdstone".

Wealdstone!!! WEALDSTONE!!! That was it!! Wealdstone, not Willesden!! Mike Babcock, I love you!!

Having soared ecstatically into the air, Sarah floated serenely down again,

"Yeah. I remember"

"Well, bottom line is, takings have collapsed and basically, we're going to have to move the goal posts, formulate a whole new game plan".

"Why? What's happened? How come takings are down?"

"Well, basically we chose Wealdstone because it scored very heavily in our research data, Bit of a dump, full of Paddies – perfect strategic fit. So we bought up a couple of shops, knocked them through, opened up and we were coining it in. Now suddenly we've got competition".

"Competition?"

"Yeah from the Catholic church of all places. They've converted their old church hall and the place is packed every night. Knock on effect being that Slattery's is now deserted. No customer loyalty. It all started with this new priest who's come in. Bit of a lad, apparently. Drives a taxi".

Yes!! Yes!! I wasn't making it up. He does exist.

Mike had worked with Sarah for a long time and had always been intimidated by her laid-back intelligence, the way she could instantly grasp and solve problems about his business without ever appearing to try or, for that matter, to care. She never seemed to share his evangelical zeal for expanding the all-conquering Slattery's chain so he was very surprised by her response.

"Oh, that's terrible, Mike. There must be something we can do. Are you free later on? Say about five?. I'll come down and we'll work something out".

"Sarah", he said with deep sincerity, "You're a star. I'll see you at five. Ciao".

By five o'clock, Mike was fired up, pacing around his office. Heaven help the fat estate agent he was playing squash with tonight.

"Sarah, hi", he said, voice louder, handshake firmer than ever, "You'll take some coffee?"

"A glass of still water will be fine".

"They've got a fucking cheek, haven't they?", he began, almost hyperventilating.

"Who?"

"These priests, vicars, whatever they are. Meddling in the

licensed trade. They should stick to God bothering or whatever it is they do"

Sarah had always regarded Mike as a crass, ignorant little man but now he was plumbing new depths.

"Still, if they want to play hardball, we'll let them have it. You live by the sword, you die by the sword. And let me tell you one thing, Sarah"

"What's that, Mike?"

"Nobody fucks with Mike Babcock"

Least of all Mrs. Babcock is what Sarah was tempted to say but just managed to stop herself.

"Anyway", he went on, warming to his pathetic little theme,, "the way I look at it, marketing strategy is like military strategy. I learnt that from Trevor Soper, my old divisional sales chief in Peterbrough. That man was a legend. Focus, focus, focus. -that was his mantra. So, at the end of the day, we're going to have to go the extra mile on this one".

"I see", said Sarah, trying not to laugh.

"Now Wealdstone represents a crucial part of our core business activity. We've got to stay results-driven and that means being pro-active not re-active. We've got to bury this new church hall, parish centre, whatever they call it".

"Is it really that important, Mike?", asked Sarah gently, "Slattery's is an enormous chain. As you say, you're gaining representation in every town in the South-East. Can't you let this one go?"

Closing his eyes dramatically, Mike gave a slow condescending chuckle, "Oh Sarah, Sarah. With the greatest respect, at the end of the day, you don't operate at the sharp end. At Slattery's, we're quality-driven, customer focused and if what we're presently doing ain't cutting it out there in the big, wide world, it's me who's going to take the rap. I'm at the coalface, Sarah, where there's no such thing as a no blame situation. I need to think outside the box, get inside the people's mindsets and basically, come out on top. At Slattery's, we're not accustomed to having sand kicked in our faces".

"Well, I've got a plan", Sarah, " A rear-guard action"

"Rear –guard action", nodded Mike seriously, "Like it, like it".

"I know Wealdstone pretty well", she lied, having never been there and only just discovered where it was. "I've got some friends over that way. What |I could do is try to get into this parish centre. See what makes it tick. Then look at Slattery's, compare the two from the consumer's viewpoint and work out our game plan from there".

Mike was delighted, "Brilliant, Sarah, brilliant. You'll really do that?"

"For sure", she smiled knowing he wouldn't realise he was being mocked

He ruffled her Supershined locks,

"Hey, we'll make a marketeer out of you yet", he grinned bestowing on her the highest compliment any human being could receive,. He pressed yet another business card into the palm of her hand. This new one had not one but two e-mail addresses. He then locked his eyes on to her eyes and gave her his most serious expression, strictly reserved for urgent marketing crises.

"Call at any time. Day or night. Leave me a message and I can always get back to you. Just keep me in the loop, yeah.? Now if you'll excuse me, big meeting with the sales team".

That, thought Sarah, was one of the most enjoyable meetings she'd ever been to. Firstly because Mike had revealed himself to be a truly vindictive and spiteful little shit. Even if he hadn't meant half of what he'd said about "burying" St, Thomas's – the very fact he even said it was disgraceful. This gave her the excuse not just to laugh at his cliché-driven drivel but to despise him quite legitimately. And, obviously she now had the opportunity to double-cross the odious little prick, derail his vicious little "gameplan" by warning the parish priest of exactly what Slattery's were planning to do. And the thought of re-establishing contact with that adorable priest made her almost ill with delight.

As she drove back to London, she realised that in all the excitement, she'd completely forgotten to play "Buzzword Bingo". Bugger! She must have let at least three full houses slip from her grasp.

TWENTY

It was an unusual sound and it resonated from the back office right through the big empty hall. Frank was alone in the office, playing a private game called "Peggy Sue". He'd been playing it on and off for about twenty years and had never once got it right. It had started when he'd seen a documentary about Buddy Holly which revealed that the famous drums that form the rhythm of "Peggy Sue" weren't drums at all, they were cardboard boxes. The Crickets' drummer Jerry Allison had created that haunting, hollow sound by lightly clattering an assortment of upside-down cardboard boxes.

So, for about the five hundredth tome, Frank arranged boxes having first removed the Walker's Crisps that they'd originally contained. He then cued up the old black Coral copy of "Peggy Sue" , picked up the two big, thick knitting needles that served as drumsticks and began – this time was going to do it. He was doing very well, he'd reached the bit about half-way through where Buddy affects that silly girly voice, without missing a beat when he thought he heard a couple of extra beats. Turning round, he realised that they had been gentle, apprehensive taps on the office door. He looked, stared, blinked, stared again, blue eyes as wide as they'd ever been in his life. Involuntarily, he dropped one of the two big knitting needles to the floor.

He swallowed hard, absolutely speechless.

"Sorry, Father", said the girl at the door, "Have I interrupted you? I could always come back"

That dazzling smile, a joint venture from the gorgeous wide mouth and the heavenly brown eyes.

"No, no – not at all. Please...um....I was just.....you know I wasn't expecting anyone....er....least of all....."

"I know, I'm sorry. I should have phoned but I lost your mobile number.... Thought your church was in Willesden. You know, London, NW10 but.....um.....anyway.....

A priest who drove a taxi and amused himself by drumming with cardboard boxes and knitting needles. It just got better and better.

"Yeah. Drumming. My secret passion" explained Frank to his other secret passion who then noticed the thousands of old 45's boxed and shelved on the other side of the room.

"My God. All those records".

"Yeah, I've been collecting them since I was a kid . Go on, have a flick through, pull out anything you want. It's all alphabetical – Abba to ZZ Top".

While Sarah, like a kid in a toy shop, started rooting through the boxes, Frank segued up his other knitting needle classics – "Let There Be Drums" by Sandy Nelson and "Wipeout" by The Surfaris,. Thrashing away on his upturned boxes, he wondered which tracks Sarah would select. This quick examination of musical taste was an almost foolproof guide to the somebody's character.

The omens were good. Sam & Dave's "Soul Sister, Brown Sugar" Tom Jones doing "Love Me Tonight", The Valentine Brothers' original version of "Money's Too Tight To Mention", and eerily appropriate, "Temptation" by Heaven 17.. Sarah hadn't thought about the title of this one but as it was playing, she and Frank found it impossible to look at each other. Frank, remembering the Sheffield sound of the early eighties, mixed it seamlessly into Hard Times by the Human League.

"Anyway", said Frank, the shock over and relaxing into his usual confident manner, "What a lovely surprise. I thought I'd have to loiter around the Fulham Road if I ever wanted to see you again. What brings you to Wealdstone?"

"Bit of a coincidence, really" and she told him about Babcock and his gameplan.

Far from being perturbed, Frank laughed out loud.

"Dear me. Is it really that important to him? Poor little man, he's clearly ill. Come on, let me show you around".

They sat and had a quiet drink and Frank proudly recounted the tale of the Parish centre, how everyone mucks in and works for nothing. It's wonderful at night. Come and see for yourself. People love being here and there's nothing Slattery's can ever do about that.. Come over next Sunday night. That's Sunday week. Big Irish night out, Sundays, always has been and it's the feast of St.Petronella.

"Saint Who?"

"Saint Petronella. Early Roman martyr, allegedly. I say allegedly because nothing is actually known about her life and death but somebody said she was a martyr and that was that. Canonised forever, feast day 31st May".

"Why are you celebrating it?"

"Well, we have this little custom here called the Any Excuse Club. And a little known saint's feast day seems a good excuse for a knees-up. I mean. we all celebrate the feast of St. Valentine".

"You celebrate Valentine's Day? But you're a priest".

"Well, I don't send cards out or put a message in The Sun to my huggy little snuggle bunny. But we'll have a big dance here on the night"

Frank, his mind flashing back to the Freshers' fair at Oxford with all its weird little societies, had just invented the Any Excuse club as a ruse to see Sarah again but the more he thought of it, the more it struck him as marvellous, cash generating idea,

"Look, she said, "I've got to get back to work".

"Well, if you can hold on for ten minutes, I've got a

diocesan meeting in Westminster. I'll drop you off at Golden Square or did you drive?"

"No. I came on the tube. I wouldn't have known the way".

"Great. On the house this time. No donations please. I was going anyway. I'm a bit early, but at least I won't have to rush".

Another cab ride. They didn't stop talking, they didn't stop laughing, again neither of them wanted the journey to end. Frank found himself driving more and mores slowly simply because he didn't want the journey to end. He was even overtaken by an old man in a hat driving a Deewoo. This was becoming a problem. Each had unwittingly colonised the other's mind. This was more than physical attraction, more than mental stimulation, far more than the initial intrigue of infatuation. Foundations were being laid. Deep, deep foundations and concrete was being poured into the footings. Something was going to be built on those foundations but neither Frank nor Sarah quite knew what. When the journey ended at Golden Square, they gave each other three numbers each – home, work and mobile. Neither could bear to lose touch again. Frank pulled out on to Regent Street and was hailed by two Japanese tourists whose command of English was rather rudimentary

"Hallods" was all they seemed capable of saying.

"Harrods?" asked Frank, just to be sure.

They nodded. "Hallods".

There was absolutely no point in going through the "I am not a cab driver, I'm a Roman Catholic priest". They wouldn't understand, it would only confuse and frighten them. Just take them down to Knightsbridge and get a tenner in the box.

The diocesan meeting in Westminster was, of course, a lie but since Frank was now in the West End, he decided to spend a couple of hours cabbing.

And when Sarah got back to her desk, she was troubled by just one thought: How on earth was she going to get up to Wealdstone tonight to get her car back?

TWENTY-ONE

Doctor Geoffrey Clarke finished his cursory examination and gave his considered opinion.

"Danny", he smiled, "You re the perfect weight".

Danny Power, suffering from sporadic chest pains, was standing in the surgery in vest and underpants and smiling nervously. He was certain this couldn't be true.

"The perfect weight", the doctor continued in a tone of exasperation, "for a man approximately thirteen feet tall".

Danny felt himself blush. A huge powerful man in every sense of the word. The gaffer who could strike terror into anyone who worked for him was standing there, fat and vulnerable, being ticked off like a naughty schoolboy. It is often said that the best way to tell people's class is by the way they treat their doctor. The working classes are very respectful, very deferential, almost in awe – Yes, doctor, no doctor, anything you say, doctor. The middle classes see the doctor as an equal , "John's a friend. He comes round for supper" and the upper classes regard the doctor a mere tradesman who comes round to fix them when they break. Danny Power, despite everything, was still very firmly in the first group. Dr. Clarke liked and respected Danny, he'd known him for years. Danny had re-plastered his whole house and surgery and done a fabulous job. Even with five children to feed and clothe, Danny's disposable income would be at least three times that of his own. And yet, despite all this, he called Danny "Danny" and Danny called him "Doctor".

"Danny – for God's sake, for your sake, for Rose and the children's sakes, this over-indulgence was got to stop and it's got to stop now. If you continue eating, drinking and smoking the way you do, you are going to die. Quite soon".

He paused.

"You're not actually fat"

"Am I not?" said Danny, really confused now.

"Oh no", the doctor went on, "you're not fat, you're now statistically obese. Twenty-two stone eight pounds, Danny. Twenty-two stone eight! You're a big man but the very most you should weigh is sixteen, maybe sixteen and a half. You are going to have to lose six and half stone immediately or you'll be dead by Christmas""

This frightened the life out of Danny though Dr. Clarke, always truthful, didn't actually say which Christmas.

"Six and a half stone, Doctor. How am I going to do that?"

"It's very simple. I'm not saying it's easy but it's fairly straightforward. There are a lot of faddy diets around through which you can lose weight very quickly but for you, and for most people, the best and most reliable way is just calories in, calories out.

Danny had a rough idea what calories were but had never seen fit to count them.

"Put simply, if you burn up more calories than you consume, you will lose weight. If you burn up fewer, you will put it on."

"But, Doctor, it could be my glands".

"It could be but I think you know perfectly well that it isn't. Glandular problems are responsible for obesity in about 2% of cases. I'm afraid you're one of the other 98"

"Worth a try, though, wasn't it?", said Danny with a wink.

Despite affecting his most serious schoolmasterly manner, Dr. Clarke couldn't help laughing. His features then had to re-arrange themselves into a pose of stern concern before he continued,

"Danny, I'm not joking when I say that this obesity is putting your life at risk. There is now so much fat around your heart that the heart itself is being pushed out of position and this will severely weaken it. No wonder you've had chest pains. Six and a half stone, Danny, now"

"Now?"

The doctor sighed, "Well obviously not now. I mean, you didn't put on six stone overnight, so you won't lose it overnight either. But as I say, calories in, calories out".

Danny looked at the doctor. He was pushing sixty but, trim, tanned and with a full head of salt & pepper hair, he looked a picture of health, a splendid advertisement for his profession, a man who clearly practised what he preached. He wasn't a fat, wheezing alcoholic like Dr. Griffiths and because of this, Danny would take heed of what he said.

"If you're sensible and determined, the first four stone will just fall off. The last bit's always the hardest. Now you're not silly, you know all the things which are bad for you, the beer, the fry-ups, the eating late at night. That's the great tragedy with builders, From an physical point of view, you all lead extremely healthy lives. Plenty of fresh air and vigorous exercise but you completely negate all that good work with your dietary and drinking habits. And you are without doubt the worst example I've ever seen. Cut out the red meats. Grilled chicken or fish instead and plenty of fruit and vegetables".

Danny nodded obediently.

"And remember the old maxim", said the Doctor, teeing up a truism he had teed up many times before, "breakfast like a king, lunch like a lord and dine like a pauper".

"What about exercise, Doctor?"

"Well, you get quite a lot in the course of your work but a bit more wouldn't go amiss".

"I don't have to join a gym or anything like that?"

"No, but didn't you once tell me that you did a lot of cycling in Ireland?"

"I did, yes" said Danny, meaning I did tell you that, Doctor but I was lying.

"Good, well why not take it up again. I want you to come back and see me in a month's time and if you're not at least a stone lighter, I'm going to kill you myself.

The following day was the first of Danny Power's new regime. Never one to do anything by halves, he'd driven his van straight from the doctor's to Buntings bike shop in Wealdstone and bought himself a brand new 21-speed racer. When he got on it, the saddle and indeed the whole bike almost disappeared up the crack of his arse but after a few weeks, he assured himself, this would not be the case. He slipped on his jogging pants which never had and never would jog in their lives. Pulling on a T-shirt the size of a marquee , Danny thought how much the apparel of the builder had changed in the thirty-odd years he'd been doing it.

When he first started it was quite normal to see a navvy digging the road wearing a suit. Old, threadbare and covered in muck but, nonetheless, a suit. This gave way to jumpers and jeans and now it was sweatpants and fleeces. So much more comfortable especially if, like Danny you possessed a slightly fuller figure.

At 6.40 am he was, as usual, in Jack's café in Masons Avenue.

"Morning, Dan" said Jack Sands, the proprietor who judging by the size of his girth, was his own best customer, "Usual, is it?"

"The usual" was four sausages, about half a pound of bacon, black pudding, three fried eggs, beans, fried bread, mushrooms and fried tomatoes, all drenched in brown sauce and served on a plate the size of a satellite dish. Cholesterol at Jack's was measured in hectolitres.

"No, thanks, Jack. Thought I'd try something different. Just beans on toast. Wholemeal toast, no butter.

Jack waited for him to continue.

"Beans, wholemeal toast, no butter", he repeated, "That's it, Jack. That's it".

Jack stood motionless.

"I'm a bit slow this morning, Dan", he replied scratching his head, "Is it April Fool's Day or something?"

"No, Jack", said Danny, his iron resolve already wilting under a vicious assault from the smell of frying bacon, "I'm on a diet, Strict one".

"You're having a laugh, aren't you? Danny Power on a diet? Next you'll be telling me you've given up the booze".

Danny couldn't bear to even think about this. He had given it up and the fortunes of the Guinness family were set to plummet as a result.

Still, he was determined to do it, buoyed up by his wife's back-handed compliment.

"Danny", she said. "this diet of yours is like when you and the lads go in to restore an old house. You often knock away a lot of the old shite and find some lovely original features underneath. Well, you've got some lovely original features too. Buried under that mountain of flab, there's a very handsome man".

Whenever this handsome man got the urge for a pint of Guinness or a family sized pork pie, he'd get on that 21 speed racer and pedal it for all he was worth. His big, powerful legs were going like pistons one evening as he raced down a little country lane in Bushey

Perhaps it was because he was cloaked in the half-light of dusk but the driver of the Volvo estate just didn't see him. It would be easy to dismiss the man as a typical Volvo driver, cocooned inside the tank-like security of his own vehicle, completely oblivious to the plight of other road users., particularly cyclists , but this may be very unfair. Even his ABS brakes couldn't stop him in time and for months afterwards he would wake in the night, sweating and screaming at the horrific memory of the mangled bike and the huge innocent cyclist being smashed up into the air.

As Danny's head hit the tarmac, the lives of one wife, five children and innumerable friends and relatives just didn't seem worth living anymore.

TWENTY-TWO

Frank was again alone in the back office, having one of his early evening single sessions before going into the Parish Centre to open up. This time he had with him a large yard broom, a prop he had been using since 1971 for his secret impressions of Rod Stewart and The Faces. Their bluesy classic "Stay With Me" was the best track for this performance. He placed the needle on the original green Warner Brothers single and waited for the guitar intro to begin. At this point he put the head of the broom down by his hip, pole in the air and really believed he was Ronnie Wood. Then, as Rod's rasping vocals kicked in, the broom was swiftly turned up the other way and his gravelly impression of the plume-haired singer who, in the early 70's was very zenith of cool, began.

He'd whacked the volume up fairly high and had only just managed to hear the phone.

Twelve minutes later, he was sprinting through the swing doors of the A&E department of Queen Elizabeth's Hospital Danny was still alive but wasn't expected to remain so for much longer. Unable to look at his friend's body, bloody and maimed, Frank gave him the Last Rites, anointing his head, his lips and the palms of his hands. Rose, Danny's soon to be widow to be seemed relieved. At least that the big man was in a state of grace, ready to meet his maker.

She fell sobbing into the priest's arms and he held up his neck to accommodate her head beneath his chin. He bit his lip and tried his best to choke back his own flood of hot, salty tears. He had to be strong, he had to assure her that everything would be fine, Danny was going to a better place but it was hard, so very, very hard. He couldn't do the standard soliloquy about suffering being over because until about twenty minutes ago, Danny wasn't suffering. He never suffered. He was a maelstrom of garrulous bonhomie – eating, drinking and laughing to excess.

Frank's father had always said that the human race is made up of drains and radiators. The drains are the takers, the people who sap your emotional resources and give very little in return, Danny Power, however, was the archetypal radiator, dispensing kindness, coarse humour and rounds of drinks to everyone who knew him.

Frank closed his eyes and silently begged for God to intervene. Don't let this man die. No purpose will be served and so many lives will be decimated. Danny was clinging on to life by his fingernails and, with the other twenty-odd stone hanging over a sheer drop into the eternal abyss. His chances did not look good. He'd fractured his skull, broken two arms, one leg and several ribs but most worryingly, suffered massive internal haemorrhaging. The doctors said nothing to Rose but confided to Frank that they didn't expect him to last until morning.

Frank stayed at the bedside all night, Rose had asked him to and Frank was quite prepared to accede to her wishes. She drew great comfort from his presence, somehow believing that if the good Father Dempsey was there, then the good Lord was too. Together, they prayed. Frank wasn't convinced that this would do any good but it certainly wouldn't do any harm.

When dawn broke, Danny was still breathing. The life-support machine was still switched on and nobody had approached Rose and told her in hushed tones that it might as well be switched off.

Way down in the depths of a coma, Danny was now clinging to life by one hand, Somehow he had to make it two and then, with the odds stacked heavily against him, try to heave his enormous bulk back up on to the edge of the cliff.

TWENTY-THREE

A couple of weeks later, when Frank dropped into the church, he saw a twelve year old boy kneeling there all alone. It was Sean Power, praying desperately for his father's recovery. When he saw Frank, he turned round with a start, seemingly ashamed of what he was doing. Frank raised his hand gently,

"No, no, Sean, you carry on. Don't let me interrupt you".

The boy turned, his eyes, puffy and red-rimmed, and gazed up at Frank. "It's OK, Father, I wasn't praying".

"Just thinking, were you? Great place to gather your thoughts, focus your mind, especially when there's no one around. I'll leave you to it".

"No, Father, there's something I want to tell you, something that's been bugging me ever since my Dad had his accident".

"Oh, right", said Frank with a warm smile, "Well, fire away then.. That's what I'm here for".

Sean fidgeted awkwardly, mad e a couple of false starts then blurted it out, "It's about the altar servers, Father.".

Frank knew what was coming but gently encouraged the boy to explain.

"Oh, I see. You want to tell me about your reasons for being one? Well, of course I know you serve mass to help me and Father Lynam and Father Conlon"

"Yes"

"Thing is, that's all very well, isn't it Sean, but it's the weddings, isn't it? The weddings and the funerals".

Sean nodded.

"The extra pocket money you make from doing weddings and funerals".

Sean stared at the floor and gave another guilty nod.

"Well", said Frank with a quiet chuckle, " I was exactly the same when I was a boy".

Sean couldn't believe this and his eyes widened at the priest's admission.

"Oh yeah", Frank went on, "Weddings and funerals – Ch-ching!. Weddings were all right but they always took place on a Saturday when there were other things to do. But funerals? Always during the week. A morning off school and a ride in a Daimler to Kensal Green cemetery. And then, I know it won't seem much to you now but 50p or even a pound. Remember, this would have been around 1971 or 72. Funerals – I used to love them".

Sean couldn't speak but Frank continued

"I bet you take an almost unhealthy interest in the sick list, don't you? Those poor sick people for whom the congregation's prayers are asked? Don't worry, all altar servers do. I remember when I was an altar boy, once somebody had clocked up six weeks on the list, I started rubbing my hands together, working out what I was going to spend my 50p on.".

"Are you angry, Father?"

"'Of course I'm not angry. A lot of people have to make their livings from the misfortunes of others. Dentists, undertakers, plumbers., priests..."

There was an awkward pause.

"Oh yeah, we can get a much bigger tip for doing a funeral than you do", said Frank smiling before letting his expression become a little more solemn, "Trouble is", he intoned, "You tend forget that the person whose death you're so looking forward to is somebody's wife, somebody's husband,....."

"Somebody's father", said Sean starting to cry.

"Exactly", said Frank, "And now because your Dad is top of the list, you feel guilty"

"Yeah and I bet the other altar servers are looking forward to doing his funeral, just so they can earn a fiver"

"Oh, I'm sure they're not", said Frank who was sure they were, "most of them are your friends. They don't want to see your Dad die any more than you do. And shall I tell you something?"

"What?"

"I don't think he's going to die. I don't think Heaven is in need of re-plastering just yet".

It would have been a very trite thing to say to a boy whose father was dying but Frank had just returned from his Queen Elizabeth's Hospital visiting afternoon. And for once he'd enjoyed it.

Danny Power was off the critical list.

TWENTY-FOUR

Once Danny was sitting up and taking soup, Frank made even more regular visits.. One evening, quite early on when the patient was still on the critical list, Frank's quiet discussion with Philip Nowell, the consultant surgeon was interrupted.

"Oh, good evening", said a spotty youth with a weak smile, ironed jeans and a pair of Marks & Spencer's trainers,

" I wonder if you'd like a record played on tonight's Colin Liddell show".

Frank turned slowly and fixed him with the sort of cold hard stare that priests aren't supposed to be capable of. He was just about to speak when Philip Nowell, a big, normally gentle man with hands the size of shovels, took over.

"Now, listen to me, you little prick", he said with controlled and powerful anger, "I've had just about enough of you and your silly little hospital radio volunteers, all pretending to be Tony Blackburn. You're nothing but a nuisance, nobody wants a hospital radio station here at Queen Elizabeth's, you do no good whatsoever. If I ever catch you up here on the High Dependency Unit, I'll have the whole station closed down, Do you understand".

The youth nodded.

"Oh God", thought Frank "Any second now, those huge hands are going to become fastened around that scrawny neck and I'm going to have to call security".

"And anyway", Nowell finished, "What sort of request do you think a critically ill patient wants to hear – Help Me Make It Through The Fucking Night – Now piss off.

Beetroot with anger, he turned back to Frank. "I'm sorry, Father but here we are trying to do our jobs. Help people, cure people. We're desperately under-funded and sometimes the odds seem almost insuperable and these people are no help at all. Patients aren't interested. Not even the children. They've all got their Walkmans and Gameboys. Hospital radio is like a sick joke. Have you seen their studio?"

Frank nodded, a trace of disgust on his face.

"Better equipped than most operating theatres", said the seething surgeon, " If it were up to me, I'd close the bloody place down".

"Why don't you?"

"Because it isn't up to me. And John Banks, the chief administrator, can't be seen to do that".

"Why not?"

"Well, there'd be an outcry"

"Who from? Nobody listens to it anyway".

"Oh, not from the patients, no, from the people who run it. Have you met that Colin Liddell?"

Frank nodded again, this time with more than a trace of disgust on his face.

"Pompous little man", said Nowell, "Oh, he'd go to the local papers, Newsroom South East, badger people with a petition which they'd sign just to get rid of him. Thing is, it doesn't actually cost us a penny. It's all funded by donations. People give because they like to feel they are contributing to the local hospital but the money isn't going where it's needed".

"Do you really want it closed down?" said Frank, that hardness returning to his face which made Nowell wonder whether the priest was going to call upon a team of heavies to go in and smash the studio up,

"It would make me a very happy man".

"Leave it to me then".

The following day, Frank made an appointment to see

John Banks. This was one of the advantages of wearing the collar. People, no matter how busy or high-powered, feel a moral obligation to see you.

John Banks was a decent enough man but the obvious stress of the way he earned his living was etched into the lines of his face. He was squeezed uncomfortably into a navy suit which no longer fitted him. Although probably still in his forties, looked ten years older. Frank could imagine him raiding the hospital pharmacy for Valium, Prozac, Haliborange, anything to help him cope.

He welcomed Frank into his large but sterile, featureless NHS office,

"Father Dempsey", he smiled, offering his hand, "John Banks – good to meet you at last".

"Good to meet you too", said Frank, "I must say, you seem to be doing a splendid job".

Praise was sweet music to Banks's ears. He couldn't remember the last time he'd received any.

"Well, that's very kind of you", he said warmly, "because, you know, hospital administration can be a pretty thankless task".

"I'll bet," said Frank sympathetically, implicitly inviting him to continue. He was an old hand at hearing confessions.

"Yes, you're forever being pulled in two directions", he went on "Constantly expected to provide more resources at the sharp end whilst trying to stay within the budgets set by the Area Health authority which, as you can imagine, are not over-generous".

"Well, you seem to be juggling it all very well", said Frank, "I've been involved with a lot of hospitals over the years and they're not as well run as this place".

"Well, that's very gratifying", said Banks "Because it's almost impossible to tell from the inside".

"Well, the staff seem happy, the patients are very well cared for and some of the facilities are wonderful".

"Facilities? Wonderful?" said Banks. What was he talking about? The facilities at Queen Elizabeth's could hardly be described as wonderful.

"Oh yes", enthused Frank, "Your hospital radio station, for instance, it's unbelievable".

Banks's expression darkened into a heavy frown and Frank waited for him tot he was about to reach for the blood-pressure pills,

Yes, it is, isn't it?", he sighed, "But between you and me, Father....."he said, taking on a conspiratorial tone, "I'd like to close the whole thing down".

"Close it down?" said Frank, trying not to overdo the incredulity,

"Close it down", he confirmed, "This hospital needs every penny it can get just to provide essential care for the patients. QEFM, as they call it, serves no worthwhile purpose. The volunteers are just a nuisance. I mean, they're pretty harmless but nobody listens to that station, these people use it to further their own ambitions to become disc-jockeys on radio stations, They never will, of course, because if they were any good, they wouldn't be on hospital radio, would they?"

"I suppose not",

"We need the space taken up by the that big studio and the money donated to keep it going could be put to much better use elsewhere".

"Well, why can't you close it down?"

"It would just look bad politically. Not just at this level but the health authority, even the government couldn't be seen to do it. The newspapers would lap it up – another savage attack on the NHS, on patient care. Colin Liddell, he's the chap who runs it would wheel out the one patient in the last six years who actually asked for a request and listened to it. Never mind the other 99.9% of people who would throw a party if it closed down".

"Oh dear", said Frank oozing empathy, "I see what you

mean now. You've made me feel uneasy about all that money going to waste ".

"Oh no, no, Father", said Banks, backtracking and desperate not to appear uncharitable, "We'll manage. At Queen Elizabeth's, we always do".

He gave a rather weak, unconvincing little chuckle.

"But what if", suggested Frank, "You could come up with a plan which allowed you to close down the radio station and it reflected badly on no-one, least of all you. In fact, it reflected very well on you".

"Impossible", said Banks with a miserable sigh of defeat "Believe me I've thought about it. Laid awake at night thinking about it. Can't be done".

"No, I agree", said Frank, trying to keep the Machiavellian mischief from his tone, "Not without the help of a clergyman".

TWENTY-FIVE

"Ah, Colin. Good to see you".

John Banks, a week later, was warm and avuncular as he welcomed the fly in Queen Elizabeth's ointment into his office. Colin Liddell walked in, toothy grin followed by wet handshake.

"You know Father Dempsey, don't you?"

"I do indeed", Frank's turn to see the snaggled teeth. "Hello, Father"

"Colin", nodded Frank with a benign clergyman's smile.

Colin sat down, confident and smug. Well, the hospital chaplain was here too. He had obviously been brought in for a pat on his anoraked back. To be congratulated on the splendid work he was doing at QEFM in alleviating the suffering of the sick. Deep down, however, he must have known that this wasn't the case. He surely didn't believe that the thousands of pounds squandered on a ridiculous, un-listened to radio station staffed by "presenters" who would never get a real job in radio, couldn't be better spent elsewhere. Maybe he did. Maybe he believed he'd pulled the wool over their eyes for so long that his position and that of his radio station were unassailable.

He was in for a nasty shock.

"Colin", sighed Banks with an air of resignation, "There's no easy way of saying this".

"Of saying what?" Colin darted out a little too quickly, almost as though he'd been expecting this moment for years.

"I'm afraid the time has come to pull the plug on QEFM".

"You can't do that", he bristled.

John Banks was being very calm and reasonable but Frank was wondering how long he'd be able to keep this up without either losing his temper or just gloating vindictively.

"Of course we can. The administrators and trustees of this hospital have regular and lengthy consultations about its future. How best to utilise our budgets, how to provide optimum care for our patients and I'm afraid the question of the hospital radio station has begun to feature more and more prominently. It is felt, quite reasonably, that too few patients tune in to warrant its existence. We desperately need the space and – to be honest – the funds for proper patient care".

Colin, like a cornered rat, was defiant...

"But patients do listen to it. We get hundreds of requests".

"Only because you have legions of volunteers out on the wards collecting them. Patients ask for a request just to be polite, often, I'm afraid just to get rid of you. They seldom tune in to hear those requests being played. Many patients and a lot of our medical staff find the volunteers a bit of a pest"

Colin couldn't argue with this.

"Hospitals nowadays, what with the Patients' Charter, have to be a lot more, if you like, customer-focused. So, for instance, when a doctor does his rounds he not only enquires about the patients' medical condition, he'll also ask how they're finding their stay in hospital, the treatment, the facilities – that sort of thing. Lately the patients have been asked whether or not they listen to the hospital radio station and, out of five hundred and twenty seven patients, Colin, do you know how many said yes?"

Colin shook his head.

"Three", said Banks with a note of triumph, barely able to keep the "So there!" out of his voice.

Colin was ready with a sanctimonious counter-argument.

"But surely if we bring comfort and enjoyment to one just one patient, doesn't that make all the effort worthwhile?"

"In a word, Colin, no" said Banks flatly. "To be honest, hospital radio has been on borrowed time for years. Ever since the invention of the Walkman".

"But how about all my studio equipment? You can't just sell it".

"It isn't your hospital equipment, Colin, it belongs to the hospital and as chief administrator, I could flog it off at a car boot sale if I wanted to".

Colin looked aghast, Oh dear, Banks was getting too animated. The Haliborange was wearing off. Frank, who had remained silent until now, decided it was time to intervene.

"I think Mr. Banks is joking", he said smoothly, "Of course it won't go to a car boot sale. Not after the enormous amount of time and effort that you and your team put in to raise the money to buy it".

"What's going to happen to it?" snapped the panic-stricken ex-presenter, "I demand to know".

Banks had recovered his composure, " Well Colin, the trustees and I have come up with a very good idea but if you have a better one we will of course be more than happy to consider it"

"Tell me what it is then".

"Well, as you know, there isn't much call for second hand studio equipment. I imagine that, generally, people who want this kind of kit have already got it".

"So wouldn't it be better", said Colin, almost pleading, "to leave it where it is?"

"Of course it would. If more than three people were listening at any given time. But they're not so Father Dempsey here has kindly offered to help us out".

Colin looked over at Frank. who took his cue to elucidate.

"You and I, Colin, are kindred spirits", he began, "Both devoted to raising funds for worthwhile causes. At St. Thomas's, we recently completed the renovation of the old church hall which we've turned into a thriving parish centre.

We hold regular discos and dances there and the money raised is distributed among various charities. Trouble is, our PA system is ancient and the sound quality is awful. Luckily, by about ten o'clock, most of the crowd are too drunk to notice".

Colin chuckled along with Frank's "witty" observation.

"So, if that QEFM equipment were to find a new home at St.Thomas's, it could continue doing its sterling work".

Colin knew he would have a hard job pitching an argument against this one. Frank continued "Now since it was always used for the benefit of the patients here at Queen Elizabeth's, I would suggest that once a month we hold a big dance at the parish centre and each time donate all the profits to the hospital".

Colin slumped further into his chair. The game was up. Frank was, however, leaving his trump card till last.

"Now with your permission, Colin, we'd like to set up a proper fund"

"With my permission?"

"Yes. If we're able to take the equipment, we realise that we would never have had it without you, so I'd want to call the fund the Colin Liddell Fund".

Not even praise of his prowess as a radio presenter could have brought a swifter flush of pleasure to his cheeks and the horrible toothy grin came out on display once again. Flatter the ego of a vain and pompous man and you can take several thousand pounds' of studio equipment from under his nose and he'll even thank you for doing it,

"Well, thank you, Father", said Colin. proffering that limp lettuce leaf of a handshake. Frank felt almost sorry for the sad and deflated little creature but he knew that the Colin Liddell Fund would bring him more recognition and satisfaction than hospital radio ever could. His mother was going to be very proud. Colin left the room thanking Frank once more. When he closed the door. Frank exhaled deeply and raised an eyebrow to Banks who, having finally managed to close down QEFM, was dancing round his desk with joy.

"Father Dempsey", he beamed, "I hope you won't be offended by this but you're an absolute fucking genius".

TWENTY-SIX

Ginger Tom was on the door that night Frank had given him Sarah's name and told him to let her in free. She was an old friend, the priest had explained, she worked in advertising and was doing some research into the on trade. It was a good job Frank had told him because it was, to quote an old proverb, easier for a camel to pass through the eye of a needle than for an uninvited guest to get into one of St. Thomas's Sunday night hoolies Members of the "Murphia" who looked after the door were not noted for their easy-going affability. Ginger Tom, for example, had worked the door at the Galtymore in Cricklewood and the Garryowen in Hammersmith. It had been his weekly duty to wade in and break up some spectacularly violent altercations. Not much frightened him.

At about 9.30, Sarah arrived.

"Hi" she said, "er...my name's Sarah Marshall".

"Ah, right", Tom smiled, "Father Dempsey is expecting you. Go on in".

"How much is it?" she asked, taking out a navy Mulberry purse from her bag.

Tom waved his hand to waive the entrance fee

"Sure you're a guest of Father Dempsey", he informed her, "Go on in".

"It's in aid of the hospital, isn't it?" said Sarah, "Please. I'd like to contribute".

Tom was impressed, "Well it's £10".

"Fine" she said, handing over two five pound notes.

"Very good of you", he smiled, "Come on, I'll take you in"

She couldn't help but notice the extraordinary sound quality of the music. So sweet, so crisp and even at these ear-splitting decibels, not even the slightest fizz of distortion. She'd been involved in the production of dozens of TV and radio commercials and this was professional quality. How on earth had they managed to acquire a sound system like this?

"The Hucklebuck" a guaranteed floor-filler at any Irish function was in full swing and for a moment, Sarah couldn't see Frank at all. Tom, however, picked him out on the packed dancefloor, hucklebucking – linking arms and swinging round with dozens of his parishioners.

After a couple of minutes, the record finished and the DJ decided to calm things down. On went Jim Reeves and "Welcome To My World" and the frenetic reeling was replaced by slow waltzing.

Sarah tapped Frank on the shoulder. He turned round and smelled again the freshly washed hair, lost himself in the gorgeous brown eyes and felt the staggering force of that wide-mouthed smile. He felt his knees start to sway and knock tried to persuade himself that it was the result of a little too much Hucklebucking.

Frank was rendered speechless again, too deliriously happy to form a coherent sentence. All he could do to greet his guest was gesture with an outstretched hand towards the dancefloor, "Together they joined the other couples 1-2-3-4-ing their way around.

Frank, despite a walloping heart beseeching him to the contrary, made sure he held Sarah's body a respectful distance from his own. He also made a perfunctory attempt at proper waltz steps. He longed to pull those lithe curves closer but more than anything, he was embarrassed by the fact that his heart was now thumping more loudly than Cozy Powell pounding out "Dance With The Devil".

"Glad you could make it", he said, slipping into the old

clockwise slow dance routine for the first time in more years than he cared to remember. .

"Well, I was very curious", she replied, "Is it always like this?"

"At weekends, yeah"

"Oh dear", she laughed, "Slattery's haven't got a prayer".

"Well", said Frank, trying to be charitable, "they're just aiming at the wrong market. Irish people have a great sense of community. Many of the people here come from small, close-knit towns and villages. This place gives them the chance to re-create that lovely warm feeling. They'll never get that at one of those Slattery's places".

Jim Reeves gave way to Faron Young with "It's Four In The Morning" – the perfect old-time waltz. Frank and Sarah made no attempt to release each other and continued their rather amateurish voyage around the dancefloor. Frank had never been so happy and so unhappy at exactly the same time

He listened to Sarah's description of her day. Reading the papers in bed, long leisurely bath. Over to some friends in Richmond for Sunday lunch. EastEnders omnibus, stroll by the river. Another quick bath, change, and over to Wealdstone. He felt for the very first time that he was missing out. Sunday was his busiest day. Two masses to say, lunchtime shift behind the bar, Sunday evening benediction then back to the parish centre to prepare for tonight's big thrash. He'd have sold his soul to Satan, or "Stan" as Frank always referred to him, for just one Sunday with Sarah.

Another couple were waltzing very close by and if you looked closely, you'd see that the woman was doing the man's steps, leading her compliant husband around. Her lips were pursed and as she looked over at the parish priest, it was clear that she did not approve of what she saw.

"Pat, who's the girl?"

Pat Walsh gave a weary sigh.

"I don't know and I don't care"

"Look at the way he's carrying on"

"They're doing the old time waltz. Same as we are"

"But we've been married for twenty-nine years"

"There's nothing that says that a priest can't have an old time waltz. He's the best parish priest we've ever had. You wouldn't begrudge the fella an old time waltz"

"I'm just not sure about him. Not sure of his motives".

"Motives. The man is completely honest. All he wants to do is make people happy.. Remember, I handle all the finances. There isn't a penny I couldn't account for".

Anne Walsh lapsed into a stony silence and Pat got the feeling that this was not over yet. Her reproving stare made it's way across the dancefloor and Frank could feel her eyes boring into the back of his head. So, when Faron Young had finished, he thought it best to go over.

"Mr and Mrs Walsh", he smiled, "I'd like you to meet Sarah Marshall – old friend of mine"

Pleasant nods were exchanged and Anne momentarily let the scowl fall from her face.

"This place" explained Frank "wouldn't exist without Pat. Financially, he runs it. He's the money man – sharp enough to shave with"

Pat was beaming like a buttered crumpet so Frank diplomatically felt he ought to say something nice about Anne.

"And Anne here does a lot of sterling work for the parish".

He wasn't quite sure what – something to do with the flowers, wasn't it? He looked over at the bar where drinkers were standing three or four deep. Big Eddie and his team of volunteers were under siege, almost unable to cope.

"Better go and help Uncle Eddie" he winked and then came out with possibly the worst thing he could have said.

"Perhaps you could give us a hand", he remarked lightly

to Anne, only trying to be friendly, "Pat tells me you were a fantastic barmaid".

The scowl returned. "That", she replied icily, "was a very long time ago".

Silence.

Cold, seemingly endless silence.

"Er…I'll give you a hand, Father" Pat suddenly piped up, more to fill the awkward gap than anything else. "I'm not bad with figures".

"Oh, Pat, are you sure?" said Frank, more grateful for the diffusion of a horrible moment than for the actual offer of help.

"Sure I'm sure. Come on, otherwise there's going to be a riot".

"Er….Father Dempsey?" asked Sarah, "Would it be all right, if I stood behind the bar, just to watch, you know, for research".

"Yes, of course" said Frank and the three of them went off, leaving Anne all alone with just her scowl for company..

"Ladies and gentlemen", said Frank to the assembled throng, jostling towards the bar, "May I introduce our new temporary barman, Mr. Patrick Walsh".

A big cheer went up. Big Eddie drew Pat aside for a couple of minutes and briefed him on the bar prices and Pat was away.

To see Pat over the next hour or so was to witness something extraordinary. A man in his element. A man returning to his element, having been so cruelly forced out of so for too long. He re-discovered the old patter, the old elan, the natural knack he'd always had with people that had made him so brilliant on the Number 16. He re-discovered the happy man he used to be. Add to this, his phenomenal grasp of figures, his ability to add up two or three rounds at the same time and you had the ultimate barman. Watching him at work, Big Eddie whistled through his teeth and remarked to

Frank that in forty-seven years, he'd never seen such a prodigy.

Pat was enjoying every second, the way you always do if you ever discover that you have a talent for something. Moreover, at last he felt that he was one of the lads. This time not in the capacity of cautious and sensible accountant, but right here in the very centre of their world, getting the beers in. Here he felt liberated from the impeccably tidy, swirly-curtained, double-glazed prison cell he called home.

Sarah watched fascinated, drawn more than ever towards the handsome, charismatic priest. To her great sorrow, she now understood why he did it. Here was a man truly happy in his work, truly fulfilled in his life. Every day, he was doing something good. He comforted the sick and dying, he organised these dances, even drove a taxi to raise money for those less fortunate than himself. How could a relationship with her, with any woman for that matter, possibly compete with this?

Just before eleven, Frank ordered a break in the music and got up on to the stage and took the microphone.

"Ladies and gentlemen. Thank you all for celebrating the feast of St.Petronella. Now you may feel that getting drunk and dancing is not perhaps the most suitable way to commemorate the life and death of an early Roman martyr but believe me, it is. Because you were good enough to come along tonight, we've raised a lot of money for Queen Elizabeth's hospital. Pat Walsh will add it all up and I'll let you know the final figure at mass next Sunday but Pat's already told me that it won't be less than five thousand pounds"

A big cheer went up followed by a round of spontaneous applause.

As it died down, Frank continued "Now I'm sure you'll agree that the evening was enhanced by the fantastic new sound system we've just installed".

Sarah had been wondering about this.

"As some of you may know, it was donated in a gesture of stunning generosity by QEFM, the hospital radio station which, sadly, had to close down last month. Now the very least we can do is re-pay that kindness by putting this equipment to good use. I suggest we make the Any Excuse Club a regular feature in the parish calendar"

Another huge cheer went up.

"I'll take that as a yes then. Now I'd like to invite Colin Liddell the former programme director of QEFM whose idea it was to give us this fabulous equipment, up on to the stage so we can show our appreciation for what he's done".

An even bigger cheer greeted Colin's horrible toothy grin. And Frank concluded,

"From now on, these little Sunday night events will take place on a regular basis, all proceeds to the Colin Liddell fund. Thank you, ladies and gentlemen and goodnight".

Two more records, Ella Fitzgerald's "Every Time We say Goodbye", and "The Last Waltz" by Engelbert Humperdinck and five hundred people staggered home.

Frank was busy mopping up, locking up and clearing away so Sarah felt it was time to make an exit.

"Er....I'll be off then. It's been a wonderful evening. Thanks for inviting me".

"Not at all", said Frank, "Thanks for coming."

This time, Sarah really had driven over and couldn't pretend otherwise. Frank would have loved to have provided another cab ride home but could not leave Eddie and Pat to do all the clearing up while he disappeared to Fulham.

So that was it. They'd run out of legitimate excuses to meet up. They wouldn't be seeing each other ever again.

No reason to now, was there?

TWENTY-SEVEN

TO: mbabcock@Unibrew.com
From: Sarah.marshall@cdp.co.uk

Mike,

As promised, I inveigled my way in to St. Thomas's parish centre last night. It was very busy because, as you know, Sunday has always been a big Irish night out. It's a members only club and every Irish person in the area seems to be a member. They are an unswervingly loyal clientele. They all know one another, drinks are cheap and all profits go to charity so there is a very warm community spirit there.

I'm afraid this whole package is something with which, in my view, Slattery's can never compete.

There are plenty of other people in the area for whom you could cater with perhaps one of the other brands in your theme pub portfolio but it looked to me like the Irish vote is already pretty sewn up.

I'm happy to meet up to discuss this further. Give me a call.

Regards,

Sarah.

Mike Babcock stared at his laptop for a minute. Then he stood up and paced around. He sat back down and put on the headset and jaw-line mouthpiece which was an essential accoutrement of the busy executive and punched out one of the thirty-six two digit quick dial numbers stored in his telephone's memory.

His tone was grave, urgent, almost as though he was starring in a particularly tense episode of ER.

"Sarah, hi, Mike. Listen, got your e-mail, thanks. Need to sit down. Can you get down here? I'm in meetings till about 1.30, can you make, say,1.35?"

"Yeah, sure, Mike, 1.35".

"Good, see you then then. Ciao"

"Ciao", said Sarah before putting down the receiver and bursting out laughing.

At 1.33, she was at Mike's office on a characterless business park just off the M4. He kept her waiting. He always did. Page 47, probably, in some awful American management textbook, "How To Get Ahead In Your Career" – always keep people waiting for a few minutes. It won't hurt them and will serve as a reminder of just who is in control of this situation. This was fine by Sarah. The less time she had to spend in a *person to person interface* with Mike Babcock, the better.

At 2.03, the receptionist called over

"Ms. Marshall, Mr. Babcock will see you now. You know the way, don't you?"

Sarah and her Visitor's Badge made their way to the sixth floor where Mike and his over-firm handshake were there to greet her.

"Sarah, hi, thanks for coming. Sorry to keep you waiting. Monthly divisional sales meeting. Overran, as per usual."

Oh, the pressures of being a captain of industry.

"Anyway, cut to the chase. Got your e-mail, very interesting, Very grateful for what you've brought to the party but for me, there were only two really crucial words"

"Which were?"

"Cheap drinks", Mike crowed triumphantly as though he'd just found a cure for prostate cancer.

"Cheap drinks?"

"Cheap drinks", he confirmed repeating the words to confirm his position as an incisive marketing genius, "Basically at the end of the day, all that stuff about community spirit is bullshit. In the final analysis, all these people care about, all anybody cares about, is the bottom line. We've got to hit these people where it hurts and we've got the financial clout to do it. We've got to make our drinks cheaper than theirs. Go the extra mile, do whatever it takes to bury them".

Sarah was disgusted, "I'm sorry, Mike but I don't agree. This place is the centre of these people's lives. It's not about money. This is a battle you can't win and to be honest, it's a battle you shouldn't want to win".

Sarah may as well have pulled out a big red handkerchief and waved it at the nearest bull.

"Sarah", he fumed, "It's pretty clear to me that you don't understand. Mike Babcock is a winner. Mike Babcock is not accustomed to coming second".

Sarah had a witty riposte on the tip of her tongue but wisely decided to keep it there.

"We carry out a lot of detailed research before deciding on a site for each Slattery's unit. Our knowledge base is phenomenal and Wealdstone scored very, very highly. This is one of our flagship units. It has to succeed. If it is seen to fail then the knock-on effect could be catastrophic"

"I understand what you're saying", said Sarah, "but wouldn't it make more sense to re-open it in a different guise and target different people who aren't so well catered for already?"

Mike shook his head with a patronising sigh, "Sarah, Sarah, Sarah. No branch of Slattery's can ever be seen to fail. Basically, because the whole brand would be seen to fail with it. This is war, so I've formulated a strategy which will see them off once and for all. Now, we don't need to worry too much about Friday and Saturday nights but we're losing out heavily on Sundays so starting in a fortnight's time, it's free drinks all night on Sundays".

Sarah's reaction was instant and frank, "You're mad".

Mike took this as a great compliment,

"That's what they said to Isaac Newton, that's what they said to Christopher Columbus".

Sarah couldn't help herself "No, Mike", she explained, "I don't mean mad in a commercial sense because as, you say, you do have the financial clout to do this. When I say mad, I mean you must be mad to want to win this badly, to close down a little parish centre which gives all its profits to charity. It's so...so....unsporting"

Mike shifted his tone to one of worldly -wise calm and experience "Sarah", he explained, "in the dog eat dog world of business, sportsmanship does not figure on the radar. Basically, if they want to play with the grown-ups, they're going to have to suffer the consequences. Free drinks on Sundays, Sarah. That's the way we're going to do it. Beers and soft drinks, obviously, not spirits, my MD would never wear that. Now we'll need a tactical ad campaign pretty pronto, tell the world what we're up to. Trust me, Sarah, I know what I'm doing".

TWENTY-EIGHT

"This is St. Thomas's Church, Wealdstone. If you'd like to leave a message for Father Lynam, Father Conlon or Father Dempsey, please do so after the tone"

"Father Dempsey, it's Sarah.. Er......sorry to bother you but I need to speak to you quite urgently. I'll try you on your mobile".

Frank was in the cab, ferrying a fascinated film producer between Hoxton and Soho when his mobile rang.

"Father Dempsey, it's Sarah".

His heart leapt. The relationship had moved a few millimetres forward. It was now, "Hi, it's Sarah" instead of " Hi, it's Sarah Marshall", the next stage was "Hi. it's me". He'd love her to drop the "Father Dempsey" in favour of "Frank" but could only dream of moving up to that exquisite level where lovers don't need to call each other anything.

"What a surprise", he said, nearly mounting the pavement.

"Look, I've left a message for you at the presbytery. I need to talk to you about Slattery's".

"Oh, right"

"Where are you?"

"Holborn. POB, that's passenger on board, on my way to Soho".

"Oh, that's handy. Can we meet up?"

Is the Pope a Catholic?

"Yeah. I'll give you a ring in about ten minutes when I'm free".

"Fine"

Ten minutes later. Frank turned into Golden Square and Sarah jumped into the cab.

It was a bright afternoon and Frank headed north up towards Regents Park. He left the cab on a rank on the Inner Circle and together they strolled into Queen Mary's Gardens and sat on a park bench. For Frank, this was almost a date. He'd only ever seen her either in his cab or at the Parish Centre. Sitting in the sun in Regents Park, he felt delightfully uncloistered – almost part of the human race.

"Slattery's are out to bury you"

"Oh, really?" grinned Frank, metaphorically placing his outstretched hand on the top of a midget's head while the midget swung wildly and vainly in an attempt to hit him.

"Yes, really", she said, "They've been losing money hand over fist since you opened that Parish Centre and they're not happy at all".

"So what are they going to do about it?"

"Well, in a fortnight's time, they're launching "Sunday Best", their best night out on a Sunday scheme which means free drinks all night.

Frank let a long slow whistle out through his teeth.

"Free drinks?" he said. For a split second, he seemed almost concerned.

"Well, beers and soft drinks. Not spirits".

"Dear me. They really are serious, aren't they?"

"Yes they are. And the thing is, Slattery's is part of a huge multi-national corporation. They've got an awful lot of money on their side"

"And we've got God on ours".

This was the first time that Sarah had ever heard him say anything remotely religious. So, under that sassy, streetwise façade he was just another naïve cleric, honestly expecting to be able to pray his way out of this one. The candles of passion she felt for him were suddenly all being snuffed out. Nonetheless, she tried not to be too disrespectful.

"God?"

"Yes, God"

"What do you mean?"

"Well, I don't mean that the Almighty is going to come down and smite Slattery's from the face of the earth. Let's just say that at times like this, you can use God to your advantage".

He looked up at the sky and grinned.

The candles were being re-lit again.

Frank really did have a diocesan meeting in Westminster so, much as he wanted to stay in Regents Park all afternoon with a picnic, go off and see a film, grab a late bite to eat and go home with Sarah to Fulham, it was out of the question.

As he dropped her back at Golden Square, he had one last question, "Two weeks on Sunday, you say?"

"That's right."

"Okay, phone me two weeks on Monday and we'll discuss what happened".

What happened? Did he know in advance what was going to happen? What was he going to do? Use God to his advantage? How? He'd just unwittingly made himself more attractive and mysterious than ever.

Two weeks on Monday? Sarah wondered how on earth she was going to wait that long. Those two weeks were going to feel like two years.

TWENTY-NINE

"So who is he then?" said Nessie, in between mouthfuls of Marks & Spencer's double chocolate cheesecake.

Sarah tried, rather unsuccessfully to look puzzled "What are you talking about?"

"Who is he?" Nessie repeated, "This bloke?"

"What bloke?" asked Sarah.

"Oh come on, don't go all Miss Innocent on me. The left side of your neck's going red".

Shit! Sure-fire sign. Sarah was a terrible liar. Not a consummate, habitual liar – a genuinely terrible, incompetent one, always let down by the reddening of one side of her neck. Once that had happened, there was no point prolonging the pretence.

"Well, nothing's happened"

"Yet", said Nessie, shovelling another bit of cheesecake in, "Do you want some of this?"

"Yeah, save me a bit"

"Look, you know I can't do that. Have as much as you want now but don't ask me to save you any".

"Anyway", said Sarah, between mouthfuls and quite relieved to be able to tell someone, "Nothing's happened – he's completely unsuitable"

"Plus ca change" said Nessie with a laugh, "Is he married?"

"No"

"Going out with someone?"

"No."

"Is he gay?"

"Wouldn't have thought so"

"Is he over sixty?"

"No"

"Under sixteen?"

"No"

"Then how, pray, is he unsuitable?"

"Well", said Sarah, taking a deep breath, "Funny you should use the word 'pray'?"

"Why?"

"Well.......because he's a...a..a.. Roman Catholic priest".

There was an involuntary splutter of chocolate cheesecake all over the sofa.

"A what?"

"A Catholic priest"

"So he's taken a vow of celibacy?"

Sarah nodded.

"And you've fallen in love with him?"

:Sarah nodded, this time biting her bottom lip alerting Nessie to the fact that she might he about to cry. Oh dear, best proceed with caution.

"Are you sure", she began, taking the most obvious route, "that you're not attracted to him simply because he's unattainable?"

Sarah sighed, "I wish that were the case but no, It goes a lot deeper than that".

This had Nessie worried. Sarah wasn't daft. She wasn't a love-struck teenager. She was nearly thirty and had had more than her share of boyfriends. She was quite able to identify in her own mind the feelings and emotions of friendship, of intrigue, of infatuation, of good old-fashioned lust. She knew what it was like to fall in love, to fall out of love, to become heartbroken, to become gradually disappointed. She was intelligent and mature enough to know whether these feelings were for real. And from where Nessie was sitting, picking up the crumbs of her cheesecake, the answer seemed to be yes.

"Well, come on, tell Auntie Nessie, how did you get yourself involved with a Catholic priest. Was it up at that wedding in Wilmslow?"

Sarah shook her head and started from the beginning – the taxi on Golden Square and poured out every detail. It was like a plug had been pulled out and there was no stemming the deluge of intimate revelations. Sarah felt like a Bolivian ex-torture victim, freed by Amnesty International, suddenly opening up for post-traumatic stress counselling. And Nessie was the ideal sounding board. A kind, understanding, very bohemian opera singer with a vast experience of the opposite sex gleaned from extensive field research

Between them over the years, they'd had dozens of these EBM's or Emergency Bloke Meetings, often stretching until three or four in the morning and fuelled by chocolate, cigarettes and bottles of red wine. This time was very different. .As Sarah recounted the little meetings, the cab rides, the feast of St.Petronella,, Nessie no time to do anything but listen, leaving that second piece of chocolate cheesecake ignored and untouched on her plate.

"..........and you know me, Nessie", said Sarah, bringing the tale to a close, "I don't have a particular type. I've been out with tall blokes, short blokes, fat blokes, thin ones, rich, poor, dark, fair – it doesn't matter. I never really fancy that many men but if they press the right buttons, that's it for me, there is nothing I can do.

"And", said Nessie gently, "This priest – he's pressed them harder than anyone you've ever met".

Sarah looked up, nodded silently and burst into tears.

Nessie cradled her friend's head in her arms. It was always fairly easy to dispense good advice on another person's love life from the comfortable position of slightly detached concern. But as Sarah kept saying – this was different, very different. Nessie for once was fresh out of good advice. She didn't know what to suggest. She felt genuinely sorry for Sarah. So sorry, she almost wanted to cry herself.

Sarah's state of mind was not helped by her work. She'd always loathed working on Slattery's, detested her dealings with Mike Babcock. The novelty of Buzzword Bingo could no longer compensate. Worst of all, she was now being asked to produce ads to promote Slattery's Sunday Best, the free drinks give-away. Dreadful, crass press ads saying things like "Slattery's has become a real Free House" and "Drinks Are On The House" with an awful picture of a group of Irishmen sitting drinking Guinness on the roof of a pub. Ha bloody ha.

The radio commercials were even worse; featuring the obligatory diddley-dee music and a "versatile" voice-over affecting an unconvincing Dublin accent. And all designed to destroy the good work and livelihood of the man she adored.

She went to Peter Clay , her boss and resigned, citing "creative differences" between herself and her client. She explained her objections to Mike Babcock's plans to "bury" St. Thomas's Parish Centre, omitting of course to mention her friendship with the parish priest.

Peter could see her point but was in a difficult position. The agency made a colossal amount of money not just from Slattery's but form the other pieces of business in the Unibrew portfolio. To upset the client at this crucial stage could be a disaster. On the other hand, he knew that Sarah was right and admired her integrity. After all, a principle isn't a principle until it costs you something and Sarah was quite willing to let it cost her her job. Replacing such a brilliant and intuitive account director would be almost impossible.

"I hear what you're saying but", he began.

This is one of those phrases like "I love her *dearly* but….." or "*I'm not a racist* but….." which is invariably followed by a statement to the contrary

"I hear what you're saying but can't you just stay on the

account for a couple more weeks? Just until this "Sunday Best" promotion is over then I'll put you on something else – more responsibility a bit more money as well".

"Peter" she protested "You're not listening. The Sunday Best promotion is the reason I'm leaving".

Peter was listening but thought it was worth a try.

"Sarah", he said, "We don't want to lose you and if you feel that strongly, how about this? Just take a couple of weeks' extra holiday from tomorrow. Fully paid, of course. Just phone in sick tomorrow. Don't tell a soul. Well not here, anyway. Come back when this Sunday Best thing is up and running, by which time I'll have sorted out something else for you to work on".

"With more responsibility?" she enquired, not that she particularly wanted it.

"Of course" he smiled, delighted not to be losing his star account director,

"And er.......?" she ventured,

"Yes of course, more money", he confirmed.

Sarah smiled back. "Thanks".

Peter Clay was accustomed to people in his department threatening to resign, trying all sorts of levering tricks to secure a pay rise. He seldom gave in but Sarah was different. He knew that she didn't want the extra responsibility or even the pay rise. Which, of course, was why he gave it to her.

"Just one more thing", he said, "What are we going to say is wrong with you?"

"Just say girly problems", said Sarah, "No-one ever wants further details. Least of all Mike Babcock".

She closed Peter's door behind her and didn't know whether to laugh or cry. A pay rise, the promise of never having to work on Slattery's again and two weeks' extra holiday. Two weeks? Without even the monotony of work to take her mind off her forbidden friend? It was going to drive her insane.

Still two weeks away from Mike Babcock, that had to be good news. What was she going to do? A fortnight in the sun somewhere cheap and cheerful? But who with? Nessie was touring with Tosca and wouldn't be back for another month. Helen would probably be going somewhere with Graham. Or more likely, they'd be putting their money into a joint account to save up for a new dishwasher. No, she'd stay in London and do all the things she never got time to do. Catch up on her reading. Those unread copies of Flaubert, Tolstoy and Dostoevsky could finally come down from the bookshelf. Or more likely, those unwatched tapes of Blind Date and EastEnders could come down from the video shelf. She could go to the gym outside of the busy early morning and early evening times and enjoy the luxury of not having to queue for a shower. She could try some recipes from that Nigel Slater cookbook that Nessie had given her three years ago. No fun on your own though, is it? Nothing really is. Except shopping. She'd go shopping. She wasn't one of those cliched girly shopoholics but she did enjoy buying things. You went to work, you got money, you bought things, That was the circle of life. As her mother always said, "Darling, you can either have money or you can have stuff. Frankly, I'd rather have stuff".

New York was the place for stuff and her brother Nick did live out there. Sarah liked to tell people he was a drug dealer, which was true – he worked in the marketing division of a huge pharmaceutical company. She could get a cheap a flight over to New York, stay a couple of days with Nick and his wife in Manhattan. Perhaps treat herself to a night in the Alchemy Suite at The Dylan. But that really would be no fun on your own. All she really wanted to do was phone Frank. Surely he could use some help at that parish centre of his. She'd love to have another root through his records but no, he'd said he'd call her in two weeks. He obviously didn't want to see her before then. Best to leave it. She'd heard of

God-botherers and had no desire to become a priest-pesterer.

She decided that what she needed was a few days enveloped in a good, sobering dose of normality and headed up to Wilmslow to visit her parents. They were delighted to see her. Business was booming and David was very excited about getting his first website complete with funky graphics of claret being poured into a glass.

"You know, darling" he said to his daughter over dinner, "if you ever get bored in London. You could always come and work for me, I mean, with me. Your advertising expertise would be invaluable. We've just taken delivery of loads of new wine. Would you mind tasting some of them? You always seem to know what's going to go down well"

Sarah could think of few things worse than becoming enmeshed in that parochial Cheshire lifestyle where everyone knew everyone else's business. She loved the anonymity of London. She lived three inches from her next door neighbours and still had no idea who they were

It was, however, always good to come home, especially with all these wines to try and so, for the next couple of hours, she became accustomed to the moist creak of yet another cork being removed from yet another bottle. She found one Chilean Chardonnay irresistibly gluggable but tried not to glug too much of it. She had to retain some semblance of sobriety because if she didn't, she could be in trouble. Her mother, who was also sampling Marshall's finest and becoming increasingly squiffy, was bound to ask that euphemistic question,

"So how are things?" which meant, "Are you ever going to settle down and get married?",

If Sarah's guard was washed away by a wave of Chardonnay, she might let it all out and wail uncontrollably about the love she felt for a man who was forbidden by his vows to reciprocate.

THIRTY

After three months in hospital, Danny Power was finally ready to come home. It had been a slow and faltering recovery but, if ever you were looking for evidence of God working in strange and mysterious ways, this would be it.

His miraculous escape from the Grim Reaper provided three separate levels of irony. Firstly, Danny's cycling, taken up to improve his health had actually come within a hair's breadth of killing him. Secondly, the huge casement of flesh which had been threatening his life turned out to be what saved it. He'd hit the road with such force that if he hadn't had that extra six and a half stone of flab to cushion the impact he would have been killed instantly. And finally, during those months in hospital, he was fed a saline drip and then a revolting cabbage soup which apparently provided all the nutrients \a bed-ridden patient would require

They weighed him just before discharging him and the hospital scales confirmed that he had lost six and a half stone, exactly what Dr. Clarke had told him to.

So, on a bright, sunny Tuesday morning, Frank picked Rose Power up in the taxi and took her up to Queen Elizabeth's to bring the (not quite so) big man home.

The following Sunday was 3rd July, the feast of St. Thomas, unofficial patron saint of Wealdstone, the best excuse the Any Excuse Club could have for a party.

It was to be a double celebration, St.Thomas's feast day and Danny Power's homecoming. In his sermon, Frank whipped up the excitement including a veiled, almost subliminal implication that God would be taking a dim view of anyone not attending. His all-seeing eye would rest upon those guiltily guzzling the free Guinness at Slattery's. He knew that certain members of the congregation would be tempted but also knew that the threat of Our Lord following them up to the bar would more than enough to discourage them.

The parish centre was full to bursting that night. After hearing Brendan Shine's "Catch Me If You Can, Me Name Is Dan" played in his honour, Danny took to the stage and paid a moving tribute to his family, his friends, everyone at Queen Elizabeth's Hospital and to his special friend, Father Frank Dempsey, who had made St. Thomas's the best parish in the world. A tumultuous cheer greeted this and Frank, genuinely overcome, took a modest little bow. That cheer was then followed by an even bigger one when Danny announced that everybody's next drink was on him.

All the time Frank kept hoping Sarah would appear to witness perhaps the finest moment of his life. He was desperate to share it with her. Never mind, he had an excuse to ring her tomorrow and boast about the fact that Slattery's Sunday Best night hadn't made even the tiniest dent in his profits.

Mike Babcock had been away on a golfing weekend in the Algarve. He'd flown out on Friday afternoon and hadn't returned until late on Sunday night. His "Driving Rock " CD had been playing in the Vauxhall Vectra all the way back from Gatwick. His mobile was switched off and when he got home, he was too tired to notice the flashing red light on his answering machine. When he woke up, he headed straight for the gym then on to the office for 8.48, Phil Collins' Greatest Hits accompanying him all the way. He hadn't tuned in to the news. If he had, he'd have heard something along the lines of::

"Violence erupted at a bar in North London last night. Slattery's in Wealdstone High Street had been offering free

beer all evening as part of its so-called Sunday Best promotion and the place had become dangerously over-crowded. Trouble flared when drunken revellers couldn't get to the bar for more drinks. A near riot broke out and the interior of the bar was completely destroyed. All the windows were smashed and the whole scene looked more like Belfast or Beirut than London. Twenty-six people, including five policemen were injured, four of them seriously. The bar is part of a nation-wide chain owned by Unibrew PLC but their chief executive, Christopher Powell has so far declined to comment.

Powell was deathly white and visibly quivering with rage.

"So, Mike" he seethed, "this Sunday Best promotion was all your idea. Or "your baby" as you called it. Well, in terms of PR, you've done this company irreparable damage. That branch of Slattery's will almost certainly now have it's licensed revoked . The whole chain – that's 128 units will now be tarred with the same brush. I've already had to field dozens of calls from the BBC, GMTV, all the radio stations, national newspapers and Alcohol Concern. This promotion is the best thing you could have done for our competitors who are now leaping on the bandwagon to point the finger. Free alcohol? It's commercially stupid, socially irresponsible and this is what you call an intelligent marketing strategy."

"Well, basically, at the end of the day...." was all Mike could manage before Powell rounded on him again.

"There is nothing you can say that can possibly justify this. As far as I'm concerned, Mike, your position here is untenable. Now. If you'll excuse me, I've got the Daily Mail waiting outside".

Christopher Powell swept angrily from his office and left the nation's newest addition to the dole queue standing all alone and silent.

Mike, however, hide like a rhino, still couldn't see the seriousness of what he had done.. Powell would calm down, this whole episode would blow over, become yesterday's news. The Vauxhall Vectra would remain safe in the carport.

Unfortunately, the light zephyr became a hurricane when, later that day, the strategy behind the Sunday Best promotion came to light. To destroy the competition. The competition being a little Catholic social club which gave all its profits to charity. Somehow, Christopher Powell managed to stop this leaking out. If it had become public knowledge, investors, especially those from staunch Catholic countries such as Italy and Spain, would have withdrawn their backing in disgust and hundreds more Unibrew employees would have had to follow Mike Babcock to the Job Centre.

As it was, the City was less than pleased and Christopher Powell was forced into drastic action to erase forever the foul smell of what Mike Babcock had done. Almost overnight, all Slattery's branches were closed down and turned into equally awful institutions each known as "Ye Olde Pig & Whistle", the speciality of which was fairly inedible "Traditional English Fayre"

THIRTY-ONE

When Sarah returned to work, there were 38 messages on her voice-mail, 37 of which were of no interest to her at all. Message number 22 was the one she'd been waiting for.

"Sarah, hello it's Frank Dempsey", his tone suggested he was just a little uneasy about calling himself Frank, "I'm....er.....Father Dempsey to my parishioners and since I've yet to see you turn up for mass on Sunday, I don't count you among them so it's seems a bit daft for you to call me Father".

Roughly translated this meant, "*When I find someone as sexually attractive as I find you, I really don't want to be reminded that I am a Catholic priest who has taken a vow of celibacy. Please call me Frank so that I can at least pretend to myself that I might one day stand a chance of getting off with you*".

"Anyway", he went on, "that shocking business with Slattery's. Um... fancy a chat? I'm out in the cab all morning so you can get me on the mobile. Speak to you later. Bye".

At one o'clock, she was once again in the back of the taxi.

"Where to, luv?" said the driver with a grin.

"Anywhere", Sarah replied, "where I can talk to your face rather than the back of your head. Are you hungry?"

"Yeah", said Frank, " I am, as it goes."

"Good", she said, "Let's go and have lunch. My treat. I'll put it through on expenses"

"That would be great but......er....", said Frank, pointing to the dog collar which he always wore whilst driving the cab to prove he was a priest and elicit more generous donations from his passengers. I know a lot of people in London, it'll be just my luck to bump into one of them".

Sarah was disappointed, "But you're not doing anything wrong", she reasoned, "just having lunch with a friend".

"I know that, you know that", he replied, "but a priest enjoying any sort of pleasure is always frowned upon. Except, oddly enough, drinking. A priest pissed out of his head is somehow considered all right. That makes him a good old boy".

"Like your friend Father Conway?"

Frank stared blankly at her for a second before remembering the drunken cleric now seem-retired in Greenwich whom he'd invented a few weeks ago,

"Exactly", he said, almost wiping his brow with relief, "Father Conway. The Good Old Boy's Good Old Boy".

He had a sudden thought. "There is one place we could go, if you don't mind roughing a bit".

"Where?" she asked,

"Little Venice", he said and swung the taxi northwards.

Little Venice is a tiny corner of London sandwiched between Maida Vale and Paddington, so called because the Grand Union Canal runs through the middle of it. It's quite pretty, with his handsome stucco villas and houseboats moored on the canal. To compare it to Venice, however, is a little fanciful but that's estate agents for you. Apparently, there's a French restaurant in Leytonstone so the area could soon be known as "Little Paris" And isn't there a dry ski-slope in Uxbridge? Well, there you are then – "Little Zermatt".

As a name, however, "Little Venice" had entered common parlance so Sarah knew exactly where it was, though she didn't recall the area being over-stocked with restaurants. Frank pulled up outside a little green hut set in the middle of the road just by Warwick Avenue tube station. It was a cabman's shelter. There used to be hundreds but now they have all but disappeared

"Ever been in one of these before?" he asked, rhetorically.

Sarah laughed and shook her head., "Not this week, no"

"The cabmen's shelter fund", he informed her, "was set up for the purpose of supplying cabmen with a place of shelter where they can obtain good and wholesome refreshments at very moderate prices, apparently".

"And". Sarah suggested "for supplying priests who aren't even cab drivers with a bolt hole from nosey parishioners".

The place was tiny because, as Frank, in his new role as tour guide would explain, the Victorian police decreed that the shelter should take up no more space than a horse and cab. Frank was on a nodding terms with Monty the proprietor and the menu chalked up on the blackboard behind Monty's head comprised the usual English stodge. Mind you, since Frank's last visit, Monty had gone a little continental and was now offering Chicken Kiev with the usual fat chips and processed peas.

Over this delightful meal, the atmosphere wreathed in steam and smoke, they began to talk.

"So.... what happened?" was Frank's opening gambit, delivered in genuine innocence.

"I was going to ask you that", she replied with a grin.

"Me?"

"Yes, you. You were in Wealdstone last night about two hundred yards from this riot".

"We didn't know anything about it. Huge bash last night. Feast of St. Thomas, It was fantastic. I wish you could have been there".

Sarah's face involuntarily turned soft and serious, "Do you mean that?"

Frank's blue eyes met her brown ones, "Yes, I do".

The two pairs of eyes gazed at each other for a few seconds longer than was strictly necessary. Sarah was first to break off. Frank was brought up in Kilburn, where staring people out is almost an Olympic sport. "Anyway, I had a suspicion that that big fight was started by a few of your heavies from the parish centre".

Frank assumed moral indignation, "How dare you?" he laughed, "What do you think I am?"

For the second time in thirty seconds, Sarah's face went soft and serious and she seized the opportunity to grill him,

"That's just it", she said, "I don't know. I really don't know what I think you are. You're a priest but you're nothing like a priest"

Frank went into his well-versed counter argument, having had to answer this charge many times before,

"How many priests do you know?"

"Er....none"

"Right. So how do you know what a priest is like?"

" I don't, I suppose, but...."

Instead of throwing up the usual smokescreen, Frank, to his own surprise and relief, cut Sarah short and found himself giving rather than receiving a confession.

"You're right", he conceded, "I'm not like a priest. I know hundreds of them but I've got very little in common with any of them, except, obviously what we all do for a living".

Sarah had been desperately hoping that he would now admit that he wasn't a priest at all and the whole thing had been an elaborate joke. But no, he was a priest. A priest who, for the first time since becoming one, was admitting to another human being exactly how he felt about it.

"I'm not saying I don't like other priests – far from it. Almost without exception, they are good, unselfish people who devote their lives to helping others. How can you not admire people like that?. It's just that........"

"You don't have much in common with them?" Sarah gently reminded him.

"No, I don't. They all claim to have received some sort of

calling from God, some divine compulsion to go and spread the word of the Lord. I never did. I've never felt personally invited into the priesthood and I sometimes feel as though I've gatecrashed the party".

"But are you enjoying the party now you're there?" she wondered. Please say no, please, please say no.

"Well, yes ", said Frank, "I suppose I am. I've always enjoyed it. For me, the personal rewards are so much greater than in any other walk of life. You can really make a difference to people's lives".

"Is that why you went into it?"

"I suppose so. I think I said to you once before, it wasn't so much a case of getting into the priesthood, more a case of getting out of more conventional ways of life".

"So you never wanted to marry or have children?"

"Well, I thought I did. I assumed I would , but as I got older and it became a more realistic option it also became a less attractive one".

"So you had girlfriends?"

Frank recognised the euphemistic nature of this question immediately,

"What you mean is, am I gay?"

Sarah was about to insist that this wasn't what she'd meant at all but, feeling the left side of her neck reddening as usual, she knew it was pointless.

"No, " Frank told her, "I'm not gay". If only you knew, he thought, exactly how gay I'm not.

"It's funny", he said, "how so many people assume that most priests are. Believe me, if you're gay, the priesthood is just about the worst thing you could go into You can't have a relationship. You can't frequent gay bars and clubs, you can't be promiscuous. Though, strictly speaking, you wouldn't be breaking any of your vows if you did".

Sarah was confused, "Really?" she said. "How about the vow of celibacy?"

"Celibacy just means being unmarried. Chastity means not having sex but since the Catholic Church forbids sex outside of marriage, celibacy effectively means abstention from sex anyway".

He paused and grinned

"Supposedly"

Sarah was just about to ask whether he had remained chaste but realised that if he were the sort of priest to flout the rules in this way, he'd have no qualms about denying it. Instead, she repeated her original question.

"Have you had girlfriends?"

"Yes, I've had girlfriends"

Sarah gazed for a moment at his kind face with its strong handsome features and thought, "I bet you have".

She asked for the bill but found her company credit card was precious little use here. She was embarrassed to discover that she had no cash but Frank was more than happy to pay. St. Thomas's could bear the loss of twelve pounds eighty-five without calling in the receivers.

They walked out into the sunshine, the marvellous smell of Sarah's freshly washed hair was now permeated with chip fat. They strolled by the canal, under a bridge to a little-known open space, too small to be called a park and sat together on a bench. Frank, as a canoodling sixteen year old had sat on this bench many times before with an assortment of girls. They were, after all only about ten minutes from Kilburn.

Sarah, by now, was more fascinated by Frank than ever, and felt happy and relaxed enough to carry on interrogating him..

"Do you believe in God?"

The question rocked him. No-one had ever asked him that before. He was a priest, what a stupid thing to say to a priest. Except that, from the moment she met him, Sarah had never really seen him as a priest. She saw him more as an ordinary man at a fancy dress party. Questions hardly came more fundamental than this: Do you believe in God?. Frank was suddenly sitting in the hot seat on "Who Wants To be a Millionaire" the first contestant ever to be asked the £500,0000 question.

Was the answer

a) Yes?

b) No?

c) Don't know?

d) Yes with a great big asterisk?.

A or D? A or D? The truth or a downright lie? He went for the truth.

"D, Chris. Yes with a great big asterisk".

"I do believe in God", he said slowly as the weight of twenty years of hypocrisy fell away from his shoulders, "But not in the way a Roman Catholic priest is supposed to".

Sarah's chocolate brown eyes were wide open with intrigue.

"I'm supposed to believe in transubstantiation. When I bless that little round wafer biscuit known as the Holy Eucharist, I'm supposed to believe that it actually becomes Christ's body. Doesn't just symbolise it, it is it. Same with the red wine. It's actually sherry, by the way, wine doesn't keep. When I bless that, I'm supposed to believe that it really is Christ's blood."

He paused, staring blankly at the canal in front of them. . Sarah waited for him to continue

"And do you?" she probed gently.

"Of course I don't. Because it isn't.. If you took a sample of that sherry to a lab for analysis and insisted it was the blood of a two thousand year man, they'd have you sent to the funny farm. I'm also supposed to believe that the Pope, as God's representative on earth, is infallible and I don't believe that either. You might as well say that as the Pope's representative in Wealdstone – which I am – that I'm infallible, which

I'm not. I'm supposed to believe in Adam and Eve when the whole story has been completely disproved by Darwin. Until recently, I was expected to believe in the authenticity of the Turin shroud until it was scientifically proven to be a fake. You only have to read Albert Schweitzer, Ernest Renan or any of the definitive accounts of the life of Jesus to realise that there are too many conflicting stories for us to ever really know the truth, I'm not even convinced that he rose from the dead. I'm not saying he didn't but it's very hard to believe that he did. I had to study theology at university. Possibly the worst thing for an aspiring priest to do".

"But you still believe in some sort of God?"

"Yes, I suppose I do. Only because, like most people, I can't think of a rational scientific way to explain things. It's far easier to just attribute it all to something mysterious, something beyond our comprehension. If there is a God, I just believe he wants us to be nice to each other. Not fuck each other over".

It was the first time Sarah had ever heard him swear. She found it strangely alluring. He was a human being just like her. Thank God for that, she now felt free to swear herself.

"Like Slattery's tried to fuck you over?"

Frank found Sarah's fist foray into profanity strangely alluring too. Every other woman he'd ever met since taking Holy Orders had patronisingly assumed that he would be offended by bad language.

"Yeah, I suppose so", he laughed, suddenly remembering that it was the fracas at Slattery's not his theological misgivings that they were supposed to be talking about. "That was one of the few times I've ever thought I saw the hand of God at work".

"God?" she laughed. "Behind all that bar-room brawling?"

"Oh yeah, " Frank said "The Almighty is not averse to a

bit of argy-bargy. Eye for an eye, tooth for a tooth, forty days of flooding, plagues of locusts"

"I thought you didn't believe any of that".

Frank winked,

"You're taking the piss, aren't you?" she laughed and thumped him playfully on the arm which sent to a fizz of sexual excitement shooting around his body like a ball round a pinball machine. Lights were flashing, klaxons were going off. "It's just so hard to know with you. I mean, you're a priest. I don't want to offend any of your religious convictions".

"I've told you", he replied quite seriously, "I haven't really got any. And I can't bear people who think they have. How can anyone possibly presume that 'they know'? I mean, how can they? It's just so ignorant, so arrogant. In that sense I'm probably as religious as you are. Just treat me as you would any other bloke".

Sarah longed, truly longed to treat him like any other bloke. Now it was her turn to feel surreal. She was twelve years old again, teetering with apprehension on the high diving board at Wilmslow Baths. It was a long way down, her heart pounded and her pulse raced at the fear and excitement of it all. But she was scared. She turned to go back down the steps but a queue of impatient people were telling her to hurry up, just jump. So she turned, closed her eyes and jumped,

"Does that mean we can meet up again?"

"I do hope so", said Frank, already bobbing up and down in the deep end..

THIRTY-TWO

They did meet up again.

And again and again and again.

On one particular occasion, Charlie, Sarah's rather plummy neighbour had seen Frank get out of the cab and ring her doorbell. He took a couple of paces back from the bay window so he wouldn't be seen. He watched Sarah get in and was still gazing, mouth agape long after the taxi had disappeared down the street.

His wife, Caroline came in to the sitting room, "Darling?" she enquired, "What are you staring at?"

Still staring, he replied quite slowly, "Just seen the damndest thing", he explained, "Chap I was at Oxford with – Frank Dempsey. Have I ever told you about him?"

Caroline shrugged.

"Bloody good man.. Came from a working class Irish family over in North London somewhere, he was a real hoot. Did theology, same as me, didn't give a shit about anything."

"Same as you. Anyway, what about him?"

"Well, I think I've just seen him outside. First time in about twenty years but he's hardly changed at all"

"What was he doing outside?"

"He's a taxi driver. Just picked up that girl next door.. Bloody sad, tragic really. He could have done anything. How the fuck did he end up driving a cab?"

"Probably wasn't him then"

"Oh it was him all right. Just shows you, doesn't it? It's still not what you know but who you know. And when it came to it, poor old Dempsey didn't really know anyone.

Not anyone that could have been any use to him anyway. So even a degree from Oxford wasn't much use to him in the end. That's a real shame. – Frank Dempsey driving a fucking cab".

Charlie Morgan was visibly upset, "It just doesn't seem right", he said bitterly, "Life can be so unfair"

His wife just laughed, "Oh come on, darling, she said breezily, "don't go all left wing on me". She went off to the kitchen and left Charlie still gazing out of the bay window.

Charlie's pity was mis-placed. If you were to dig out the old matriculation photograph of the Christ Church intake of 1977, you'd be hard pushed to find an undergraduate who was now happier, busier and more fulfilled than Frank Dempsey. Frank had very little spare time. His days were consumed by pastoral duties, his evenings by holding court at the parish centre, any free bits in between were usually spent fund-raising at the wheel of his cab.

And now in the form of Sarah Marshall, a beautiful extra dimension had entered his life and he would always try to make time to meet up with her

He had come to terms with the fact that she was the sexiest woman in Christendom but had grudgingly accepted that he would never have first-hand experience of this.

Nonetheless, he started to take a bit more care of his body. Most people have one reason for trying not to let themselves go, for watching what they eat, and going down the gym It's was nothing to do with health or fitness, it's simply because they expect, at some point in the future, to have sexual intercourse with another human being. Now, as a priest, you have made a solemn, non-retractable vow never to have sex again. So what's the point of denying yourself that extra pint of lager, that huge fried breakfast, that nice big helping of jam roly-poly? What's the point of trying to keep yourself in shape? Frank, who had been just about to give in, accept his lot and grow a belly the size of a space hopper, suddenly found himself jogging round the park in the mornings. and replacing prayers with press-ups just before he went to bed.

Sarah's feelings for him were identical but they were able to silently console themselves with the fact that each found the other good company. Really good company and this was incredibly rare, especially between members of the opposite sex from dramatically different backgrounds. They made each other laugh and could communicate almost telepathically with little more than a glance or the raise of an eyebrow. For the first time in years, Frank felt he had a real friend. He knew hundreds of people whom he liked and who liked him but people like Danny Power and Pat Walsh weren't really his friends. They couldn't be, they wouldn't ever allow themselves to be. He was a priest, he was holy, almost messianic so it could never be an equal friendship, there would always be that deferential distance between them. Sarah was different. She had little interest in Father Dempsey the priest principally because it broke her heart to think of his vow of celibacy, its attendant chastity and the fact that he could never be hers. She concentrated instead on Frank Dempsey, the human being. The warm, kind, funny, intelligent and unbearably attractive human being. Because of this, she became the person Frank would talk to in his head, the person who, if he had seen or heard something interesting or amusing that day, he would be dying to tell.

A priest can be like a lonely child who makes up imaginary friends to play with. Except that the priest falls back on God – the ultimate imaginary friend.

Frank and his real live friend had a number of dates – always peculiar. They avoided restaurants and bars because Frank could never really relax for fear of being recognised by one of several thousand ex-parishioners. Furthermore, he was quite old-fashioned and felt awkward about Sarah's gold Amex paying for his nights out. And, although he had access to plenty of money of his own, he felt it would be a misappropriation of parish funds if he spent a big slug of them taking a gorgeous girl out to dinner at The Ivy. Fortunately, it didn't mater where they went, they always had a good time.

One night, they were enjoying a take-away curry in a secluded spot on the Highgate side of Hampstead Heath. Frank had found a foldaway picnic table in the storeroom at the Parish Centre and set it up in the back of the cab, complete with cutlery, candles and bottles of lager. It was here, over two lamb passandas, one pilau rice and two onion bhajis that Sarah asked him the question that no-one had ever asked him before.

"Would you ever give it up – the priesthood, I mean?"

Frank was back on the set of "Who Wants To Be A Millionaire?". This time it was the million pound question.

The four possible answers:

a) No
b) Yes
c) Don't Know
d) Depends.

Once again, a or D, the truth or a lie.

"Can I phone a friend, Chris?"

"Yes, of course. What's your friend's name?"

"God. He's my imaginary friend".

Frank dialled his imaginary friend in his imaginary phone and got the imaginary answering machine.

A or D? A or D? He'd have to make up his own mind.

He went for A.

"No, I could never give it up. Not now. I've finally got my own parish and it's even better than I thought it would be. All right, so I'm not exactly religious but they don't know that. I pay lip service to the Nicene Creed. It doesn't make me any worse at my job. If anything, it makes me better. I'm not doing it for God, I'm doing it for me and I'm doing it for the parishioners. I can't think of a job in the world that I'd rather do. Anyway, I'm knocking forty, this is all I've ever done. What other career could I have now?"

Frank was surprised to see Sarah's mouth fall slightly agape with shock and disappointment. There was real sorrow in her eyes and her features seemed momentarily to sag. She was absolutely crestfallen. So too were the imaginary studio audience. Frank had been the first contestant ever to be asked the million pound question.

And he'd got it wrong.

THIRTY-THREE

It was just after midnight when Pat Walsh got home and, pointing his plipper at the remote-controlled garage door, he noticed that his bedroom light was still on. He slid the silver BMW 318i into its nocturnal resting place and went upstairs via the interconnecting door to the kitchen.

Ann was propped up in bed reading the latest Danielle Steel. She wasn't happy.

"You're very late", she pouted .

"Had a couple drinks with Frank and Eddie after closing", he explained, "'twas a grand night".

"Oh, 'Frank' now, is it?" she sneered.

With a weary sigh, Pat decided not to rise to the bait. He began to remove his navy polo shirt and beige chinos. He'd bought these himself. He was now seldom seen in the "outfits" his wife had always selected for him. Since becoming St. Thomas's star barman, Pat was his own man. Next stop would probably be ripped jeans and biker's boots.

"You just don't like him, do you?"

"I don't dislike him", said Anne, " I just don't trust him. You mark my words, he is not what he seems. He reminds me of one of those crooked American evangelists – anything for money".

Pat was tired of this insinuation, "How many times have I got to tell you? All the cash he makes goes through me, there's not a penny I couldn't account for. The fella isn't interested in money. He gives it all away and I can tell you when, where, how much and to whom.".

"Yeah, well" was the best she could muster in response

before continuing sourly, "Anyway, it's his whole attitude. It's all a big ego trip for him."

Pat remembered how his wife had said exactly the same thing about Bob Geldof during Live Aid. Never mind about his phenomenal achievement, the millions raised, the lives saved, Geldof was nothing more than a show-off.

All I know is that Frank Dempsey is the best parish priest we've ever had", he said "He's just not pious enough for you. That's what all this is about".

"You're wrong, Pat" she scowled and he was indeed wrong. The real reason Anne Walsh did not warm to her parish priest was plain, simple jealousy.

Since meeting Frank and performing behind the bar at the Parish centre, Pat had wriggled out from under her thumb. He was happier, more confident and a lot more relaxed, just like the bus conductor she had fallen in love with. However, like so many people do; once married, she then set about changing the very things that had attracted her in the first place. Since stepping behind the bar at St. Thomas's, Pat had re-discovered his old self, a quick and witty personality which had been submerged, all but forgotten, for the best part of thirty years. Pat's personality no longer belonged to his domineering wife and she just couldn't bear it. She'd do anything to stop him turning up for his shift.

"You do all the books for that parish centre", she'd moan, "Don't you think that's enough?"

The old Pat in his colour co-ordinated casuals would probably have given in, but the new one answered back,

"And since when", he'd retort "was there a limit to how much a person can do for charity? We've done well out of life. Isn't it nice to be able to give something back?"

"You've only done well because I pushed you", she'd remind him spitefully. "If it hadn't been for me, you'd be no more than an unemployed bus conductor".

"You're quite right", he'd acknowledge calmly, "so

shouldn't you be especially pleased. Anyway, I'm going to be late. See you later. Pop down if you want".

She never did. Prevented, as always, by some non-existent illness

Later on, Pat would change into his flannelette pyjamas and say goodnight to his wife's turned back. He closed his eyes and consoled himself with the thought that although, he was still lonely and unfulfilled within his marriage, at least he was no longer lonely and unfulfilled outside of it.

THIRTY-FOUR

Saying goodbye was always the most awkward moment. Frank and Sarah would have the most fantastic night out together but when it came to valediction, neither of them knew quite what to do. They couldn't shake hands and neither would allow themselves or each other so much as a peck on the cheek. Frank knew that if his lips ever touched any part of Sarah's anatomy, well.... that was just it, he didn't know what would happen, how he would feel, what cataclysmic effect it might have on him. And he was terrified of finding out.

Sarah, of course, felt exactly the same way. She couldn't even allow herself to give Frank a "Fulham Kiss" which would have involved placing her cheek on his and kissing the air whilst exclaiming "Mwa" then repeating the process with the other cheek – "Mwa, mwa". It was practised every day by at least half the female population of Fulham, but Sarah felt it was somehow inappropriate, almost indecent to do it to Frank. She too was terrified yet at the same time, gut wrenchingly curious to think where it might lead.

Fortunately, Frank always dropped her at the door and they simply played out a taxi driver/passenger relationship.

"Goodnight"

"Yeah, goodnight and thanks".

Neither ever promised to phone the other one because, in truth, neither really intended to. Whenever people indulge in any form of illicit pleasure – whether it's a skinful of booze, a noseful of coke, or a double portion of chocolate fudge cake , they tend not to make immediate plans to do it again. Quite the reverse. They usually vow that will never happen again even though they know damned well that it will.

And so it was with Frank and Sarah. Within a couple of days, one would have called the other with some spurious reason to meet up and the other would always accept the invitation.

The nights had drawn in and Christmas wasn't far away. December was a busy time for both of them. Sarah had various client parties to attend and Frank had the biggest feast in the Catholic calendar speeding towards him like a runaway train. His father had always insisted that Easter was a far bigger deal than Christmas. "Anyone can be born", he'd say, " but how many people do you know who've risen from the dead?"

"None", Frank was often tempted to reply, "Not even Jesus".

As far as world was concerned, Christmas was the big one. Frank, like a secret Santa was busy, through Pat Walsh, distributing all the spare cash in the coffers so he could start again in January with a completely clean slate. Their joint signatures were on cheques received by charities all over the world.

It was because of this seasonal workload that Frank and Sarah broke their usual spontaneous, casual arrangement and booked each other a fortnight in advance for their very own Christmas party. They were to meet at 8.30 in the lobby of the London Hilton on Park Lane. Frank had been out in the taxi for most of the day. For him, like any other taxi driver, bogus or otherwise, this again was the busiest time of the year. With passengers overflowing with the compliments of the season, he simply couldn't afford not to be out there.

At 8.20, he parked the cab round the back of the Hilton and strode into the lobby, carrying a small holdall. He made his way to the Gents and underwent a quick Clark Kent style transformation. He was already wearing a black two piece suit with his dog-collar. The latter was removed and replaced with a crisp white shirt and an old Scott Crolla tie which, incredibly, he'd picked up at the last Parish jumble sale. As he straightened it in the mirror, he suffered a momentary crisis of identity. Who was he? What was he? In the space of a minute he'd been a priest posing as a cab driver now posing an ordinary civilian. Tomorrow he'd be a priest again and probably a cab driver too whilst all the time remaining an ordinary civilian and a priest at the same time.. Never mind. He returned to the lobby, feeling sinful and excited just in time to see Sarah arriving through the revolving doors.

"Cheryl?" he beamed solicitously

"Oh, Mr.Reynolds", she giggled in an Essex. Accent.

"Shall we?"

He took her arm and escorted her to the twenty-eighth floor to a bar called Windows to The World for a spot of role-playing. Despite its fabulous location and majestic views over Hyde Park and across most of London, this was the sort of place where lecherous personnel managers took tarty, impressionable typists, Frank and Sarah had dressed for the occasion. Frank found it incredibly liberating. His dog-collar had always hung round his neck like a millstone, almost pulling his facial expression down until it was one of pious solemnity. Without it, he felt free to laugh, to muck about, to place his hand jokingly on his companion's knee

"You look after me, Cheryl", he leered, "And I'll look after you".

"Oh, Mr.Reynolds", she cackled , "You are a one".

"Cheryl's" skirt was a little too short, her heels a little too high, her make-up a little too generously applied. . Her black bra was also a little too visible under her white cotton shirt.

"Mr.Reynolds" was transfixed,

"Show me a man", thought Frank, "who doesn't find a tarty girl attractive (assuming she's moderately attractive in the first place) and I'll show you a liar".

"Oh, look", he said, "Bet you wish you were going there tonight". He gestured over to a line of guests filing into the function suite next door. It was the sort of party both would have considered frightfully smart when they were children. The "gentlemen" were in dark suits with satin lapels, frilly shirts and velvet bow-ties, the "ladies" resplendent in long evening dresses. Now, as adults, they could see that most of the ill-fitting tuxedos were hired and the evening dresses were from Littlewoods catalogue.

"Accountants", said Sarah with some certainty, expecting to see JJ, the oh so wacky one with whom her friend Helen had tried to fix her up. He would no doubt be the joker in the pack, with a multi-coloured waistcoat and one of those hilarious bow ties with the flashing lights.

She was right. It was an accountants' party and one of the guests had just left the function suite to answer a call of nature.

After a couple of wildly over-priced drinks (lager for Mr. Reynolds, Malibu and pineapple for Cheryl) Frank and Sarah descended the twenty-eight floors back out on to Park Lane.

The temperature had dropped and there was a very light dusting of snow on the roof of the taxi. If the cab hadn't been black you probably wouldn't have noticed it but it leant a very Christmassy feel to the air. Frank slotted in the Christmas tape that he played almost non-stop from the first to the twenty-fourth of December before putting it back in its box for a year. It opened with Sinatra doing Jingle Bells followed by Dean Martin's "Winter Wonderland" and The Pogues' "Fairytale of New York", the three greatest Christmas records ever made.

For Frank, Christmas simply wasn't commercial enough. Yes, of course, as a priest, he always had to concentrate and expand upon its religious element. The congregation were always reminded of why they were there – the deep religious significance of it all but that was about as far as he wanted to go. We live in an increasingly secular society. Christmas was more about giving and receiving gifts, eating, drinking and having a good time. The part on which Frank always placed great emphasis was the fact that it was the "season of goodwill to all". Goodwill to other people was his raison d'etre, and had always been the whole purpose of his vocation. At Christmas, more than at any other time, he could witness his ideas in action. And if the birth of Our Lord Jesus Christ tended to get a bit lost in the midst of all this, well, so what?

To the sound of "Sleigh Ride", he and Sarah were swirling around London taking in the city in all its seasonal splendour. The lights, the decorations, the displays adorning the windows of Harrods and Selfridges, the drunken revellers, paper hats askance on the sides of their heads, ties undone, trying in vain to hail the bogus taxi.

However, the light was out and the driver was off duty. Very off duty. Off duty from both his occupations. He'd never felt so off duty in his life.

"Can I have a go?" said Sarah suddenly, "I've always wanted to drive a taxi"

"Well", said Frank, "Er....."

"Oh go on", she pleaded, "Christmas treat. I'm not over the limit. I don't think those Pina Coladas had any vodka in them at all".

Frank, a little reluctant at first, pulled over, got out and climbed into the back. Sarah's first manoeuvre was a spectacularly tight U-turn.

"Wh-hey!" she whooped, " I've always wanted to do that" and the cab sped off towards Regents Park

"Where are you taking me?" asked the passenger, still not sure whether this was a good idea,

"Don't worry, guv", replied the driver, "Scenic route".

Sarah pulled up at the bottom of Primrose Hill and together they strolled to the top.

"This is one of my favourite views", she said wistfully as they looked down upon the lights of London, gleaming and twinkling beneath them. The wind blew and without even thinking, Sarah snuggled up to Frank and without thinking either, he wrapped his arms around her. One second later, he realised what he was doing. He tried to justify it by remembering that this is what people in Siberia did to survive. They snuggled up to keep each other warm. But this wasn't the frozen wastes of the tundra, this was a reasonably mild night in London, NW1, what the hell did he think he was doing?

Surely God would appear now. What did he have to do before the Almighty would make his presence felt?

" Oh God", he silently cried out, "She's drawing her face away from my shoulder, those brown eyes were gazing right into mine. Those delicious full lips are slightly parted – half playful, half deadly serious. She is almost involuntarily tilting her head slightly to the right and, almost involuntarily, so am I".

Oh God! Oh God! Where are you? Aren't you supposed to stop me? Having I asked you thousands of times to "lead me not into temptation" Oh God!!" Is this some sort of test? Are you listening? Can you hear me up there? Can you????

Silence.

Then, with the sound of Glen Campbell crooning "Have Yourself A Merry Little Christmas" still ringing in their ears, it happened. They kissed. Gently and tentatively at first and then both thinking that you may as well be hung for a sheep as a lamb, more passionately. A lot more passionately. Oh Christ, they really meant it. It was though an unseen hand were holding a giant sprig of mistletoe high above Primrose Hill. It seemed the most natural thing in the world, a truly life-affirming moment and Father Francis Dempsey, to his simultaneous delight and horror, couldn't bring himself to experience even the faintest feeling of guilt.

THIRTY-FIVE

The devout Catholic indulges in a very thorough preparation for Christmas. This involves a lot more than wrapping presents, decorating the tree and stuffing the turkey, There is supposed to be some spiritual preparation too which normally entails a trip to confession to get rid of all those niggly little sins that have been staining the soul so it's pure white for Christmas.

For some, it is the only time they go and for Frank, listening to their insincere and perfunctory contrition, it was as dreary as hell. If only they'd do what he was always tempted to when he was on the other side of the grille. He would always want to invent a whole list of outrageous sins that he hadn't really committed. Murdering three people, masterminding a gold bullion heist, having a torrid affair with a novice nun, finishing, of course with "..........and I told lies"

But no. Same old stuff., week after week, year after year. There were three confessional boxes each with the name of the priest printed on a little wooden plaque above the door. "Fr M. Lynam" "Fr F. Dempsey" and "Fr. W Conlon". Frank would dispatch his customers with such alacrity that you could be forgiven for thinking that the door marked "Fr. F. Dempsey" was, like a supermarket checkout, for people with "five sins or less".

Having dished out the twelfth mandatory penance of two Our Father's, four Hail Mary's and a donation to the CAFOD box, Frank was considering a far knottier problem. How could he eat his four-fingered Kit Kat during the next confession without the confessor hearing him unwrap it or break it or realise that he had his mouth full?

He heard the door swing open, then shut and felt the familiar sound-proofed silence close in around him. It would be hard to imagine a worse place to try and scoff a secret Kit-Kat. He heard the usual creak of the little wooden platform being knelt upon but it was the next sound that made him drop his Kit Kat and nearly fall off his chair.

"Bless me, Father for I have sinned". He recognised the voice, he recognised the words, but each was utterly out of context. What could he say? He was a priest, a professional, and this was a very important part of his work.

"How long is it since your last confession?"

"I've never made one before"

" I see. So what's troubling you? For what are you asking God's forgiveness?"

"Well, last night, I did something I really shouldn't have done".

" Okay. Do you want to tell me what it was?"

"I gave into temptation", she explained slowly, "Temptation of the flesh".

" I see. And why was this wrong? Are you married?"

"No?"

"In a relationship? Have you deceived a loved one?"

"No".

"Right. And the man, I'm assuming it's a man, with whom you gave in to temptation, is he married?"

"No"

"In a relationship? Was he deceiving a loved one?"

"No"

"Well, as you know, sex outside of marriage is forbidden by the church. Is....that.....what you did?"

"No".

"So what did you do that was so wrong?"

"Well", she struggled to explain, "I've become emotionally and now sort of physically involved with a man whose line of work forbids him to marry, forbids him any sort of intimacy with women"

"Does it forbid him to be friends with women?"

"No but I feel we've gone way beyond that. Well, I know I have anyway. I don't think I could ever be just friends with him again".

"So what would you like him to do?"

She paused, caught her breath and in the soundproofed booth, Frank could hear the beating of her heart. And, for that matter, his own The silence was finally broken by her slow and faltering explanation.

"What I'd like him to do and what I know he ought to do are two different things", she said, "And that's why I'm asking forgiveness. He's a wonderful man, I've never met anyone like him and I know I never will again. He does so much for other people and by my actions last night, I hope I haven't.....um....impeded his ability to carry on doing that. I should have shown more restraint".

It was Frank's turn to struggle for words, "There's an old saying" he began, "Not really a biblical one but very appropriate nonetheless: And that saying is "It takes two to tango". Now, this man was clearly not an unwilling participant, he knew exactly what he was doing. He's always known that he could never marry, never become intimate with you and yet he wantonly allowed your friendship to develop in this way. Perhaps he should also have shown more restraint. It strikes me that he is equally to blame.

He paused

" If, indeed, blame is even the right word in this context".

A lump was forming in his throat and he was glad he was hidden behind a grille or she would have seen the tears in his eyes.

"I'm sure God will forgive you for this". He paused again. "I just hope he'll forgive your friend".

"Thank you, Father", she said, getting up, "Goodbye".

Those waiting outside Father Dempsey's normally quick box had become very curious. In the time she'd been in there, Father Lynam and Father Conlon had absolved the sins of three parishioners each. That girl must have had a litany of serious sins to confess.

At that moment, Frank wanted to abandon the box, abandon his vows, abandon the last twenty years of his life and go racing after her but, completely numbed, he remained dazed and rooted to his chair, his Kit- Kat still lying on the floor. The door opened and closed, the kneeling platform creaked again.

"Bless me Father for I have sinned" . It was an old Irishman., George Breen by the sounds of it. George could have confessed to fourteen counts of rape, murder and robbery with violence and Frank would still have given him two Our Fathers and four Hail Marys.

He simply wasn't listening anymore.

THIRTY-SIX

Dear Cardinal Hayes,

This is a very hard letter to write but after a lot of soul-searching, I felt it had to be written.

Last week, I accompanied my husband to the Society of Certified Accountants' annual Christmas function at the Hilton Hotel in London. In the cocktail bar, I was astonished to see our parish priest, Father Dempsey, wearing a suit and tie, drinking and canoodling with a young lady. I watched them for some time. It was definitely him. I saw him put his hand on her knee which suggested to me that their friendship was far more intimate than would be right and proper for a priest. I then saw them leave together arm in arm.

I am a great admirer of Father Dempsey and of the work he has done at St. Thomas's in Wealdstone but I feel that this sort of behaviour is an insult to the Catholic Church and to all the people who he is supposed to set an example to.

I trust you will treat this letter in the strictest confidence but I just felt you ought to know.

God bless,

Yours sincerely,

Anne Walsh (Mrs.)

THIRTY-SEVEN

The passenger got out in Vincent Square, poking a ten pound note into Frank's donation box.

"Thank you, Father" he smiled, "and Merry Christmas".

The mobile rang. Oh please be Sarah, please, please be Sarah.

"Frank?" said a familiar deep, cultured Irish voice, "It's Tom Hayes"

"Oh God", thought Frank, "What does he want?"

"Cardinal", said Frank, apprehensively, "What a pleasant surprise. What can I do for you?"

"Frank, I was wondering if you could drop by next time you're passing"

Uh-oh.

"Are you in that taxi of yours?"

"Yeah, just round the corner, as it happens, I could call in now".

"Ah, that'd be grand. Just a little matter I need to discuss with you. About five minutes then?"

"Yeah, fine, said Frank, pointing the cab towards Westminster Cathedral, "Five minutes".

The Cardinal's tone was very relaxed and friendly but Frank had a hunch that something was up. A guilty conscience needs no accuser.

Cardinal Hayes took one more look at the letter. He'd been in two minds. He wasn't even going to mention it to Frank. After all. it was hardly the most serious of sins. Not really on a par with the sort of bacchanalian orgies indulged in over the years by generations of popes. He was just going to write back to this Mrs. Walsh, thanking her for bringing the matter to his attention. He would promise to speak to Father Dempsey about his conduct and try to ensure that this sort of thing didn't happen again.

To have a priest in the diocese like Frank Dempsey was a very rare privilege. Frank had it all – charm, charisma, a razor-sharp intellect and a selfless devotion to his flock.. He had done so much to enrich the lives of virtually everyone he came into contact with. Although the priesthood is not a career which officially offers any sort of fast-track, there will always be the gifted ones, those marked out for the mitre and Frank was probably the most obvious candidate of them all.

Also, vocations were down. Fewer and fewer young men were proving willing to take Holy Orders. Now was not the time to upset an exceptionally gifted young man who had, just because of a minor indiscretion.

However, that would be the coward's way out. Cardinal Hayes had never lacked courage and felt a moral obligation to Mrs. Walsh to at least investigate her allegation. He also felt a duty to Frank to find out if this little incident was indicative of a struggle he may be having with his vows.

Frank was shown in and the Cardinal greeted him with a warm smile and a firm handshake.

"Ah, Frank, thanks for coming. Now this is a little embarrassing but...well...I'm not going to beat about the bush"

Oh shit. He knows. He bloody knows.

This was confirmed as the Cardinal continued, "You were apparently seen out with a young lady last week at a hotel on Park Lane. Is this true?

Frank surprised himself with his reaction.

"Yes". The word was delivered without a trace of embarrassment, without a trace of remorse, without even a trace of defiance. Just a simple confirmation of fact.

After a pause, the Cardinal spoke again, "Do you want to tell me about it?"

"No", said Frank, "but we both know that I'm going to have to".

The Cardinal nodded and let a sad, silent chuckle exhale through his nostrils.

"Her name is Sarah Marshall, I first met her a few months ago when she was a passenger in my cab. She then booked me to take her to Heathrow one morning and we just got chatting. We get on really well and she's just a friend".

"So that's all she is? A friend?"

Frank suddenly found himself unable to answer this question. The Cardinal noted this and continued,

"Frank, I've been a priest now for forty six years. In that time, I've known quite a few priests strike up, shall we say, inappropriate relationships with women. But as I recall, they were all terribly discreet about it, going to the most ridiculous lengths to conceal these 'friendships'. You, on the other hand, were apparently laughing and drinking in a crowded bar in a big hotel in the West End, blithely unconcerned about the fact that somebody might see you and somebody clearly did".

Frank had his excuse ready and waiting but the Cardinal beat him to it.

"Now to me that suggests one of two things: Either that this is no more than an innocent friendship and you therefore have no reason to hide. Or, that you didn't really care who saw you. Subconsciously, you may have even wanted to be seen".

Frank thought for a moment before speaking.

"There is nothing in my vows that forbids me from enjoying close friendships with members of the opposite sex. If anything, my friendship with Sarah has given me another dimension, made me more able to cope with my work. Men living lonely, celibate lives can lose touch. The whole concept is absurd. I'm expected to give marriage guidance and advice on bringing up children when I have no practical experience of either. The days are long gone, particularly in London, where a man can expect automatic respect and obedience just because he is a priest. He has to offer a lot more than that".

He went quiet and the Cardinal, aware that he may be about to hear the Christmas Confession to end all Christmas Confessions, waited for him to continue. Frank began to unburden himself.

"It's all a load of bollocks anyway", he said.

"What is?" asked the Cardinal gently

"Oh, you know as well as I do, all the stuff we're supposed to believe in. Transubstantiation, papal infallibility, the Old Testament, the Gospels, these things are simply not true. It's no different from pagans worshipping trees. By professing to believe in it all, I'm just living a lie.

"How long have you felt like this?"

"Since I was about ten or eleven"

"And yet you chose to become a priest? Why?"

"Because I enjoy it. I cannot think of a more rewarding way to spend my life. I get real satisfaction out of helping other people and from being the catalyst for people to help one another. And last Friday night, I felt like doing something for myself. This diffuses any resentment that might build up inside of me. Makes me much more able to cope".

"Frank, you are an exceptional priest. You don't need me to tell you that but you went into the priesthood with your eyes wide open. Much wider, as I recall, than most of your fellow trainees. Aren't you now being a little naïve? You knew the rules before you started".

"Perhaps some of those rules need to be relaxed"

"Well, that's a whole separate issue. At the moment celibacy is compulsory and to be honest, I can't see that changing. A wife and family deserve and demand so much of a man's life, so much of his time, leaving far less for him to give to his parishioners, the ones who depend on him for spiritual guidance. They are his family. Your parishioners are yours.".

Frank shook his head wearily, "I know all that but the fact remains that we are becoming out of touch. It's nearly twenty years since I first enrolled at Allen Hall and in that time there's been a hell of a lot of social change. As I say, I'm expected to give marriage guidance, advice on bringing up kids when I don't know the first thing about it. Who the hell am I to tell these people what to do?. It's a joke. They're not going to take any notice of me. Why should they? What do I know about real life?"

"I understand that, Frank. but you haven't really answered my question. Why so public? The London Hilton, for heaven's sake".

"I just wanted to feel part of the human race. The way we live isn't natural. Why do you think so many priests turn to drink and suffer from depression in later life? Because they still crave love and companionship when life has passed them by. It's all right for you. You're Cardinal Hayes, you're famous, important and powerful. Your life is very rich and fulfilling but for other priests of your age, it's a very different story".

"Is that what you're frightened of, Frank? Growing old and lonely?"

"Not really. If, as you say, I'm an exceptional priest, I'll probably end up as a bishop. And that just goes to show what a load of old cobblers it is because, I don't actually believe any of the teachings I espouse. And has it made me any worse as a human being, any less effective as a priest?"

"No, Frank, it hasn't", sighed the Cardinal sadly, "but by your own admission,, you're living a lie and the priesthood isn't like other jobs. You can't just chuck it in because you don't like it anymore. Once you're ordained, you are a priest until the day you die. Now, I want you to go away and think about your vocation. Refresh yourself, re-charge your batteries. You've been working incredibly hard. There are a number of sabbatical programmes, there's a particularly good one in Massachusetts. I'd be more than happy to send you".

So one last time, just in case, Frank called out to God. "God, they want me to think about my vocation, They want to send to the States on some sabbatical programme. What should I do? What the hell should I do?"

Silence.

More silence.

And to Frank, that silence spoke volumes.

THIRTY-EIGHT

The news spread like wildfire. Grossly exaggerated wildfire. Father Dempsey had been caught in a hotel room with a young girl. He'd been sacked and had fled to America.

Some parishioners, huge fans of their parish priest only a few days before, were suddenly hedging their bets. Father Dempsey had sinned, he had done wrong, he had offended Our Lord. By sympathising or siding with him, they too would be offending Our Lord and putting their places in Heaven at risk. Best to disown him, best to denounce him. Never liked him anyway. Never trusted him. Wasn't like a priest, was he? Too worldly, too flash. Good riddance to him.

The vast majority, however, felt a deep sense of sadness, a deep sense of loss. They tried to be sanguine, reasoning that it was only a matter of time before a handsome man of the world like Father Dempsey, grew bored of the constraints placed upon him by the priesthood . They were content to count their blessings and give thanks for the fact that they'd had him as a parish priest at all.

It was a Wednesday night and, although business at the Parish Centre was fairly brisk, the atmosphere was sombre and subdued. almost like the aftermath of a terrible tragedy. There were posters on the wall advertising the Any Excuse Club's next big charity bash. Saturday 22nd December, obviously a Christmas dance but billed instead as a celebration of the feast of St. Frithelbert, the 8th Century bishop of Hexham. It was already a sell out but without Father Dempsey, nobody really felt like turning up.

Big Eddie and Pat Walsh were behind the bar. Pat was without his usual cheer and sparkle, just pouring the pints, taking the money and giving the change with nothing more than a polite, perfunctory smile. Big Eddie knew exactly what had happened. Frank had phoned his uncle just before disappearing to "think about things". He was recounting the tale to Danny Power and a few other shell-shocked regulars who had gathered at the bar.

"Apparently, he was seen having a drink with a girl up the West End", he explained, "I mean, there are hundreds of quiet little pubs he could have gone to but the fucking Park Lane Hilton? Jesus".

Pat Walsh, just along the bar from Eddie, drying a pint glass, almost dropped it in horror.

"What was that, Eddie? Where was he?"

"The Hilton in Park Lane. I mean.......Pat? Pat?"

Pat didn't hear him. He had already flung down his bar towel and was striding purposefully towards the door.

Ten minutes later, he put his key in the front door. Anne wondered what was up. It wasn't even half past eight. Why was he back so early? She didn't hear him replace his shoes with his slippers at the front door.

"Shoes" she called out from in front of the mock Queen Anne cabinet which housed the new TV.

"Never mind fucking shoes", growled her husband, stomping over the carpet in his new Timberland boots. He was puce with rage, "It was you, wasn't it?"

"What was me?"

"It was you who ratted on Father Dempsey. It was you who ruined that man's life, you vindictive little bitch".

This was the moment Pat had been waiting almost thirty years for. The opportunity to hit back. He had always felt very grateful to his wife for transforming him from a struggling bus conductor, to a fairly wealthy and successful accountant. He was by nature a cheery, easy-going man who had endured her moods, her ailments, her piety, her frigidity for the sake of his marriage. But lately, he had become less cowed, more assertive and thirty years of anger and resentment were boiling over right now. Anne had expected him to find out sooner or later but Pat had always been so nice, weak and timorous that the consequences hadn't really bothered her. She hadn't expected him to react in this way and she was, for the very first time, almost frightened of him.

"How could you do it?" he spat.

"I was going to tell you, Pat........"

"But you knew what I'd fucking say so you did it behind my back. You did it behind everybody's back and it's not just his life you've ruined. That man helped thousands of people and would have gone on to help thousands more but now you've taken all that away. You've ruined my life too. Running that parish centre, doing the books, distributing the money to charity gave me so much pleasure, gave me a real interest outside of this fucking house. I never set out to be an accountant but I went along with it so that I could provide for you and the girls. Now, for the first time, I was really glad to be one, really proud of what I was able to do. Instead of going to mass and just going through the motions, I was doing something really worthwhile. I can't tell you how happy that made me. But you just couldn't stand it, could you? Me giving anything to anyone but you. All you care about is your so-called holiness and keeping this house clean and tidy like a fucking laboratory".

He swung his arm round with chilling ferocity and violently swept a shelf full of tasteless ornaments to the floor. With the cry of a banshee, he then leapt on to the sofa with his boots on and ripped the big swirly, swagged curtains from their pelmet. Anne could take no more and threw herself at him, yanking his hair with one hand and clawing his face with the other. With a strength he never knew he possessed, Pat pulled her off then fastened his little fat hands around her throat and began to squeeze. He would have carried on squeezing until she turned limp and lifeless in his grasp had he not been interrupted by the sudden sound of Vivaldi chiming out from the doorbell..

THIRTY-NINE

Saturday evening mass was introduced in the mid-seventies when the Catholic Church, first started to get really concerned about falling attendances. It was decided that if people came along on Saturday night, then their Sunday obligations would be fulfilled. It was never that popular at St. Thomas's because, on a Saturday night, most people had better things to do. However, since Frank's arrival, its popularity had soared because the congregation could then pile straight into the Parish centre and drink until they passed out, secure in the knowledge that they wouldn't have to get up for Mass the following morning.

This particular Saturday evening mass would boast the biggest attendance ever seen at St. Thomas's. Frank had apparently been in touch with Father Lynam and would be making an appearance at the 6.30 mass to explain himself. People began taking their seats over an hour early like pilgrims at Lourdes, desperate to catch a glimpse of the Virgin Mary. By 6.15, you couldn't get in the door. There seemed to be quite a lot of faces that the regulars didn't recognise. Who were they? What were they doing here?

The church looked fabulous. Frank had made it one of his first tasks to have the place restored to its original Victorian splendour and tonight, none of the lights were turned on. The whole place, the arches, the statues, the translucent stained glass, everything was illuminated by the light of two hundred candles

At 6.30, the bell was rung and several hundred people got to their feet. The familiar looking priest followed his two acolytes out on to the altar and several hundred faces registered visible disappointment that the familiar looking priest was Patrick Lynam not Francis Dempsey. Father Lynam began the mass as normal, not acknowledging the enormous number of people crammed into the pews, down the aisles, into the porch and out on to the street. He gave a reading from the gospel according to Luke.

"This is the word of the Lord", he concluded.

"Praise to you Lord Jesus Christ", they responded.

Time for the sermon. For once there was complete silence, every ear in the church was tuned in.

"This evening", he began, "I want to devote the sermon to a quite remarkable man. Not Jesus Christ whose birth we will be celebrating next week, not even St. Frithelbert whose feast we are celebrating today. No, I want to talk about the reason we are celebrating the feast of St. Frithelbert, the reason we even know that there is a St. Frithelbert. I want to talk about Father Frank Dempsey.

When he came here at the beginning of the year, I handed him the helm of a happy and harmonious parish but a parish, I will be the first to admit, that had 'room for improvement'. His commitment, his imagination, his drive and his energy brought about improvements beyond our wildest dreams. He was behind the fabulous restoration of this church and the dramatic transformation of our old church hall into the magnificent parish centre it is now. This place is now the hub of our community and has been the venue for so many memorable evenings which have generated thousand s of pounds for charitable causes all over the world".

He paused for effect. He had seen this rhetorical trick work often enough for Frank. Now it was working for him.

"Now in the last few days you may have heard a number of stories about what he did and what has subsequently happened to him. Let me tell you what actually happened. Over the last few months, Father Dempsey became friendly with a girl called Sarah Marshall. No vows were broken. There is nothing that forbids a priest from having friendships with women. They were enjoying a drink together at a bar in the West End of London when they were spotted and Father Dempsey was reported to Cardinal Hayes.

Now you may believe that this is not the sort of conduct we should expect of our Parish priest. You may believe that perhaps this friendship had become a little too close. You may, indeed, be right but I would ask you not to judge Father Dempsey too harshly. Technically no sin was committed. But even if you do not approve of what he did, please try to balance it up against the extraordinary amount of good work he has done, the wonderful way he has helped and cared for others

I have, of course, spoken at length to Father Dempsey about what happened and he explained that recently he has been having great difficulty with his vow of celibacy. Now, a lot of people under a mis-apprehension about the word 'celibacy'. Celibacy isn't simply the abstention from with sexual intercourse. To be celibate originally meant just being unmarried. Father Dempsey had a problem with this part of his vow. He had a problem with not being married. He often preached about the sanctity of marriage and I know many of you here have enjoyed the benefit of his counselling and have felt your marriages go from strength to strength because of it so I suppose it's understandable for a man to want to practise what he's preached.

Another pause. Much longer this time. Truly dramatic effect. And just before the sharper members of the congregation realised what was about to happen, Father Lynam made the announcement,

"Dearly beloved, we are gathered here today to witness Francis John Dempsey finally break his vow of celibacy……"

FORTY

Frank had left the Cardinal's office not quite knowing how he felt. He knew how he was supposed to feel. Wretched, ashamed, depressed, his life's work brought to a sudden and ignominious halt. This was surely how he was going to feel any minute. He was just dazed, shocked, numbed. It was delayed reaction. Any moment now, the pain and shame would kick in and he would sob and howl like a wounded animal.

He waited. He waited a bit longer but he simply didn't feel that way. He even put on his Misery Tape to try to get the tear ducts going. Gilbert O' Sullivan's "Alone Again Naturally", Kevin Johnson's "Rock'n'Roll, I Gave You All The Best Years Of My Life" Brian Protheroe's "Pinball". Nothing. No effect at all..

He started to feel guilty about not feeling guilty.

So surely God would turn up now. Either to castigate him, remind him that those vows were unbreakable and threaten him with eternal damnation. It would be quite nice if he turned up to say thank you, pat him on the back, wish him all the best, present him with a metaphysical carriage clock. But no. The former Father Dempsey was waiting in vain.

Even before his conversation with Cardinal Hayes, Frank knew that he loved Sarah far more than he could ever love his job. It was no contest. The Cardinal had been right. Frank had subconsciously wanted to be caught and when he was, it was a blessed relief. He could easily have squirmed and apologised his way out but had chosen not to.

But what if she didn't feel the same way? What if it had

been a bit of a giggle for her but no more than that. After all, they'd had nothing more than the equivalent of a quick snog at the office party. People don't generally alter their whole lives on the strength of that. And could he bear to put that sort of pressure on her? It may be flattering to tell a woman that you're giving up a lifetime's vocation because of her but unless she adores you and cannot contemplate living her life without you, this may not be what she wants to hear.

Oh God.

No point asking him for guidance, thought Frank. Even if he does exist, he's probably got the right hump with me now.

Frank carried on thinking about his dilemma. Was it such a dilemma? He could either have the woman he loved or the job he loved. Either way, he was going to be happy. Wasn't he? Trouble was, he loved one much more than the other. He looked at his watch and realised that he'd been sitting there on the south side of Westminster Bridge for nearly two hours. This was the longest he'd ever thought about anything. His gaze fell upon St. Thomas's Hospital. He still hated hospitals. They made him uncomfortably aware of his own mortality. At this very moment, he thought, somebody will be dying in there. Somebody's life will be ending. He couldn't let his own life end without finding out the one thing he really needed to know. He started the engine, swung the cab round towards Vauxhall Bridge and headed for Fulham.

Within twenty minutes, he was outside Sarah's flat. He took a deep breath, closed his eyes and rang the buzzer. An unfamiliar voice, Nessie's, replied,

"Hello?"

Oh no, she's moved, she's gone, she's emigrated. I'll never see her again.

"Er...hello? Is Sarah there please"

"Who is it?"

Frank paused, not knowing quite what to say

"Just tell her her taxi's here".

The buzzer sounded and, for the first time ever, Frank went inside.

Nessie welcomed him in, "Hi, I'm Nessie"

"Frank", he smiled and the two shook hands with an awkward sense of over politeness.

"Sarah" Nessie called out, "Someone to see you"

Sarah emerged from the kitchen, not quite prepared for her visitor – hair tied back in a pony-tail, old sweatshirt, tracksuit bottoms, bare feet. It was the most beautiful sight Frank had ever seen in his life. Sarah let out a stifled sob and the two fell once more into a passionate embrace.

Nessie tiptoed backwards.

"Er...." she said awkwardly, "I'll think I'll just go and...er.....make a cup of coffee"

She paused

"At Robert's house"

Neither Frank nor Sarah noticed her leave. They simply held each other. Without coming apart they eventually fell on to the sofa and held each other some more, neither saying a word.

They didn't make love. Or perhaps they did. It depends how you define "making love". If you go for the standard definition – having sex – then they didn't. If you go for the Doris Day definition, then they did. In her 1964 hit "Move Over Darling", Doris repeatedly implores her beau to "make love to me". Bearing in mind, Ms. Day's squeaky-clean image, it is highly unlikely that this would have meant "shag me till I'm sick". It would have meant no more than a kiss and a cuddle. So when Frank and Sarah had finished "making love", they had to talk. Heart to heart, soul to soul, cards on the table.. Sarah was intuitive enough to know that this would be particularly hard for a man who had never been completely honest with anyone. Least of all himself.

"Yes?" she began, "Can I help you?"

"Help me do what?"

"You tell me"

"I'm sure you could help me become very, very happy", he replied, "but the question is, could I help you?"

"Oh, I know you could. But do you really want to? Just think what you'd be giving up".

"You're right", he conceded, "I'd have to give up a lonely celibate life, sharing a house in Wealdstone with two priests. Personal poverty, feeling increasingly useless and outdated as more and more people realise that what I represent, theologically at least, is.....well...not to put too fine a point on it....crap".

"Look, it isn't quite like that and you know it. I've never seen a man more successful and fulfilled in his work. Those people worship you".

"No they don't. They worship God. I just make it easier for them. But I'm making it harder and harder for myself. I now know I can't go on doing this forever. It's been great but I'd like to pack it in now and do something else. I don't want to be on my own any more"

"How can you say you're on your own with all those adoring parishioners?"

"Very easily. I think the world of them but there'll always be a distance between a priest and his parishioners. As there should be. I'm not really close to them or intimate with them. As a priest, I can't be intimate with anybody and that can be very lonely. The more I think of it, the more I now realise that I only took those vows because I hadn't met the right girl and assumed I never would"

"And have you now?".

"I think so"

"But you're not sure?"

"I'm as sure as I've ever been about anything"

"Well, that's not saying very much"

"True".

“And anyway, you always said you weren’t the marrying kind”.

“I wasn’t”

“And are you now?”

Frank paused. This time not for dramatic effect but simply because he was about to answer the most important question of his life.

“Yes”.

This time, he’d got it right. He’d won the million pounds. Chris Tarrant was hugging him and the studio audience were going wild..

FORTY-ONE

So that was it. They decided there and then to get married. There was no agonising, no questions, no wondering whether or not they were doing the right thing, They were both intuitive, intelligent and impulsive enough to, as the unlamented Mike Babcock would have said ,"go for it".

Frank had no desire to invite God to his wedding, he was in favour of quick registry office ceremony with a couple of friends as witnesses. Sarah, however, insisted that due tribute was paid to the years he'd devoted to the church. Together they sought and were granted special dispensation from Cardinal Hayes to marry in a Catholic Church – St. Thomas's Wealdstone, naturally. They'd caught him in a mood of Christmas clemency. .Sarah wanted to make her wedding the most significant and memorable moment in her life and Frank, the consummate show-off, was more than happy to oblige.

One thing was bugging him, though. Who was the grass? Who had set this whole chain of events in motion? To whom did he owe his eternal gratitude for releasing him from his vows into the arms of the woman he loved?

It took just one call to the Hilton in Park Lane, to enquire about the function held in the rooftop suite on Friday 15th December. The Society of Certified Accountants Christmas dinner and dance, apparently. Pat Walsh was the only certified accountant he knew and, come to think of it, he vaguely remembered Pat mentioning that he wouldn't be able to work his usual Friday night shift – "posh do up the West End" Pat was no Judas, the man was a sound as a pound. It could only have been his po-faced wife.

With Sarah up in Wilmslow, gently breaking the news to her parents that she was about to marry a penniless, unemployed ex-Roman Catholic priest, Frank walked up the drive of "Patanne" and was a little perturbed by the sight of Pat's BMW, haphazardly parked, lights on and the driver's door still open, as though its owner had rushed out in a state of some urgency.

He rang the doorbell. Pat answered, red in the face, his hair dishevelled with fresh blood and scratch marks down one cheek. Speechless and rooted to the spot, Pat simply stared.

"May I come in?" asked Frank. Pat nodded and Frank walked through to the half-wrecked sitting room where Anne Walsh stared at him too. She now believed that her husband's attempt to murder her had been successful. Surely she had died and gone to hell. Pat had strangled her, her precious ornaments and swirly curtains lay destroyed on the floor and now Father Dempsey, the man she had betrayed, was standing in front of her looking very serious indeed.

Pat went to say something. Frank held his hand up to stop him before turning to Anne with a benevolent smile.

"Anne", he beamed, "I've come to thank you".

Still believing she might be in Purgatory and some tears of contrition could tip the balance and get her into Heaven, Anne broke down and wept.

"Oh , Father", she sobbed, "I'm so sorry".

Frank pretended to be bemused.

"Why are you apologising? I've come to thank you", he repeated and put a comforting arm around her shoulders

"I know what you did", he said "And I now understand why you did it".

Anne could do nothing but sob helplessly while Pat simply stared, shiny-eyed and slack-jawed at the drama that was unfolding in his sitting room.

"Anne", Frank went on "You're a very perceptive person, aren't you? I've often watched you watching others. I've watched you watching me and you were the only one sensitive enough to spot a man who, despite appearances to the contrary, was unhappy in his work. You knew something that I didn't even know myself – that I was never really cut out to be a priest. That I would be much happier leading a more conventional life. So when you saw me at the Hilton doing just that, you were good enough to tell someone who could help me. Someone who could persuade me to face up to my feelings and find the courage do something about them. And for that, I can never thank you enough"

Anne was no longer sobbing. Too stunned, too dumbfounded for that. She was unable to sob, unable to speak, unable to move, her gaze fixed to the floor.

Frank, really enjoying himself now, continued,. "I want you to think back and remember how you felt when you first met Pat. On the Number 16 bus, wasn't it?"

Anne sniffed, wiped her eyes and looked up. How did he know this?

"Pat's told me all about it. The magic he felt when he first met you. And I've always really envied him. To feel that depth of love for a woman. I'd never felt it, couldn't appreciate it until now. Now I feel truly happy, truly liberated. Now I understand what all the fuss is about. It's finally happened to be and that's all down to you.. So...."

He took her face between his hand and placed a big kiss on her forehead,

".......thank you. Thank you from the bottom of my heart".

Still she couldn't speak.

Frank smiled once more, "I'll see myself out and by the way", he said gesturing towards the wrecked curtains and broken pelmet, "I'm glad you've taken those curtains down. I was never very keen".

FORTY-TWO

The candlelit wedding was a triumph. The congregation had burst into spontaneous cheers and applause when the bride and groom, breaking just about every nuptial convention, strolled up the aisle together arm in arm. Father Lynam joined them together in Holy Matrimony. Then, to the strains of Mendelsohn, they walked down again to even more tumultuous applause. The whole congregation were then invited to the biggest party ever held at the Parish centre. St. Frithelbert had never realised how popular he was.

Frank finally made it to the Lake District. Twenty years after setting off on the train from Euston, holdall full of theological textbooks, he finally arrived. For the first time in its life, the taxi headed up the M1, on to the M6 before arriving at an impossibly beautiful cottage in a breathtaking location right on the shore of Lake Ullswater.

It was here, for a few days, that Mr & Mrs. Dempsey decided to take their belated honeymoon. It was that peculiar time between Christmas and New Year, a time when London always seems well below par – running on two cylinders. Many of its inhabitants are away and the whole city seems to resemble a pale and sickly patient convalescing after an operation. The drama and excitement of Christmas has gone, though the decorations still hang around, outstaying their welcome. The patient won't regain its full colour, fitness and vitality until the first week of January and so Frank and Sarah opted to leave it alone until it was back to its best.

Far better to decamp to a village which has very little life and vitality anyway and very few Christmas decorations, a place where they could just sit down, relax and take stock.

Frank was only now beginning to take in the enormity of what he had done. Given up on his vocation, reneged on his vows, reneged on his whole life.

His days as the garrulous, gregarious yet intensely private priest couldn't have lasted forever. He knew that the game was almost up. It was only a matter of time before his maverick activities reached a wider audience. Only a matter of time before a commissioning editor from Channel 4 hopped in the back of his cab, bringing him unwanted celebrity and spawning a host of imitators. The Licensed taxi drivers tolerated him firstly because they liked him and secondly because he was a one-off. They would not have taken kindly to having their ranks swelled by a rash of trendy vicars all trying to raise money for the church roof.

Nothing stays the same forever, time to move on.

But move on where? Practical considerations were starting to rear their ugly heads.

What was he going to do? His years as a priest had allowed him to take on the roles of counsellor, teacher, youth worker, accountant, nightclub manager, DJ and taxi driver but, as far as the outside world was concerned, he was qualified for nothing.

He felt just as he did when he left school, just like he did when he left Oxford, except now it was far more serious. The best part of two decades had disappeared. He was married. He and his new wife might want to start a family. How was he going to earn a living? He was, in real terms, no further on with his career than he had been on that sunny August morning in Mr. Bracewell's office.

Sarah had been expecting this. Nessie had brought it to her attention at 3.15 one morning when they'd spent yet another night sitting up and talking about it.

"It's all very well, darling", she'd said, "I don't doubt that he is the most marvellous man in the world but what's that old saying? Beware of your dreams. They might just come true. What if he did chuck in the priesthood? What if you did end up together? What would he do? Who'd earn the money? And you don't exactly run on two-star, do you?"

It was about five o'clock. Frank and Sarah had just returned to the cottage after a glorious day spent walking, talking and laughing. They were still getting to know each other, each still intrigued by the other's autobiographical anecdotes. Frank had just finished telling another one, this time about the time he had gone rushing into Queen Elizabeth's hospital and mistakenly given the last rites to a man recovering from an ingrowing toenail.

She crossed the room and unplugged the laptop she had brought, ostensibly to check her e-mail.

"Write it down", she told him.

"Write what down?" he asked, assuming she was referring to that one little tale.

"All of it. Your childhood, the way you blagged into Oxford, your time as a priest – all of it. It's a great story and if you can write as well as you talk, well, who knows?".

Those gorgeous brown eyes stared at him, the arms held out the laptop. He looked a little unsure of himself but slowly, almost timidly, he took the laptop from her hands. What the hell? It wasn't as though he had anything else to do.

"I'm going upstairs for a long. leisurely bath", she said, "Now get typing".

Frank sat down and plugged it in

File....New.....Blank Document.

His fingers hovered nervously over the keyboard for a moment and then, after a few false starts, some words began to appear on the screen.

"The church was packed. Of course it was. This was Kilburn, 1970, home to the largest Irish community in Britain and the big Catholic Church in Quex Road was its epicentre...... "